THE PLEDGE

"Have you remembered the promise?" Maurice asked in his low, appealing voice.

And Evelyn answered as low, "Yes," with her eyes down.

She looked up in time to see the light of joy in his eyes and then down again as she felt the tightening of his clasp on her hand when he said in tones almost triumphant:

"I knew it. I knew you would. And, may I know, is it being answered yet?" His voice was yearning, anxious, as if he could not bear to go away without his answer.

She answered in a slow hesitation: "I think so."

The confession meant much to her and revealed much of her own heart to herself. Then she looked up to see the light of joy in his face, for she seemed to know it was there, and to realize that the sight of it would soon be a memory she must fasten now or lose perhaps forever.

Bantam Books by Grace Livingston Hill
Ask your bookseller for the books you have missed

An Unwilling Guest

Grace Livingston Hill

From henceforth thou shalt learn that there is love
To long for, pureness to desire, a mount
Of consecration it were good to scale.
                                    —*Jean Ingelow*

BANTAM BOOKS

TORONTO · NEW YORK · LONDON · SYDNEY · AUCKLAND

AN UNWILLING GUEST
*A Bantam Book / published by arrangement with
Harper & Row, Publishers, Inc.*

Bantam edition / January 1985

PRINTED IN THE UNITED STATES OF AMERICA

H   0 9 8 7 6 5 4 3 2 1

Contents

An
Unwilling
Guest

1

Outside Quarantine

The gray horse stopped by a post on the other side of the road from the little wooden station as if he knew what was expected of him, and a young girl got out of the carriage and fastened him with a strap. The horse bowed his head two or three times as if to let her know the hitching was unnecessary but he would overlook it this time seeing it was she who had done it.

The girl's fingers did their work with accustomed skill, but the horse saw that she was preoccupied and she turned from him toward the station a trifle reluctantly. There was a grave pucker between her eyebrows that showed that her present duty was not one of choice.

She walked deliberately into the little waiting room occupied by some women and noisy children, and compared her watch with the grim-faced clock behind the agent's grating. She asked in a clear voice if the five-fifty-five New York train was on time, and being assured that it was she went out to the platform to look up the long stretch of track gleaming in the late afternoon sun, and to wait.

Five miles away, speeding toward the same station, another girl of about the same age sat in a chair car, impatiently watching the houses, trees, and telegraph poles as they flew by. She had gathered her possessions about her preparatory to leaving the train, had been duly brushed by the obsequious colored porter who seemed to have her in charge, and she now wore an air of impatient submission to the inevitable.

She was unmistakably city bred and wealthy, from the crown of her elaborate black chiffon hat to the tip of her elegant boot. She looked with scorn on the rich farming country, with its plain, useful buildings and occasional pretty homes, through which she was being carried. It was evident, even to the casual onlooker, that this journey she was taking was hardly to her taste. She felt a wave of rebellion toward her father, now well on his way to another continent, for having insisted upon immuring her in a small back-country village with his maiden sister during his enforced absence. He might well enough have left her in New York with a suitable chaperon if he had only thought so, or taken her along—though that would have been a bore, as he was too hurried with business to be able to give time and thought to making it pleasant for her.

She drew her pretty forehead into a frown as she thought the vexed question over again and contemplated with dread the six stupid weeks before she could hope for his return and her release from exile. She pouted her lips in annoyance as she thought of a certain young man who was to be in New York during the winter. She was to have met him at a dinner this very night. She wondered for the hundredth time if it could possibly be that papa had heard of her friendship with this gay young fellow and because of it had hustled her off to Hillcroft so unceremoniously. Her cheeks burned at the thought and she bit her lips angrily. Papa was so particular! Men did not know how to bring up a girl, anyway. If only her mother had lived she felt sure she would not have had such old-fashioned notions, for her mother had been quite a gay woman of fashion, from what people in society said of her. There was nothing the matter with this Mr. Worthington either—a little fast, but it had not hurt him. He was delightful company. Fathers ought to know that their daughters enjoyed men with some spirit and not namby-pamby milk-and-water creatures. Probably papa had been gay in his youth also; she had heard it said that all men were, in which case he ought to be lenient toward other young men and not expect them to be grave and solemn before their time. Mr. Worthington dressed perfectly, and that was a good deal. She liked to see a man well dressed. Papa was certainly very foolish about her.

With this filial reflection the young woman arose as the train came to a halt and followed the porter from the car.

Several passengers alighted, but the girl on the platform knew instinctively that the young woman in the elegant gray broadcloth skirt and dainty shirt waist, carrying on her arm her gray coat, which showed more than a gleam of the turquoise blue silk lining, and unconcernedly trailing her long skirt on the dirty platform, was the one with whom she had to do.

Allison Grey waited just the least perceptible second before she stepped forward. She told herself afterward that it made it so much worse to have that shining black porter standing smiling and bowing to listen. She felt that her duty was fully as disagreeable as she had feared, yet she was one who usually faced duty cheerfully. She could not help glancing down at her own blue serge skirt and plain white shirt waist, and remembering that her hands were guiltless of gloves, as she walked forward to where the other girl stood.

"Is this Miss Rutherford?" she asked, trying to keep her voice from trembling, and hoping her mental perturbation was not visible.

The traveler wheeled with a graceful turn of her tall figure that left the tailor-made skirt in lovely curved lines which Allison with her artist's eye noted at once,—and stared. Evelyn Rutherford's eyes were black and had an expression which in a less refined type of girl would have been called saucy. In her it was modified into haughtiness. She looked Allison Grey over and it seemed to Allison that she took account of every discrepancy in her plain little toilet before she answered.

"It is." There was that in the tone of the answer that said: "And what business of yours may that be, pray?"

Allison's cheek flushed and there came a sparkle in her eye that spoke of other feelings than her quiet answer betokened:

"Then will you come this way, please? The carriage is on the other side of the station. Your aunt, Miss Rutherford, was unable to meet you and I have come in her place. If you will give me your check I will see that your baggage is attended to at once."

"Indeed!" said the bewildered traveler, and she followed

the other girl with an air of injured dignity. Was this some kind of a superior servant her aunt had sent to take her place? Her maid, perhaps? She certainly did not speak or act like a servant, and yet—— Then her indignation waxed great. To think that her father's sister should treat her in this way, not even come to the station to meet her when she was an entire stranger, and had never even seen her since she was three years old! In New York, of course, she would not have expected it. Things were different. But she had always understood that country people made a great deal of meeting their friends at the station. Her aunt had spoken of this in her letters. A fine welcome, to be sure! She could not be ill or this person would have mentioned it at once.

She entirely forgot that a few moments before one of her greatest grievances had been that she feared her aunt would bore her with a show of affection, for she remembered the many caresses of her babyhood indistinctly, and her nature was not one that cared for feminine affection overmuch.

Allison showed the colored porter where to deposit the bags and umbrellas on the station platform, and taking the checks given her she left the elegant stranger standing amid her belongings, looking with disdain at the pony phaeton across the road and wondering where the carriage could be. She was growing angry at being left standing so long when she became aware that the girl across the road untying the pony was the same one who had gone away with her checks, and it began to dawn upon her that she was expected to get into that small conveyance with this other girl.

She submitted with what grace she could, as there seemed to be nothing else to be done, but the expression on her face was anything but pleasant, and she demanded an explanation of the state of things in no sweet manner.

"What is the meaning of all this? Is this my aunt's carriage? Where is her driver?" she asked imperiously. Having made up her mind that this girl was a servant she concluded to treat her accordingly.

It was characteristic of Allison that she waited until she had carefully spread the clean linen robe over the gray broadcloth skirt, gathered her reins deliberately, and given the pony word to go before she answered. Even then she did not speak until the phaeton was turned about and they were fairly started spinning over the smooth road under the arching trees. By that time her voice was sweet and steady, and her temper was well under her control.

"I am very sorry, Miss Rutherford, that you should suffer any inconvenience," she said. "It certainly is not so pleasant for you as if your aunt had been able to meet you as she planned. No, this is not her carriage. It belongs to us, and we are her neighbors and dear friends." She forced herself to say this with a pleasant smile, although she felt somehow as if the girl beside her would resent it.

"Really!" interpolated Miss Rutherford, as one who awaits a much-needed explanation.

"Yes, your aunt was expecting you, 'looking forward with great pleasure to your coming,' she bade me say," went on Allison, reciting her lesson a trifle stiffly, "and only two hours ago she discovered serious illness among her household which they are afraid may be contagious. They cannot tell for some hours yet. She does not wish you to come to the house until they are sure. She hopes that it will be all right for you to come home by to-morrow, or the next day at most, and in the meantime we will try to make you as comfortable as possible. Your aunt sent us word by the doctor this morning asking me to meet you and explain why it would not be safe for her to meet you. I am Allison Grey. We live quite at the other end of the town from Miss Rutherford, so you will be entirely safe from any infection should it prove to be serious. Miss Rutherford was kind enough to think my mother could make you a little more comfortable than any one else."

Allison was almost in her usual spirits as she finished speaking. It would not be so bad after the stranger understood, surely. She did not add what Miss Rutherford had said about having her niece with herself, Allison, as she hoped another girl's company would make her feel less lonely and strange, for Allison saw at once that this was not a girl who cared for other girls' company a straw, at least not such as she.

Evelyn Rutherford's face was a study. Chagrin and astonishment struggled for the mastery.

"I do not understand," she said. "Who is ill in the family that could prevent my aunt meeting me? I thought she lived alone."

"She does," said Allison quickly, "except for her two

5

servants. It is one of them, the cook. She has been with Miss Rutherford for fifteen years, you know, and is almost like her own flesh and blood to her. Besides, she has taken care of her all night herself, before she knew there was any need for caution, and if it is smallpox, as they fear, she has been fully exposed to it already, so it would not be safe for her to come to you until they are sure."

"Horrors!" exclaimed the stranger, and Allison saw that her face turned a deadly white. "Stop! Turn around! I will go right back to New York!"

"You need not feel afraid," said Allison gently. "There is none of it in town and this case is entirely isolated. The woman has been away on a visit to her brother and probably took the disease there. She came home only yesterday. She came back sooner than she intended because you were coming and Miss Rutherford sent for her. There is really no cause for alarm, for the utmost care will be taken if it should prove to be smallpox, and by morning we may hear that it is all right and she is getting well, and it is not that at all. Besides, there is no New York train going out to-night. The last one passed yours about ten miles back. You will have to stay until to-morrow, anyway."

"Mercy!" said the stranger, seeming not to be able to find words to express her feelings. She was certainly taking the news very badly, but her hostess hoped she would behave better when she was fully possessed of the facts.

Miss Rutherford asked a few more questions about her aunt, commenting scornfully upon her devotion to a servant, which brought an angry flush into the other girl's cheek—and then settled down to the inevitable. Upon reflection she decided it would be better to wait and write or telegraph to her friends in New York before returning to them. Indeed, there was no one in town just then—for it was early for people to return to the city—with whom she felt sufficiently intimate to drop down upon them unannounced for a prolonged visit, and she knew that her father would utterly disapprove of her being with any of them, anyway.

"Do your people keep a boarding house?" she asked, turning curious eyes on Allison, who flushed again under the tone, which sounded to her insolent, but waited until she had disentangled the reins from the pony's tail before she replied gently:

"No."

"Well—but—I don't understand," said the guest. "Did you not say that my aunt had arranged for me to board with you?"

A bright spot came in each of Allison's cheeks ere she replied with gentle dignity:

"No, you are to *visit* us, if you will. Your aunt is a dear friend of my mother, Miss Rutherford." She resolved in her heart that she would never, never, call this girl Evelyn. She did not want the intimate friendship that her old friend had hinted at in telling her first of the coming of this city niece.

Allison was favored with another disagreeable stare, but she gave her attention to the pony.

"Really, I'm obliged," said the guest in icy tones that made Allison feel as if she had been guilty of unpardonable impertinence in inviting her. "Was there no hotel or private boarding house to which I could have gone? I dislike to be under obligations to entire strangers."

Allison's tones were as icily dignified now as her unwilling guest's as she replied: "Certainly, there are two hotels and there is a boarding house. You would hardly care to stay in the boarding house I fancy. It has not the reputation of being very clean. I can take you to either of the hotels if you wish, but even in Hillcroft it would scarcely be the thing for a young girl to stay alone at one of them. We sometimes hear of chaperons, even as far West as this, Miss Rutherford."

Allison's eyes were bright and she drew herself up straight in the carriage as she said this, but she remembered almost immediately the pained look that would have come into her mother's eyes if she had heard this exhibition of something besides a meek and quiet spirit, and she tried to control herself. Yet in spite of the way in which she had spoken, her words had some effect on the young woman by her side. She had been met by the enemy on her own ground and vanquished. She had a faint idea that her brother Dick would have remarked something about being "hoist with his own petard" had he been by, for she was wont to be particular about these things at home. She felt thankful that he was several hundreds of miles away. She said no more about hotels. She understood the matter of chaperonage even better than did Allison Grey, and strange as it may seem, Allison rose in her estimation several degrees after her haughty speech.

There was silence in the phaeton for some minutes. Then the driver spoke, to point out a dingy house close to the street with several dirty children playing about the steps. There was a sign in one window on a fly-specked card, "Rooms to Rent," and a card hung out on a stick nailed to the door-frame, "Vegetable soup to-day."

"This is the boarding house," said Allison. "Do you wish me to leave you here?" Her spirit was not quite subdued yet.

Evelyn Rutherford looked and uttered an exclamation of horror. Her companion caught the expression and a spirit of fun took the place of her look of indignation. In spite of herself she laughed.

But the girl beside her was too much used to having her own way to relish any such joke as this. She maintained an offended silence.

They passed the two hotels of the town, facing one another on Post-office Square. There were loungers smoking on the steps and on the long piazzas of both and at the open door of one a dashing young woman, with a loud laugh and louder attire, joked openly with a crowd of men and seemed to be proud of her position among them. Evelyn curled her lip and shrank into the carriage farther at thought of herself as a guest at that house.

"I fear I shall have to trouble you, at least until I can communicate with my aunt or make other arrangements," she said stiffly, and added condescendingly, "I'm sure I'm much obliged."

Then the carriage turned in at a flower-bordered driveway with glimpses of a pretty lawn beyond the fringe of crimson blossoms and Miss Rutherford realized that her journey was at an end.

2

Contrasts

They stopped at a side door which opened on a vine-clad piazza. The house was white with green blinds and plenty of vines in autumn tinting clinging to it here and there as if they loved it. A sweet-faced woman opened the door as they stopped at the steps and came out to meet them. She had eyes like Allison's and a firm, sweet chin that suggested strength and self-control. Apparently she had none of Allison's preconceived idea of their guest for she came forward with a gentle welcome in her face and voice.

"So you found her all right, Allison dear," she said as she waited for the stranger to step from the carriage, and Evelyn noticed that she placed her arm around her daughter and put an unobtrusive kiss on the pink cheek.

"This is mother," Allison said, all the sharpness gone out of her voice.

That Mrs. Gray should fold her in her arms and place a kiss, tender and loving, upon her cheek was an utter astonishment to Evelyn Rutherford. She was not used to being kissed. Her own mother had long been gone from her, and the women in whose charge she had been had not felt inclined to kiss her. In fact, she disliked any show of affection, especially between two women, and would have been disposed to resent this kiss, had it been given by one less sweet and sincere. But one could not resent Mrs. Grey, even if that one were Evelyn Rutherford.

"My dear, I am so sorry for you," was what she said next. "It must be very hard for your journey to end among strang-

9

ers after all. But you need not be anxious about your dear aunt, she is so strong and well and has often nursed contagious diseases without contracting anything."

Allison, as she went down the steps to take the pony to his stable could not help waiting just the least little bit to hear what this strange girl would say, but all the satisfaction she had was a glimpse of her face filled with utter astonishment. She felt in her heart that the least of Miss Rutherford's concerns was about her aunt. She wondered if her mother could not tell that by just a glance, or if she simply chose to ignore it in her sweet, persistent way. There were often times when Allison Grey wondered thus about her mother, and often had she suspected that behind the sweet, innocent smile which acknowledged only what she chose to see, there was a deeper insight into the character before her than even her shrewd daughter possessed. Allison puzzled over it now as she drove to the stable, flecking the pony's back with the end of the whip that was almost never used for its legitimate purpose.

In the house Miss Rutherford was carried from one astonishment to another. The gentle, well-bred welcome, she could not repulse. It took her at a disadvantage. She was ill at ease. She followed Mrs. Grey silently to her room. Something kept her from the condescending thanks she had been about to speak, thanks which would have put her in no way under obligation to these new, and, as she chose to consider, rather commonplace strangers. Why she had not uttered the cold, haughty words she did not know, but she had not.

The room into which she was ushered was not unattractive even to her city-bred eyes. To be sure the furnishings were inexpensive, that she saw at a glance, but she could not help feeling the air of daintiness and comfort everywhere. The materials used were nothing but rose-colored cambric and sheer white muslin, but the effect was lovely. There was a little fire in an open grate and a low old-fashioned chair drawn up invitingly. The day was just a trifle chilly for October, but the windows were still wide open.

"Now, dear," said Mrs. Grey, throwing the door open, "I hope you will be perfectly comfortable here. My room is just across the hall and Allison sleeps next to you, so you need not be lonely in the night."

Left to herself Miss Rutherford took off her hat and looked about her. The room was pretty enough. The low, wide window-seat in the bay window, covered with rosebud chintz and provided with plenty of luxurious pillows, was quite charming; but then it had a homemade look, after all, and the girl scorned home-made things. She had not been brought up to love and reverence the home. Her world was society, and how society would laugh over an effect achieved in cheap cottons with such evident lack of professional decorators. Nevertheless, she looked about with curiosity and a growing satisfaction. Since she must be thus cast upon a desert island she was glad that it was no worse, and she shuddered over the thought of the possibilities in that boarding house she had passed. However, she was not a young woman given to much thanksgiving and generally spent her time in bewailing what she did not have rather than in being glad over what she had escaped.

Presently the lack of a maid, who was to her a necessary institution, began to make itself felt. Her aunt had servants she knew, for they had been mentioned occasionally in the long letters she wrote at stated intervals to them. Her father had most emphatically declared against taking a maid with her from New York. This had been one of her greatest grievances. Her father said that her aunt had all the servants that would be necessary to wait upon her, and it was high time she learned to do things for herself. All her tears and protestations had not availed.

But in this house there had been no word of a maid. Mrs Grey had told her to let her know if there was anything she needed, but had not suggested sending a servant. Of course they must have servants. She would investigate.

She looked about her for signs of a bell, but no bell appeared. She opened the door and listened. There was the distant tinkle of china and silver, as of someone setting a table; there came a tempting whiff of something savory through the hall and distant voices talking low and pleasantly, but there seemed to be no servant anywhere in sight or sound.

Across the hall Mrs. Grey's wide, old-fashioned room seemed to smile peacefully at her and speak of a life she did not understand and into which she had never had a glimpse before. It annoyed her now. She did not care for it. It seemed to demand a depth of earnestness beneath living that was uncomfortable, she knew not why. She went in and slammed her door again and sat down on the bay-window seat, looking out discontentedly across the lawn.

Presently a wagon drove into the yard carrying her two large trunks. She heard voices about the door and then the heavy tread of a man bearing a burden. She waited, thinking how she could get hold of a servant.

Allison's light tap on the door soon followed and behind her was the man with a trunk on his shoulder.

"Wal, I kin tell yew that there trunk ain't filled with feathers!" ejaculated the man as he put down the trunk with a thump and looked shrewdly at its owner.

"You ought to bring some one to help you, Mr. Carter," said Allison's fresh, clear voice, with just a tinge of indignation in it as she looked toward the stranger; "that was entirely too much of a lift for you."

Miss Rutherford curled her lip and turned toward the window till the colloquy should be concluded.

"And now," said Mr. Carter, puffing and blowing from the weight of the second trunk which was even worse than the first, "I s'pose you want them there things unstropped. You don't look like you was much more fit to do it yourself than one o' these ere grasshoppers, er a good-sized butterfly."

"Sir!" said Miss Rutherford in freezing astonishment.

"I said as how you wa'n't built for unstroppin' trunks," remarked the amiable Carter with his foot against the top of the trunk and his cheeks puffed out in the effort to unfasten a refractory buckle.

"Your remarks are entirely unnecessary," said the haughty young woman, straightening herself to her full height and looking disagreeable in the extreme.

The buckle gave way, and Carter, taking his old hat from the floor where it had fallen, looked at her slowly and carefully from head to foot, his face growing redder than when he had first put down the trunk.

"No harm meant, I'm sure, miss," he said in deep embarrassment as he shuffled away, mumbling something under his breath as he went downstairs.

"The idea!" said the young woman to herself. "What

impudence! He ought not to be employed by decent people."
Then she heard Allison's step in the hall and remembered her
wants.

"Will you please let your maid bring me some hot
water," she said with a sweet imperiousness she knew how to
assume on occasion.

"I will attend to it at once," answered Allison in a cold
tone, and it became evident to the guest that her sympathies
were all with Mr. Carter. It made her indignant and she
retired to her room to await the hot water.

She stood before the mantel idly studying a few photographs. One, the face of a young man, scarcely more than a
boy, attracted her with an oddly familiar glance. Where had
she seen some one who had that same peculiarly direct gaze,
that awakened a faint stir of undefined pleasant memories?
She turned from the picture without having discovered, to
answer the tap on the door with a "come" that was meant as a
pleasant preface to her request that the entering maid would
assist her a little, and met Allison with the hot water.

"Oh, how kind to bring it yourself," said the guest a trifle
less stiffly than before. "But would you mind lending me your
maid for a few minutes? Can you spare her? I won't keep her
very long."

The color crept into Allison's cheek as she answered
steadily: "I am very sorry to say we are without any just now,
so I cannot possibly send her to you; but I shall be glad to
help you in any way I can as soon as mother can spare me."

"Oh, indeed!" said the guest with one of her stares.
"Don't trouble yourself. I shall doubtless get along in some
way," and she turned her back upon Allison and looked
haughtily out of the window.

Allison reflected a moment and said in a pleasanter tone:

"If there is any lifting to be done or your trunks are not
right, father will help you when he comes in for supper. And
I'm sure mother would want me to help you in any way I can,
if you will just tell me what to do. Would you like me to help
you unpack?"

"Oh, no, thank you," said the guest with her face still
toward the window, "I can do very well myself."

Allison hesitated and then turned to go. As she was half

out the door she said helplessly: "We have supper in half an hour. If you want me just call. I can easily hear you."

Miss Rutherford made no answer. After the door had closed she began elaborate preparations for a dinner toilet. She belonged to a part of the world that consider it a crime to appear at dinner in any but evening attire. In her life atmosphere it was thought to be a part of the unwritten code of culture which must be adhered to in spite of circumstances, as one would wear clothes even if thrown among naked savages. In her eyes Hillcroft was somewhat of a cannibal island, but it never occurred to her that it would be proper for her to do as the savages did. Therefore she "dressed" for dinner.

It was decidedly over an hour from that time before the guest descended. Mr. Grey had waited as patiently as possible, though he had pressing engagements for the evening. The bell rang twice, loud and clear, and Allison tapped at her door once and asked politely if she could be of any assistance as supper was ready; but in spite of all this the guest came into the dining room as coolly as if she had not been keeping every one waiting for at least three-quarters of an hour, and spoiling most effectually the roasted potatoes, which had been in their perfection when the bell rang.

Mrs. Grey had been as much annoyed by the delay as she ever allowed herself to be over anything, for she did like to have potatoes roasted to just the right turn, and prided herself upon knowing the instant to take them from the oven and crack their brown coats till the steam burst forth and showed the snowy whiteness of the dry delicious filling.

But potatoes and engagements alike were forgotten when Miss Rutherford burst upon them in her glory.

She had chosen a costume which in her estimation was plain, but which by its very unexpectedness was somewhat startling. It was only a black net with spangles of jet in delicate traceries and intricate patterns here and there, but the dazzling whiteness of the beautiful neck and arms in contrast made it very effective. She certainly was a beautiful girl, and she saw their acknowledgment of this fact in their eyes as she entered the room.

But she could not know of the shock which the bare white shoulders and beautifully molded arms gave to the whole family. Hillcroft was not a place where *décolleté* dressing was considered "just quite the thing" among the older, well-established families. It was felt to be a little "fast" by the best people, and it happened that Allison had never in the whole of her quiet, sheltered life sat down to a table or even moved about familiarly in the same room with a woman who considered it quite respectable to use so little material in the waist of her dress. It shocked her indescribably. She could scarcely understand herself why it should have such an effect upon her. She was a girl who had read widely, and in the world of literature she had moved much in the society of women who dressed in this way, and so far as one can be, through books, she was used to society's ways. But she had moved through that airy world of the mind without even noticing this feature of the fashions, except to disapprove them, because her parents did. Now she looked for the first time upon a beautiful woman standing unblushing before her father in a costume that his own daughter would have thought immodest to wear in his presence. After the first startled look Allison turned away her face. It was a beautiful vision, but one that she felt ought not to be looked upon. It seemed that the girl before her must be shielded in some way and the only way she could do it was by averting her gaze.

If Allison had been a frequenter of the theatre she would not have felt in this way; but Hillcroft was not a place where many artists penetrated, and if it had been, Mr. Grey disapproved of the theatre and so did his wife.

The feeling which Allison had about the white neck and arms extended in a less degree to her mother and father. There was a tinge of embarrassment in their greeting as they sat down to the evening meal, which they could hardly have explained. It was not so much embarrassment for themselves as for their guest, for they felt that she must inevitably discover how out of place she was in such surroundings, and then what could she feel but confusion? They forgot that her home surroundings had not been theirs.

3

The Maid-of-All-Work

It was well for the Grey family that their custom was to drop their eyes and bow their heads upon sitting down to a meal, while the head of the house asked God's blessing.

On this occasion it was a great relief to all concerned to close their eyes and quiet their hearts before God for a brief instant. They were people who lived close enough to their heavenly Father to gather strength from even so brief a heart-lift as was this.

As for the guest, it was actually the first time since her little girlhood that she had sat at a table and heard God's blessing asked. There could scarcely have been brought together two girls whose lives had been farther apart than those of Allison Grey and Evelyn Rutherford. Miss Rutherford slightly inclined her head as good breeding would dictate, but she kept her eyes wide open and looked about on the group, half amused and a trifle annoyed. She did not care to have such an interruption to her little triumph of entrance. Besides, she now thought she knew why these people were so awfully placid and unusual in their behavior,—they were religious. She had never known any very religious people, but she felt sure they were disagreeable and she decided again to get away from them as soon as possible. Meantime she was hungry and she could not help seeing that a tempting meal was set before her, even though, in the housekeeper's notion, it was almost spoiled.

When the blessing was concluded she noticed, as she waited for the plate containing a piece of juicy steak to be

16

handed her, that the table-cloth was fine and exquisitely ironed, and that the spoons and forks, though thin and old-fashioned, were solid silver. She happened to be interested in old silver just then, on account of a fad of a city friend, so she was able to recognize it. This fact made the people rise somewhat in her estimation, and she set herself to be very charming to the head of the house. It had never seemed to her worth while to exercise her charms upon women.

She really could talk very well. Allison had to admit that as she sat quietly serving the delicious peaches and cream, and passing honey, delicate biscuits, and amber coffee with the lightest of sponge cake.

The guest did thorough justice to the evening meal, and talked so well about her journey to Mr. Grey that he quite forgot his hurry and suddenly looked at his watch to find that he was already five minutes late to a very important committee meeting.

Allison did not fail to note all these things, nor to admit the beauty and charm of their visitor as she from time to time cast furtive glances, getting used to the dazzling display of white arms. Her face grew grave as the meal drew to a close, and her mother, watching, partly understood.

They had just risen from the table when Mrs. Grey, stepping softly from the hall, folded a white, fleecy shawl about the guest's shoulders saying gently: "Now, dear, you must go out and watch the moon rise over the lawn, and you will need this wrap. It is very cool outside."

Allison noticed with vexation that the shawl was her mother's carefully guarded best one that her brother had sent last Christmas. Allison herself always declined to wear it that it might be saved for mother. Yet here was this disagreeable, haughty, hateful——

Allison stopped suddenly and tried to devote herself to clearing off the supper table, realizing that her state of mind was not charitable, to say the least. She went with swift feet and skillful fingers about the work of washing the supper dishes, and her mother, perhaps thinking it was just as well for Allison to have a quiet thinking time, did not offer to help, but sat on the piazza with their guest, talking quietly to her about her aunt, though she must have noticed that the girl did not respond very heartily nor seem much interested. By

17

and by Allison slipped out with another shawl and wrapped it about her mother and the stranger saw in the moonlight the mother's grateful smile and the lingering pressure she gave Allison's hand, and, wondering, felt for the first time in her life a strange lack in her own existence.

"Are the dishes all washed, dear?" said Mrs. Grey a little while later, when Allison came out and settled at her mother's feet on the upper step.

"Yes, mother, and I have started the oatmeal for breakfast. You wanted oatmeal, didn't you?"

During the few words that followed about domestic arrangements it became evident to Miss Rutherford that the other girl had actually washed the supper dishes and done a good deal of the work of the house that day. She looked at her with curiosity and not a little sympathy. She felt a lofty pity for any girl who did not move amid the pleasures of society, but to be obliged to wash dishes seemed to the New York girl a state not far from actual degradation. And yet here was this girl talking about it as composedly as if it were an every-day occurrence which she did not in the least mind. She wondered what could be the cause of the necessity for this state of things. Probably all the servants had decamped at once, it might be on account of the fear of smallpox. In that case it might be that even she was in danger of contagion. It would be well to investigate. Mrs. Grey had gone into the house and Allison sat on the step quietly looking out at the shadows on the lawn.

"You said your maid had left you, I think," said Miss Rutherford, trying to speak pleasantly. "Have all your servants gone? What was the matter? Were they afraid of the smallpox?"

"Oh, dear, no!" said Allison, this time surprised out of her gravity into a genuine laugh. "There isn't any smallpox in town, only perhaps that one case you know. No, we never keep more than one servant. I did not say she had left; I said we had none now. She's not a maid in the sense you meant; she's the maid-of-all-work. She has been with mother since we were little children, but she is away on vacation now. She always goes for a month every fall to visit her brother in Chicago, and during that month mother and I do all the

18

work, all but the washing. She only went to Chicago day before yesterday, so we are just getting broken in, you see."

"Oh!" said Miss Rutherford slowly, trying to take in such a state of things and the possibility that anybody could accept it calmly. "And you only keep one servant? I'm sure I don't see how ever in the world you manage. Why, we keep four always, and sometimes five, and then things are never half done right. I should think you would just hate to have to do the work. Don't you?"

"Why, no," said Allison slowly. "I rather like it. Mother and I have such nice times doing it together. I love to make bread. I always do that part now; it's a little too hard for mother."

"Do you mean to say you can make bread?" The questioner leaned forward and looked curiously at the other girl, as though she had confessed to belonging to some strange tribe of wild people of whom she had heard, but whom she had never expected to look upon.

"Why, certainly!" said Allison, laughing heartily now. "I can make good bread too, I think. Wasn't that good you had for supper?"

"Yes, it was fine. I think it was the best I ever ate, but I never dreamed a girl could make it. Don't you get your hands all stuck up? I should think it would ruin them forever. I've always heard work was terrible on the hands," and she looked down at her own white ones sparkling with jewels in the moonlight as if they might have become contaminated by those so lowly near by.

"I have not found that my hands suffered," said Allison, in a cold tone, spreading out a pair as small and white and shapely as those adorned with rings. Her guest looked at her curiously again. Sitting there on the step in that graceful attitude, with the white scarf about her head and shoulders which her mother had placed there when she went in, and the moonlight streaming all about her, Miss Rutherford suddenly saw that the other girl was beautiful too. The delicately cut features showed clearly with the pure line of profile against the dark foliage in shadow behind her. Evelyn Rutherford knew that here was a face that her brother would rave over as being "pure Greek." What a pity that such a girl must be shut in by such surroundings, a little quiet village wherein she was buried, and nothing to do but wash dishes and make bread. Curiosity began to grow in her. She would try to find out how this other girl reconciled herself to such surroundings. Did she know no better? or had she never heard of any other world, of life and gayety? What did she do with her time? She decided to find out.

"What in the earth do you do with yourself the rest of the time? You only have to wash dishes and make bread one month you say. I should think you would die buried away out here? Is there any life at all in this little place?"

If Allison had been better acquainted with her visitor she would have known that her tone was as near true pity as she had ever yet come in speaking to another girl. As it was, she recognized only a scornful curiosity, and it seemed an indignity put upon her home and her upbringing. She grew suddenly angry and with her habit of self-control waited a moment before she answered. Her questioner studied her meanwhile and wondered at the look that gradually overspread her face. She had lifted her eyes for steadying to the brilliant autumn skies, studded with innumerable stars. Did they speak to her of the Father in heaven whom she recognized, of his wealth and power and all the glories to which she was heir? Did it suddenly come to her how foolish it was that she should mind the pity of this other girl, whose lot was set, indeed, amid earthly pleasures, but whose hope for the future might be so lacking? For suddenly the watcher saw a look almost of triumph mixed with one which seemed like pity, come over the fair young face before her, and then a joyous laugh broke out clear and sweet.

"Why, Miss Rutherford," she said, turning to look at her straight in the face, "I would not change my lot for that of any other girl in the world. I love Hillcroft with all my heart, and I love my life and my work and my pleasures. Why, I wouldn't be you for anything in the world, much as you may wonder at it. As for life here, there is plenty of it if you only know where to look for it."

Miss Rutherford about made up her mind that the investigation was not worth pursuing. It was not pleasant to have pity thrust back upon one in this style. She straightened back in the comfortable rocking-chair and asked in an indifferent tone:

"Then there is something going on? I always thought from aunt's letters that it must be a very poky place. What do you do?"

"There are plenty of young people here, and we are all interested in the same things. I suppose we do a great deal as they do in other places," mused Allison, wondering where to begin to tell about her life which seemed so full. Instinctively she felt that she must not mention first the pursuit dearest to her heart, her beloved Sunday-school class of boys, for it would not be understood. She thought a minute and then went on.

"We have a most delightful club," she said eagerly, her eyes kindling with pleasures past and to come. "I think you would enjoy that."

"Club?" said Miss Rutherford, stifling a yawn. "Girls or men?"

"Both," said Allison. "The girls meet early and do the real, solid hard work, and in the evening the boys come and enjoy and learn and give the money."

"You don't say!" said Miss Rutherford, with interest. "How odd! I never heard the like. What do you do? I suppose you make fancy work and the men buy it for charity and then you have a good time in the evening. Is that it? What do you do? Dance? Do you give germans? Or perhaps you are devoted to cards."

She was quite at home now and began to feel as if perhaps her exile might be tolerable after all.

"Oh, no!" said Allison, almost shocked to see how far she had been from making her visitor understand. "Why it is a club of the young people of the church."

"Do you mean it is a religious society?" questioned the girl, a covert sneer on her face.

"No, not religious," answered Allison; "but it is made up of the young people in our church. It is wholly secular and we have delightful times, but it is not a bit like society. We don't any of us play cards or dance, at least a great many of us don't know how and don't care anything about those things. But we have most delightful meetings."

Then Allison entered into a detailed and glowing account of the last meeting of their unique club of young people, wherein was combined the intellectual, useful, and social.

She warmed to the subject as she went on till it seemed to her that her guest could not but see how fascinating such evening entertainments could be. She told how the hostess had contrived clever ways to make the entertainment of the evening bring in the subject which had been the theme of the afternoon's discussion; and described the dainty arrangement of tables, flowers, lights, and refreshments to suit the occasion until she felt sure Miss Rutherford would see that she understood how things ought to be as well as if she lived in New York. Then she turned at the close to meet cold unresponsiveness and hear in a tone of entire indifference the word. "Indeed!" from Miss Rutherford.

In truth the visitor had heard very little of what was said. It sounded to her like a country church sociable—though she had never attended such a gathering—and she was simply bored by the account. Her mind was not sufficiently awake as yet to appreciate the cleverness manifested by these village girls in supplying the needs of social life which in the city are ministered to by professionals as a matter of course. She had been idly studying the sweet face before her and wondering what haunting memory was awakened by the expression that flitted across it now and again. Where had she seen some one of whom these people reminded her?

Allison suddenly subsided. She was aware that she had been casting her precious pearls before—well, she was hardly prepared to finish the sentence. But she was a girl whose likes and dislikes were intense, and when she went into anything she put her whole heart into it. This young people's club was dear to her. She did not relish seeing it despised. She was glad that her mother came out just then and made it unnecessary for her to say anything more. Gladder still was she when she saw her father open the gate down among the shadows of the trees and she could flit down to meet him and come back slowly arm in arm with him, asking about his meeting and knowing that he loved to tell her all about everything. She drew a long breath of relief and felt she had gotten away from the interloper in her pleasant home for a little space.

Meantime the guest watched her in absolute amazement. She tried to fancy herself rushing at her father in that style, and walking arm in arm up the path. Why did this other girl do it? And what was the reason of that pleasant look of understanding and love that passed between father and daughter as the two reached the steps and paused to finish a sentence before sitting down?

Evelyn Rutherford felt for the second time that there was something missing from her life which might have been pleasant and wondered why it was. Whose fault had it been, hers or her father's?

4

Allison's Fears

"Mamma," said Allison the next morning, as she put on the kettle she had just filled with fresh water from the spring, "Had you forgotten that Maurice is coming next week?"

The mother looked up from the eggs she was beating as she said, with a bright smile: "Oh, no indeed, daughter! How could you think I would forget my dear boy for a minute?"

"But suppose—she—is here yet?" and the troubled expression in the dark eyes showed that this was not the first time she had pondered the possibility.

"Why there is room enough, Allison," said the mother, beating some cold rice into the milk and eggs for the delicate batter-cakes she knew how to make to perfection.

"Oh, yes, *room* enough," said the girl. "But, mother, think of it! How can we enjoy his visit with her here? She will just spoil everything and Maurice won't like it at all."

"I fancy I should enjoy his visit if there were a whole regiment of strangers here, dear," said her mother, laughing, "and as for one girl being able to spoil it, I think you are mistaken. Besides, your brother is not so easily put out as that."

Allison looked at her mother with the trouble still in her eyes. She was evidently not yet satisfied, though she went thoughtfully about setting the breakfast table. But as she placed the forks and spoons at the stranger's plate, a vision of that young woman in her bewitching black gown and gleaming white shoulders appeared and brought back her trouble in full force. She went to the kitchen door and stood irresolute a moment watching her mother, opened her mouth to speak and closed it again, and then went back to her cups and plates. She could not quite make up her mind to put her thought into words and wondered whether it was wise to trouble her mother with it, even if she could. If it could not be helped why give her mother the anxiety of thinking about it, seeing she had not yet thought of such a thing for herself? Or had she? Did the mother think of it and calmly put her anxiety aside because there seemed a duty in the way she was walking?

Allison drew her brows in thought and went to look out of the window. Twice she went to the kitchen door and began, "Mother," but when the mother answered she asked some trivial question about the table and turned away. At last however she threw down the pile of napkins she was placing and deliberately walked to her mother's side.

"Mother," she said, in a low, troubled tone, "I must tell you what I am afraid of. Didn't you notice how pretty she looked last night and how attractive she can be when she tries, with all those beautiful clothes and her city airs? I can't help thinking what a terrible thing it would be if Maurice should take a fancy to her, and—and—marry her—perhaps!" she finished desperately.

The mother stood erect and looked her daughter full in the face gravely.

"Dear child," she said, "do you think your brother is so easily influenced by a pretty face and a beautiful effect? You give him little credit of discernment. And besides, do you not recognize a higher Power in shaping our lives than a mere chance of meeting? Cannot you trust God when we are in the way of duty?"

"But is this the way of duty?" asked the daughter desperately.

"What would you have me do, dear? Refuse my old friend her request? Tell the girl to go?"

Allison turned to the window with tears growing in her eyes. "Wouldn't there be some other way? She doesn't want to stay, I feel sure, and we could just encourage her to go back home. I think that could be done without being any more impolite than she has been."

"Allison, have you forgotten her aunt? She is one of our oldest, most valued friends. She has come to our rescue in many a time of trouble and now she has asked us to help her. Is it less incumbent upon us to do it because it is unpleasant? Have you forgotten that this girl is a fellow-mortal, that your Saviour died for her? You may be doing her great injustice. You have let your prejudice influence you largely and you forget the wide difference in your home surroundings. Her ideas of what is proper in dress and everything else are built on an entirely different standard from yours. The life she has led is not Hillcroft life."

"I should think not!" said Allison, in a low, repressed tone.

"Allison, won't you try to know this girl's true character before you begin to hate her?"

"Mamma, I should think it was plain enough what her character is, and you know I don't hate her, only it is so hard to think of having Maurice's visit spoiled by her, and it would be just terrible to have her come between me and my brother. I could not bear it."

"I wish my little girl would learn to trust her troubles to her Burden-Bearer instead of carrying them herself. You may be carrying all this woe unnecessarily. It may be this sickness will not prove serious and she can go to her aunt's in a day or two. But, Allison, have you forgotten that you have been asked to make a friend of this girl and to help her?"

"Mother, I could *never* help her, and she would never take any help from me," said Allison with firm conviction.

"My daughter, you do not know what you can do with God's help, or rather what God can do with your help."

Then the fried potatoes demanded attention and Allison,

25

unconvinced but somewhat softened by her mother's words, went back and finished her work quickly.

The guest, however, did not put in an appearance at breakfast time. They waited as long as possible for her and then went on without her, thinking she was weary with the long journey. To Allison it was a relief to have her father and mother to herself. Mrs. Grey realized this and tried to make the little time spent at the table as cheerful as possible, speaking of the expected arrival of the brother and son who had been away for nearly a year and who was to give them a whole week of his precious society before entering his professional career in an Eastern city. But the sister's face was not altogether unclouded and she looked eagerly for the promised message from the doctor which she hoped would bring word that their guest might leave them soon.

But the doctor did not come and as the morning wore on and he did not send a message, Allison began to have a growing conviction that there would be no good news, else it would have been brought before. Her mother tried to make her look upon the cheerful side, insisting that no news was good news, and trying to make her see how inhospitable she was to actually desire a visitor to leave; but her usually ready smile was slow to come. The mother grew troubled over this persistent feeling on the part of her usually sunny and helpful daughter. It seemed strange that Allison should take such a dislike to another girl. Perhaps she did not realize how deeply some of Miss Rutherford's looks and tones of evident scorn had cut the sensitive nature. Allison writhed inwardly again and again that morning over remembered sentences and glances. She worked grimly, taking the utmost trouble to prepare for dinner a dessert so elaborate that it was usually saved for high occasions. Her mother, smiling, understood and let her alone.

And while she worked with foamy eggs, rich whipped cream and gelatine, she made up her mind that she would show this city girl how much a country girl could do, and how useless was a frivolous life of mere pleasure. Forgetting that her chief aim should be to show her the adornments of a meek and quiet spirit she let her eyes flash many times as, according to her impetuous habit of mind, she plunged into imaginary scenes and discussions with this new girl from another atmosphere.

It was nearly eleven o'clock before the visitor came downstairs. She wore an elaborate white morning gown fastened at the belt with a clasp of gold in exquisite design. That dainty buckle worn on a morning costume accentuated the difference between these two girls to Allison. She would have kept such a rare ornament for her best gowns, but this girl doubtless had so many that it was quite common to her. Also, the stranger carried a novel in her hand and looked as utterly care-free and lazy as Allison herself would have liked to be, therefore she felt like a martyr and was filled with self-righteousness, and made a show of much bustle and haste. She plunged herself into an unnecessary piece of work which could not be left without spoiling, so that her mother had to carry the dainty tray with the lunch of rich milk, brown and white bread and butter, and a bunch of purple grapes to the guest.

Of this lunch Miss Rutherford partook leisurely, sitting in Mr. Grey's large rocking-chair, which always stood in the dining room that he might take a brief rest whenever he came in a little before a meal, and the while read her novel. Allison could see her through the open door and was offended anew. Her frame of mind was growing worse and worse. She resented the stranger's sitting in her father's chair; she resented her lying in bed and being daintily fed whenever she chose to arise; she resented the novel and the white gown and the beauty of the girl; and above all, she resented the fear that she would be there to share in her cherished brother's smiles and conversation.

It was not that her brother Maurice was given to being bewitched by any pretty girl that came along, that she was so worried about this particular one. No, it was rather the reverse with the young man. But he had his mother's gentle, kindly way of meeting every one pleasantly and giving every one a fair chance. It hurt Allison to think that this girl, who could be so hateful to her, would be given an opportunity to show how delightful she could be to others, and Allison was quick enough at character reading to know that her brother would be more likely to receive smiles than she had been.

She began to recognize in her own feelings an element that she did not admire as the day wore slowly away.

At last, toward evening, came a message from the doctor. The symptoms were very grave. The case was decidedly smallpox. Miss Rutherford desired her niece to remain where she was until the danger was past and she could plan to take her to a safe place. She intimated that she had received instructions from her brother which made her anxious to have his daughter with her as soon as possible, and for the present she was to feel that she had put her in the safest, happiest home she knew in the world, where she hoped she would be more than contented until the danger was past.

This message was brought by a member of the doctor's family who had not been near the infected house and had received it over the telephone from the doctor; but the young lady to whom it came declined to see the messenger or to touch the paper upon which the message was written, preferring to take it from Mrs. Grey's lips. She was annoyed beyond measure at its import and retired to her room to consider plans for her own alleviation.

She was certainly in no enviable frame of mind as she sat looking out the window without seeing the glowing tints of autumn leaves in such profusion. The girl in the next room, who had also fled to a refuge to bear her disappointment, though she insisted that this was just what she had expected all the morning, had the advantage of recognizing in herself the evil spirit that was dominating her being and had a will to be free from it. Not only that, but she understood what to do in order to be free. It was not long before she knelt beside her bed to confess her sin and to beg forgiveness and strength. But her heart was yet hardened toward the intruder in her home.

It was perhaps not to Miss Rutherford's advantage that mention was made that evening of the expected home-coming of the son of the house.

It came about in this way. Mr. Grey asked his wife at the supper table about some arrangements in the house which were to be made in view of Maurice's coming and talk followed in which his name was used several times. Allison said little about him, but once or twice a sentence of hers showed the guest that whoever it was that was expected, his advent would give Allison great pleasure. She studied her curiously while she ate and the others talked, wondering if he were some commonplace rustic lover, and thought it a pity that this handsome girl should not have a chance among men who were of some account. She sat on the porch alone after supper until Allison and her mother had finished the work. It never occurred to her to offer her assistance. Indeed, she would not have known how to help if she had been so disposed. She looked upon all household tasks as menial, not for such as she.

She had decided that afternoon to write to one or two New York friends and beg for invitations. She had written several letters confiding her disagreeable position and she felt certain that the returning mail would bring her an invitation to quit this dismal place, believing that she had excuse enough to send to her father. Meantime she must while away the hours as best she might until her release. It would be but a week at most she felt sure. She yawned and wished for something to do. She had read until she was weary of it. She wondered if there were any fun to be got out of the town. She must find out who this expected Mr. Morris was, as she had settled it in her mind his name should be, though the family had spoken of him as "Maurice" merely.

Allison, in obedience to her mother's request, and in penance for her ugly thoughts of the morning, came to the piazza and dutifully sat down to talk.

"Who is this Mr. Morris you are expecting?" asked Miss Rutherford at once. "Is he interesting? Does he intend staying long? He isn't your especial property, is he?"

"Mr. Morris?" questioned Allison, puzzled, and laughing as she suddenly comprehended the mistake, then growing angry as she further realized the import of the last sentence, she said in a dignified tone: "I think you must mean my brother Maurice. He is coming home for a short visit. He will be here a week perhaps."

"Oh, indeed!" said the guest, losing interest at once. "He is away working, I suppose."

Allison hesitated before she answered, the color growing brighter in her cheeks and her eyes shining with the slightest bit of wickedness. Then she said in a strained tone:

"Yes, he is away—working."

Why she made such an answer she did not quite understand. It gave her real pleasure to feel that for a little while before he came at least this girl would not look upon her precious brother as a possible subject upon whom to exercise her charms. Ordinarily she would have resented the evident slight in the expression about his working and would have proudly hastened to state that his work was that of a physician in Bellevue Hospital, in New York, and that he was about to enter the profession for himself with a fine opening and every prospect of success in a worldly way. She was proud of her brother and would not have been willing to let this pass if he were not coming so soon to speak for himself and show this supercilious young woman that he was in every way superior to her. A little twinge of pride gave her pleasure as she thought of the surprise Maurice would evidently be. Meantime, the other girl was looking dreamily off into the garden.

"Maurice, you said? Maurice Grey. That's curious," she said musingly; "I know a man by that name and he is awfully nice too. He's fine!"

The girl on the step started almost imperceptibly. Had they then already met? There was all the more danger in their meeting in his home. And to have her call him "awfully nice!" It was intolerable.

"Where did you meet him?" she asked, in a cold tone which she forced to be steady. "My brother has been in New York."

"Oh, it isn't your brother, of course. He's quite a different person, I fancy. My Maurice Grey is quite a brilliant man. He is a young doctor and I hear his prospects for the future are remarkable. He's a good friend of mine, or was. I have not seen him for a year. I met him abroad," and in the moonlight her face took on a softened, dreamy, wistful look.

5

The Arrival of Maurice Grey

The rush of thoughts into Allison's mind was suddenly checked by the sound of the gate clicking and a strong, manly step coming quickly up the walk. She started to her feet and looked down through the shadows. It could not be that any other step could sound just that way, and after poising one instant on the step to make sure, she uttered a smothered "Oh!" and rushed swiftly down the walk.

Miss Rutherford heard the sound of subdued greeting, and knew that the steps lingered while there was the murmur of low-spoken words. Then they came on and a voice that was strangely familiar to her ear said: "Where is mother? Yes, I found I could get away a whole week ahead and I thought I would enjoy giving you a real surprise for once in my life."

The mother's quick ear had caught the sound too, and she was out on the walk before he could reach the door, and had folded the tall form in her arms, saying tenderly, but so that the guest could hear, "Oh, my dear boy!" and Miss Rutherford knew again that she had missed something by having no mother. It made her heart ache with a strange new longing for just an instant, till Allison's clear, cold voice said precisely:

"Miss Rutherford, this is my brother, Dr. Maurice Grey, formerly of Bellevue Hospital."

Dr. Maurice Grey, wondering at the coldness and dignity of his sunny sister's introduction, turned in surprise to face the beautiful girl who stood in a flood of light at the top of the steps in front of the open door.

Was it only the hall light that illumined his face, or did Allison in her keen watch really notice a sudden lighting of his eyes as he smiled and grasped the white hand held out to his, saying, with true pleasure in his tones: "Why, Miss Rutherford! This is a pleasure, indeed, to find you in my own home. How comes it about? My surprise is double, is it not, mother? I have met Miss Rutherford before."

They sat down to talk while Allison, smarting under this cordial greeting to her foe, went to prepare a hasty supper for her brother. Her cheeks were glowing with a heat that did not come from the fire, over which she was making delicate slices of toast. She was covered with shame over the introduction she had given her brother. The instant the words were out of her mouth she had felt the bad taste and the low motive which had prompted her, and moreover, she anticipated her brother's dislike to being introduced in this way. She had felt his questioning look and the surprise in his face as he turned to greet the visitor. She knew he did not like it. She knew he preferred not to have any display made of his title or achievements. But worst of all was the feeling that she had done it in revenge for what her guest had said. She feared she was beginning to hate Miss Rutherford.

There was a verse somewhere in the Bible, she could not remember the exact words, which said you must not be glad when your enemy was brought low. Allison knew she would be very glad if Evelyn Rutherford could be brought very low before her brother so that he would despise her.

The household sat up unusually late that evening. There was much to be talked about, for the son had been away so long, and they could not bear to close their eyes upon the goodly sight of him even for a little while.

Miss Rutherford had the good grace and good breeding to take herself to her room early in the evening. Allison blessed her for this even while she recognized that it would count one with her brother in favor of the instinctive delicacy of their guest. But it was good to have him entirely to themselves, for the first evening at least.

Alone in her room Miss Rutherford lighted the gas, forgetting for once to wonder how people endured it to always have to light their own gas and have no maid to attend to such bothersome details. Then she walked to her mantel and contemplated the boyish face in the cabinet picture that stood there looking with frank eyes into her own, just as the young man downstairs had done to-night—and one other time. She understood now why his face had haunted her and stirred pleasant memories. It was like his present self and yet not enough for her to have recognized him, she decided, as she studied his features closely. She knew now why the faint memories had seemed so pleasant. How strange it was that for the third time she should be among strangers where she did not wish to be and should again meet him. Who was he? Her fate? Her affinity? The prince that every girl waits for, who will sometime come into her life and fill it full of joy forever? She was not a girl who spent much time in dreaming. The eager rush of doing and being and getting pleasure out of life had crowded out the sentimental. There had been little to develop the poetical. But her meeting, or rather meetings, with this young man had been so strange and unexpected that she could but be fascinated by the unusual.

She sat down in the low window seat, the picture in her hand, to think it over. Her first meeting with Maurice Grey—she shuddered as she remembered it. Her friend, Jane Bashford, had summoned her cousin from his den to attend her home one evening when nothing had been going on worth while and the two had spent the evening together. Jane and she were very intimate and spent much time at each other's home. It was an understood thing that Jane's cousin, or an old house servant, should see her home whenever she was out late and it was not convenient to send her in the carriage.

Jane's cousin had seemed exceedingly gay as they started out and when they were fairly on the street and away from the house, Evelyn, ignorant as she was in such matters, became aware that she was being escorted by a drunken man. She had not been much frightened at first, for she had known him since they were both children, and the way was short. She thought there would surely be some one passing in a moment to whom she might appeal for help if necessary; but it was later than she realized and when Jane's cousin became affectionate and attempted noisily to put his arm about her and kiss her, she grew alarmed and started to run, not knowing which way she went. She could remember just how her heart was beating and how the houses grim and tall looked down upon her, piling up in dark perspective whichever way she looked. Not a creature seemed abroad, no one to help her. Then suddenly there had been footsteps, a hand placed upon her trembling arm, and a strong manly voice had said:

"Miss Rutherford, can I help you?"

Even in her terror she had not thought to be afraid of this man, his voice seemed so strong and trustworthy. He had led her quickly through the streets to her home, saying with assurance: "Don't be alarmed. He has not control enough over his feet to follow," and had landed her safely at her own door, rung the bell, and waited until she was safely inside the brightly lighted hall with the mere explanation that he had known her brother in college and happened to see her in his company several times. It was all over before she had gathered her wits together to ask any questions. The man was gone and she did not even know his name. The brother, questioned, could not give any clue. He declared that he had a host of friends with strong, trustworthy voices and besides he believed that his sister would have considered almost any voice trustworthy, frightened as she was. She did not seem able to give any lucid description of the man, and so he dropped away from her life again and if it had not been for Jane Bashford's cousin, whom she had occasionally to meet in her world, perhaps she might have forgotten him altogether. She had kept away from Jane's cousin as much as possible, he seeming willing that it should be so. Evelyn doubted if he realized how grave his offense had been. Sometimes, though, the dreadful night experience would come back to her vividly and she would live it over again and then hear that strong, clear voice and see the dim outline of a fine face in the darkness. She knew the face had been handsome, even though it had been too dark a night and she too perturbed to examine carefully. She felt certain she should know it again. She had often wondered why she never met any man who made her think of him and began to think she would not know him after all. Perhaps he walked the streets of New York every day and even passed her house and was kind enough not to embarrass her with having to thank him by ignoring the occurrence altogether.

It had been a year later—she started as she thought of it. It was just about a year ago now. How strange! A year apart each time. A year later she had met him again. She had known him almost at once, even before he spoke.

It was while she was traveling abroad. Her father had left her in care of friends who had a mania for seeing everything that was to be seen, and they had insisted upon dragging her with them. She hated it all. They were poky people, who went everywhere with a book and hunted up everything they saw in the book and read about it, and then told each other that it was here such a woman sat, and there such a man walked, and over yonder some one was murdered or buried or what not.

She had not cared for it. What were ancient battles and dead men and women to her? This was not what she had come to Europe for; she wanted some life and pleasure. Her father, doubtless, hoped she would imbibe some knowledge, but it had escaped from her like water off a duck's back. One afternoon they had taken her to visit a famous ruin. When they reached the ruin it was found that the excursion included a sail across a placid strip of water to a tiny island whereon was located something or other, Evelyn did not now know what, and was not sure that she had ever known. She had determined in her heart not to get into that leaky-looking boat, with the dirty sailor, and swelter in the hot sun while her guardians had all sorts of tiresome things pointed out and explained to them, and hunted out the items about them with slow, near-sighted vision in the volumes they carried. After the rest had embarked and the boatman essayed to help her in, she suddenly declared her intention of remaining where she was till their return, giving as her excuse a headache. There had been some demur. The boatman told her it might be some time. All the more reason why she felt she would not go. Her staying might hurry their return. Each of the party mildly offered to remain with her, but she had declined all their offers. She had longed to get away from them all for a little while. The day was sunny and the place entirely safe, with a comfortable seat under a tree by the water. At last they sailed away and left her.

She could remember now how unhappy she had been as she watched them go, and reflected that she must stay there alone until their return. She wished herself back in New York, wished her father had not come on this business trip, wished she ever could have anything but poky, commonplace happenings. She had longed for some adventure, and even looked about for some dangerous place to climb or some wild thing to do while they were gone. Suddenly in the midst of her thoughts there had come a tremendous storm.

She had not looked behind her until she heard the low rumble of thunder, and turning saw the whole mass of lowering ruins black against a blacker sky, with lurid flashes of lightning making great clefts and picking out every separate stone of the old castle with fearful distinctness.

She had been terribly frightened. She looked off to the place where her friends had but a moment before been a white speck on the quiet blue lake, and lo, there had been a transformation! The lake was no longer blue but a livid purple, with ghastly green lights over it, an ominous whirl and strange treacherous ripples blowing across it. The island seemed farther away, and the white sail had disappeared. Perhaps they had rounded the island. Perhaps they had landed. At any rate they were evidently not meditating an immediate return to her. She had sense enough to see that it would not be possible for them to do so now.

A terrible sheet of lightning blinded her eyes for an instant and sent her shivering from beneath the tree. She knew that a tree was a conductor of lightning. The rain began to fall in great plashing drops and she had fled to the ruin and wondered if that also were a place of danger. She had crept into an alcove with roof enough for protection from the rain and there, facing her in the companion alcove not three feet away stood a man, and his face she knew at once. She seemed to have seen his smile before, though that was impossible in the dark, and when he spoke, as he immediately did, she knew his voice. It all had been so strange. They had seemed good friends at once, as if they had known each other for years. He had seen that she was trembling, that she was afraid of the storm, and had led her inside to a place more sheltered, where the awful flashes that blazed through the whole sky could not be so distinctly seen and where the roar of the thunder and the sound of the dashing water in the thoroughly aroused little lake would reach but faintly through the great stone walls; and there they had talked.

She had told him how grateful her father was for his service to her a year ago, and how chagrined she was that she had not inquired his name, and how they had tried their best to find him and thank him. When he smiled and said he was glad she had not been afraid of him also, she felt that she had known him a long time.

Never once during the two hours they spent in the old hall of the castle, while the elements did their worst outside, did it occur to her to wonder if he belonged to the favored few who composed her world of society and who were eligible to talk and dance and play with such as she. It was only afterward that this question came to her, when her friends asked, "Who is he?" and "What is he?" for they came from the part of the world where these things count for much. Then she found she knew very little indeed from her three hours spent with him, as to either of these important questions, in the sense that these people meant. Afterward, when her brother Dick had been called in to help, she had been glad to know that he stood high in his profession, and could go anywhere, if he but chose. But he had not come her way again, though she had always been hoping that he would.

Their talk that afternoon had drifted to the old ruin and she suddenly found it peopled with real folks, breathing and walking before her, and she wondered why this man could make the people of history so interesting to her, when her friends had only bored her with talk of them.

Once when the lightning had been most vivid and she had shuddered involuntarily and covered her eyes with her hands, he had said, "Don't be afraid," in a quieting tone. Then she had looked up into his face and had known that he was not at all afraid.

She lay awake a long time that night after thinking the whole story over. A sudden thought had come to her. Was it, could it be because he belonged to this strange family and held peculiar beliefs, that he had not been afraid of that terrible storm? Or was it because he was a man? No, he had something more in his face than most men when they are merely brave. There was something in this whole family, some controlling, quieting force that she did not understand.

How very strange that he should have belonged to these people! And stranger still that she should be here!

6

Maurice Grey's Vow

There were other vigils kept that night. The mother in her own room, though she put her light out quietly enough and knelt beside her bed as usual, prayed long and earnestly for her dear boy and added a petition for "the stranger beneath our roof." Then she lay down to wonder anxiously if she had done exactly right in bringing this strange unknown quantity into the house just now, when her dear boy was coming home, and to tell herself for the thousandth time that day that it had not been her doing. She had not even known that Maurice was coming this week. Finally she laid down her burden, asking her heavenly Father to make it all work out to his glory, and fell asleep.

Allison in her room was trying to read her Bible. She was reading by course and her chapter that night brought her to the thirteenth of First Corinthians. She had read two or three verses unthinkingly, when her mind suddenly became aware of the meaning of the words. Impatiently she closed her Bible, then opened it again. She would not read in her regular order to-night. She needed special help. Her soul was weary and hungry. She needed something like "Come unto me all ye that labour and are heavy laden," or "Let not your heart be troubled." Not that sharp unbraiding, and being obliged to examine her heart again.

She had done that all day. Besides, she knew that chapter by heart, "Though I speak with the tongues of men

38

and of angels and have not charity." She knew all the latest expositions, had read and even learned it, substituting the word "love" for "charity." The whole thing searched her too keenly to-night, hence she turned away.

But turn as she would to find comfort, that persistent Bible would open again and again back to the chapter in Corinthians. At last, unwillingly, she read it through, piercing her soul with every verse, and lay down to weary contemplation of her mistakes and failures, having tried to throw off her burdens in prayer, but picking them up and shouldering them once more. It was very hard for poor Allison to give up. When her will decided a thing she simply could not bear to have things go the other way. She could not see how it was right. In theory she believed that God knew what would be best for all his children. In practice she had a strong conviction that she knew pretty well what the Lord had intended in the first place and there was danger of its getting switched off the track if she did not watch the switch and worry about it.

Maurice Grey, in his old room, among the relics of his boyhood, his college days, and his early manhood, searched for a minute or two in an old desk drawer and brought therefrom a little black book labeled, "My Foreign Diary."

He hastily turned the leaves and read:

"At last I am afloat. New York has faded from our view. The last tie to *terra firma* in the shape of a dirty little boat has left us and we are bound for another shore. How I have dreamed of this day! Yet now that it has come I scarcely realize it. I have had so much to do the last forty-eight hours. I believe I felt more that my foreign trip was actually begun when I bade mother and father and Allison good-bye last week than I do now. It was hard to have to leave them behind. In my dreams of this they have always been a happy accompaniment to my anticipated pleasures.

"There has been nothing notable in the three days I have spent in New York, with the exception of my experience last evening. I was standing at the corner of West Sixty-fourth Street looking up Fifth Avenue and trying to decide whether it was too late to make a brief call on any of the fellows in that part of town, or whether I would better go at once to the hotel and get a good night's rest. The clocks had just struck eleven and for New York there seemed to be a sudden quiet about that quarter. I could hear footsteps, a woman's and a man's. The woman's steps suddenly quickened into a run as they turned the corner below and she came in sight. I could see that the man was trying to catch her, and he did succeed in taking hold of her arm as she came nearer. Then he tried to kiss her, calling her name in loud tones, 'Evelyn.' It made me shudder to hear that lovely name spoken in the street so, and by a drunkard in a drunken voice! That has always seemed to me a name that speaks of guarded, sheltered life. I soon saw that the man was beside himself with liquor, and as they passed under the street light I suddenly recognized the girl to be Dick Rutherford's stately sister. I never met her, but have seen her many times with Dick and other college men. She is a great society girl and very beautiful. I knew her at once. Her face was white with fear. She seemed as glad to turn to me as a little child in trouble might be. I think she was too frightened to talk much. I took her to her father's door, telling her I knew her brother. Perhaps it is just as well for my future peace of mind that she did not ask my name. She will never be bothered with having to thank me for the small service I did her, and I shall not be chagrined because I am not eligible to her 'set.' It might be some temptation to me to try to become eligible if I had not decided to live another kind of life. I have consecrated everything to Jesus Christ—myself, my talents, if I have any, my all. Miss Rutherford has other aims in life probably. She would not think twice of a young medical student. I wonder if she is a Christian. I wonder what our meeting last night was for!"

He turned the pages rapidly till his eye fell on the right date and then he settled to reading once more.

"I have had an adventure. Here in this strange land of wondrous beauty, where I did not expect to see a familiar face, I have met another human being to whom, indeed, I have spoken but once before, but with whom I have been conversing for nearly three hours. I was taking my second view of the old ruin before going away; and as I stood looking at the moss-grown turrets and imagining the old days back when knights and ladies walked and talked there and looked off across the lake to the blue mountains in the distance, it reminded me of Browning's poem, 'Love Among the Ruins.' I repeated a verse aloud as I stood alone in a grassy meadow that stretched away to a bit of ruin standing by itself:

> *"Now the single little turret that remains*
> > *On the plains,*
> *By the caper overrooted, by the gourd*
> > *Overscored,*
> *While the patching houseleek's head of blossom*
> > *Through the chinks,*
> *Marks the basement where a tower in ancient time*
> > *Sprang sublime,*
> *And a burning ring, all round, the chariots traced*
> > *As they raced,*
> *And the monarch and his minions and his dames*
> > *Viewed the games.*

"Just then I noticed the heavy blackness that was swiftly overspreading the sky. I watched it grow dark all about the ruin till the gray turrets and the purply green-gray clouds blended and there were turrets and towers in the sky everywhere. Vivid flashes of lightning set forth this mighty spectacle. I withdrew to the shelter of a covered archway, and the rain began to pour down. I had not been under cover more than a minute before I heard the flutter of garments and looking out I saw—Evelyn Rutherford, Dick Rutherford's beautiful sister. The last time we met was in New York. How strange that she should be here! We talked about many things, for there was nothing for us to do but remain under cover until the rain ceased. I do not think three hours ever went with greater swiftness. She is a fine conversationalist—or—no, is she? Perhaps she is a fine listener, for I can remember hearing my own voice most of the time, now that I think of it. But if I can judge by her face we certainly enjoyed the time together. We peopled the old rooms and corridors with knights and ladies robed in rich satins, stiff with gold broidery. I repeated Browning's poem again, for it kept running in my head all day. She liked it, I think. At least her eyes seemed to say so, and her comments were well-made and to the point. She showed a keen appreciation of the poem's literary beauties, which was more than I expected from one in her position in society. But then! It was but for an afternoon. What am I? And what is she? We are as from two worlds. It may be we shall never meet again. There are other poems of Browning's which might appropriately be quoted just here, but I am too weary to-night to hunt them up, and besides, I do not care to have the charm of the day lifted just yet. I never quite believed in their sentiments either, and always revolted at the idea that two beings who seemed to be affinities should meet and enjoy each other and then be thrown apart and care no more, but I don't know but I understand better now how the necessities of life compel one to adopt such a philosophy. But somehow this adventure has unfitted me for the ordinary. It is well I am going back to work soon.

"I am reading the life of Moody. I have been making it a rule lately to do a little religious reading every day, aside from the Bible, to keep in touch with things most vital. I wonder I have never read this before. It is not a great book as books go, but it is the story of a great life, a life near to God. Last night I read that Moody made it a rule never to be alone with a person five minutes without having by some little word or action left his testimony for Christ, and found out whether his companion was a Christian. I was much impressed by the story of his walking in the rain with a stranger on the street to protect him with his umbrella and before the short walk was over asking the question: 'My friend, do you know Jesus Christ?' I do not think I could always do that way, perhaps; but I might be able to witness in some way if I tried. I could not but marvel what a difference it would make in the world if all Christians would do so. I lay awake thinking it over and resolved, after much thought and prayer, to adopt this rule for myself. I made that resolve only last evening and prayed for the necessary opportunity and courage. Behold, it needed neither courage nor opportunity. Three hours were given me in which to reach a human soul, and one with whom in all likelihood I shall never come in contact again. If I loved Christ, as I had thought, would I not have been anxious at once to do this little for him? I spoke of my father, mother, and sister, but of him whom I love better than all I breathed never a word. I cannot even comfort myself with the thought that there was aught in my conversation that indirectly showed her my purpose in life, not even so much as a hint that I ever attended church. And this because I was so absorbed in other things as to entirely forget. I do not think it would have required much courage.

"The thing I need to pray for first is watchfulness. My Master's words to his disciples apply to me now, 'Could ye not watch with me one hour?' I have been taking my ease, my pleasure, and never watching for words to say for him. And now the opportunity has passed. Oh, that I might have another! I judge this girl by her words and she does not seem to be a Christian. Does she judge me in the same way? I deserve it. Twice I have met this soul and missed my opportunity to carry a message for my Lord. I hereby pledge my word, God helping me, that if I am ever thrown in her company again I will do my humble best to show her that it is a sweet thing to have Christ as a Saviour. But so great a privilege is not likely to be awarded me again, seeing I have shown myself unfaithful. But I can and will pray for her. I will make it my daily practice, so help me God, to pray for her soul until I die or know that she belongs to Christ. She is nothing to me, perhaps; but the responsibility of three long hours misspent is upon me and I have been found wanting."

The young man closed the book which registered his vow almost reverently. He had kept that pledge for a year, and now he sat thoughtfully.

"Strange," he said, speaking aloud to himself as was his habit when alone, "strange and wonderful that I should have another opportunity given! It is a great privilege for a human soul to be given a third chance, having failed in two through utter thoughtlessness. Why I should feel so about this particular soul I do not know. There are doubtless many others whom I have passed by again and again, and never knew nor thought, but my meeting with this girl was unusual. And then, I believe one cannot pray for another without having a deep interest in that other. I am very happy. Can it be that I am to be allowed to do what I have left undone? It may be all my absurd imagination. I may not have been needed at all; but this I know, that if I live until to-morrow I shall endeavor to find out in some way if this young woman is a Christian."

He said the words solemnly as if registering a vow to an unseen witness, and then he knelt in prayer and offered a petition for this stranger beneath his father's roof, that she might know and love Jesus, and that if it were to be his privilege to show her the light that he might be guided by the Spirit.

Then he lay down with the joy of expectation in his soul.

7

A Strange Love Story

For some reason best known to herself Evelyn Rutherford chose to appear at the breakfast table the next morning.

She was not expected. Without a word being said, mother and daughter and father too had taken it for granted that their guest would sleep and leave them to breakfast alone with the son and brother.

But she came in without any apparent hurry just as they were sitting down and the brother, who did not yet understand the state of the case with regard to their guest, hastened to draw out a chair and then looking about for his own seat, exclaimed:

"Why, Allison, you have counted wrong. You forgot so soon that I had come home. I did not think it of you, sister mine. You have but four plates."

Allison, whose cheeks were flaming and whose disappointment was great, murmured something about the waffles and that she was not going to sit down, which decision was arrived at on the spur of the moment, and vanished into the kitchen to hide her confusion and dismay. She had not counted on this possibility, and actual tears came into her eyes as she bent over the waffle iron to butter it, while it spluttered at the cool butter in much such a heated way as she would have enjoyed voicing her feelings.

In the dining room the young man carried the weight of the conversation, and strangely enough it was addressed to the guest almost entirely. He did not realize it, but his whole mind was largely filled with studying this girl with a view to gaining an influence over her for good, or at least finding out whether she needed it. He was not so conceited as to think that of course all people with whom he came into contact needed his help.

He was conscious of being quite happy. He was once more in his dear home, surrounded by those who loved him and whose smiles and voices could always make glad sunshine for him, and he was being given a chance to redeem the past.

But the gentle mother was troubled. She had watched her daughter's speaking face and knew the keen disappointment she was suffering, and she was such a mother that she thoroughly suffered with her. She knew Allison's delight in talking freely with her brother, in waiting upon him and asking questions; and she knew that the visitor made a complete bar to all these pleasures, for Allison was shy and reserved beyond most girls. Her daughter's feelings filled her thoughts so entirely as to leave little time to worry about her son; but occasionally, as she caught a bright look on his face and saw the beautiful face of the city girl light up with smiles as she replied, she began to fear that after all Allison was right and there was cause for worry here.

Certainly Evelyn Rutherford was fascinating when she chose to be. She was dressed again in white, with the offending gold buckle, and as the morning had in it a tinge of frost, she had added a scarlet jacket which was exceedingly becoming. The mother could not deny that the vision was beautiful, and yet she had not thought there would be sympathy between these two. Neither could she wonder that the girl wished to please the young man seated opposite to her, as she looked with a mother's admiration on the fine form and strong, noble features of her boy.

But the boy suddenly became aware that, though the golden-brown waffles and amber syrup were vanishing rapidly and he had done his share of helping them onward, his sister, who came and went with very red cheeks, was not having any. When she came in with the next steaming plateful he suddenly arose and took it from her.

"Now sit down, Allison," he said, "and I will show you how well I remember my early training in waffle-baking, sister mine."

He took her, before she was aware of what he was going to do, and placed her in his chair, deftly gathering his own soiled dishes and placing before her a clean plate from the sideboard behind him. But his sister was in no mind to sit before the guest just now and try to eat. Swallow a mouthful she knew she could not and she did not wish the other girl to know it. She resisted her brother, urging several reasons why he must not bake the waffles, and finally followed him to the kitchen, only to be laughingly but persistently brought back and seated again. In a few minutes the young man returned with a plate of rather melancholy waffles, it must be confessed, compared with those which had gone before, but triumph on his face.

"They burned," he explained, "because I had so much trouble with Allison, but the next will be all right, now I've got my hand in," and he marched back to the kitchen looking very funny in his mother's big check apron he had donned, tied up high under his arms.

During all this pleasant home play Evelyn Rutherford looked on in amazement. It was as if she caught a glimpse of what her own childhood might have been if she had been blest with a mother and a true home. How pleasant it would be to have a brother who cared for one like that! It was not put on for show, she felt sure as she eyed him keenly. No, she had been positive from her first meeting with him that he was a man from another world than her own. Fancy Dick caring whether she had waffles or not, let alone taking the trouble to bake them for her, if he only had all he wanted for himself. As for baking waffles, either of them would be obliged to starve if it came to that, for they had no more idea than kittens what went into their make-up.

She began to look at Allison in a new light, with a lingering undertone of envy. True, this other girl had missed much of which her own life was composed; but did she not have some things that made up for their loss that were even better, perhaps?

Allison, meanwhile, was having a very hard time with her breakfast, and her mother, perceiving this, made an excuse to send the rest away from the table as soon as possible. She sent her son from the kitchen, hoping he would go at once to his sister. She told him they must get up some pleasant occupation for them all for the morning, and he, nothing loth, went to the piazza in search of Allison. She had left the breakfast room and he supposed he should find her with her guest. His heart was light at the thought of his cherished sister with this girl, who was a queen in high circles. It was what he could have wished.

But Allison had fled to her room to let fall the pent-up tears, and Miss Rutherford was standing on the piazza alone, fingering a lovely scarlet spray of the vine that covered the porch. He reached up and picked it for her, thinking what a crown it would make in her beautiful black hair. She accepted it pleasantly and fastened it in the gold clasp of her belt, where it well accorded with the crimson coat she wore with its moss-green velvet collar-facing.

The young man proposed a walk to the post office in the crisp October air, and searched for his sister to accompany them.

"Allison," he called, "where are you? Come down. We are going to the post office. Get your hat and hurry, dear. It is glorious out of doors."

A muffled voice that tried to sound natural answered from upstairs, "I can't come just now, Maurice. Don't wait for me." The while she frantically bathed her red eyes and swollen cheeks and scanned them hopelessly in the glass, her heart wrung with desire to go, and dislike of part of the company she should be in.

It may be that Maurice did not have his usual quick perceptions about him, or his mind was filled with another subject, for contrary to his custom he did not urge her and insist upon waiting, but turned to Miss Rutherford with an eagerness which would have made his sister's heart still heavier, had she been there to see.

She heard the steps go down the walk, and peeped out from the sheltering curtain to watch her brother and guest go slowly down the walk and out the gate talking and laughing together as if they did not miss her, and her much-tried soul threw itself into another abandonment of weeping, not caring now for the red eyes which would have plenty of time, she felt sure, to regain their wonted look ere they were called to meet a scrutinizing gaze again.

Evelyn Rutherford, as she walked down the pleasant shaded street with the handsome, well-built young man by her side, wondered at the beauty of the place and that she had not noticed it when she arrived. There were spacious grounds and houses comfortable and pretentious. There must be some life worth living, even in this place. Did all these homes know a life such as the Greys lived? What was it that made the difference? She meant to find out. It was interesting, anyway, and she began to be glad she had come.

And now Maurice Grey had his opportunity, long coveted, at last. He was alone with her in a quiet, pleasant place with a reasonably long walk before him, and the one for whom he thought he had a message seemed ready to listen to anything he had to say. And yet he found it was not so easy after all. How was he to begin? He had thought much about it and planned the way he should say it many times, but somehow, with her beautiful eyes upon him and her bewitching laughter in his ears, none of those solemn sentences seemed to fit. He kept thinking back to the strange surroundings of their last meeting and feeling a sort of kinship of soul with her, and yet his longing for her salvation was just as great. He must not wait. He must not waste this opportunity. Already a part of the distance to the office had been traveled. Who knew how soon something would occur to break in upon the opportunity and it would be gone forever? Was he to waste this one also? With sudden eagerness he broke off in a sentence about some mutual friends they were speaking of and said:

"Miss Rutherford, pardon me for interrupting this line of thought, but my heart is so full of something I want to say to you, that I do not feel I can wait any longer."

Evelyn turned wondering eyes upon him. She was not without experience with young men. Not a few had told her of their undying affection, and asked for hers in return. These opening words sounded almost like some of theirs. Could it be that she was to add him to the list of men whom she rather despised in her heart for pledging their life and being ready to give their all to a pretty face without knowing much about the heart that was behind it? She had not time to reason this out. The idea merely flashed into being and flashed out again as it was quickly followed by the certainty that there was something of a vastly different nature to be spoken of, with a consciousness of satisfaction that this man was different from those others.

"I have blamed myself and have suffered for a whole year," went on her companion, "that I did not speak before, and have longed and hardly hoped for this opportunity."

In wondering silence Evelyn walked by his side. All sorts of possibilities went through her brain, none of which seemed adequate for the intensity of his language. She began to think that after all it must be a proposal and a sense of pleasure filled her at the thought. Then her pride rose in arms as she realized once more that his face did not look as if he were going to ask for her hand in marriage. She must not be blamed for making this the central thought of her life. It had been the only end to be attained, set forth to her from her babyhood. Even her father had unconsciously fostered it. Her nurses and teachers had trained her for the time when she would be married; her friends and associates talked of nothing else than their conquests. Naturally it seemed to her a thing worth boasting that she had won the love of many men. She was yet to learn that the love of one true man is worth a life's devotion, and the love of the hundred who fling their hearts about to the highest bidder or the prettiest face, and then furbish them up again for the next trial as good as new, is not worth a thought.

The young man had paused and Evelyn's eyes were lifted to meet such a hungering, tender gaze that she dropped them immediately. It was a different look from any she had ever met before. What did it mean? She had never yet met one in whose eyes blazed a passion for souls, that look that is the nearest reflection of his likeness earth can give. She did not understand it and it choked her.

It was not at all what he had planned to say. The Spirit seemed to guide his low-spoken, impassioned words:

"I have a confession to make to you, and I am humiliated more than I can tell you at my shortcomings. A year ago I spent nearly three hours in your company. I talked of my family, my friends, my books, and my best life, but so far as I can remember I breathed no word of my best and dearest Friend."

The listener almost halted. Had he then brought her out here to tell her he was engaged? And for what? Did he fear she would expect his attention? Had she shown a particular delight in his society? The ready scorn mounted to her face, but melted as his words went on.

"It may seem strange to you, Miss Rutherford, that I love Jesus Christ better than my life, and have consecrated myself to his service. But I do, and I want you to know that he is a dear friend, and that his service is my highest joy. It seems incredible that feeling as I do I should allow myself to be in the company of any one for three hours without hinting anything that would lead that one to suppose that I knew Jesus Christ, and I can only say that I am ashamed and humiliated, and have resolved in future to witness for my Master wherever I may have opportunity."

If the young man by her side had suddenly burst out in an eloquent tone in the Choctaw language, or in Sanskrit, or some other equally unknown tongue, Miss Rutherford would not have been more surprised. A wild thought that he might be losing his mind flitted past her, but a look into the calm, steady eyes watching her so earnestly put that to flight. She looked down once more. There seemed to be nothing for her to say and she felt that he was not done.

"I am going to make a clean breast of it and tell you the whole story in as few words as possible. That night after I met you at the old ruin it all came over me that I had been with you so long and might never see you again, and yet I had not even found out if you loved my Saviour. We had compared notes about our tastes in books and many other things. We seemed in harmony on many questions. It grieved me more and more as I thought of it that I had not found out if you were planning to spend eternity in heaven, and that I had said no word to urge you to in case you were not thinking of it. And so I made bold to pray for you. I hope you will not feel it was presumption. And as I prayed I grew to long so for you to love Christ that sometimes I felt I must try to do something about it, though there seemed nothing I could do but go on praying. And so I have prayed for you every day since we last met." He paused and looked down at the silent girl beside him.

"Are you angry with me, Miss Rutherford, for presuming

to take such an interest in your welfare?" There was a pleading in his tone which compelled her to answer, though all the haughtiness was gone from her voice and it was quite unsteady.

"No, I am not angry," she said softly.

"And you will believe that my Saviour was and is more to me than my very life, in spite of the fact that I have done nothing to prove it to you?"

"I have known from the beginning that you were different from every one else I ever met," answered Evelyn. "But I did not understand what made it—and—I do not think I understand now."

"And will you let me try to tell you? May I have the joy of bringing to you that great, great love that Jesus has for you?"

"And so 'twas a love story after all," mused Evelyn, and one in which her experience stood her in no stead.

The tall elms dropped the yellow leaves and the maples their crimson before them as they walked down the quiet streets. The interested neighbors looked out upon them and wondered, but the destiny of a soul was in the balance and the two who were most interested thought not of anything else.

"Maria, just come here, quick!" said Rebecca Bascomb, peeping through the closed blinds of the parlor where she was dusting. "Forever! If that ain't Maurice Grey! When did he come home? Ain't he grown? I never thought he'd be so grand looking. And who's that with him? His sister? No, you never saw Allison out in any such rig as that. A white dress in the morning! and a red flannel sack! I'll be beat! She looks for all the world like a circus rider. Did you ever? Who can she be, tricked out like that? He ain't been and got married has he? Maybe she's some actress he's brought home as his bride. I should think if that's so the fam'ly 'd never want to lift their heads again, as down on the theatre as they've always been. Step out o' sight, Maria, she's lookin' this way. I think I'll run over and take that recipe for fruit cake Mrs. Grey asked for last fall, and borrow her cookie cutter this afternoon. Ours is all wore out."

If our destinies could be affected by every word that is spoken about us or every glance of misunderstanding that is thrown upon us, how precarious would be our way. And how trivial will seem some of our thoughts about others when we realize at the judgment day that at the very time we were criticising them, eternal and momentous questions were being decided.

> *God's ways . . . soon or late . . .*
> *Touch the shining hills of day.*
> *The evil cannot brook delay,*
> *The good can well afford to wait.*

8

A Promised Prayer

Meanwhile Allison in her room wept out her bitterness and knelt for comfort. Then she bathed her eyes and arranged her hair, and busied herself about little duties in her room till the traces of tears should be gone, wondering presently why her mother did not call her or come in search of her.

The loving mother, supposing Allison to be with the other two young people, patiently did the work in the kitchen, rejoicing that the shadow was lifted from her dear child's heart and hoping to see her bright and sunny when she returned. It was so unusual to have Allison other than laughing and sweet that it oppressed her. She was glad to have her out in the sunshine, and sang softly about her work the verse of a hymn which had lingered with her from last Sunday's service:

> *Spirit of God, descending,*
> *Fill our hearts with heavenly joy;*

An Unwilling Guest

Love with every passion blending,
Pleasure that can never cloy;
Thus provided, pardoned, guided,
Nothing can our peace destroy.

Perchance the evil one wished to show her that this last line of her hymn was not true, for at that moment for some reason she was moved to go into the sitting room on an errand, and raising her eyes to the window she saw walking slowly up the driveway in deep and earnest converse, her son and their guest. The glimmer of the brilliant scarlet jacket flashed between the trees, and the mother looked for the duller blue of her daughter's to follow, but look as she might no Allison was in sight, and the two who walked thus together did not seem to need a third. She wondered what it could mean. Had Allison remained at the store on some petty excuse? Was the child carrying her ill feeling so far? The song died on her lips and peace picked up her fluttering garments and fled for the time being.

The guest went straight to her room. The mother sought her son with a troubled expression which the son could not fathom, and which in his exalted mood he soon forgot. Where was Allison? In her room, he thought. She had asked them not to wait for her and they had been to the post office. He was reading letters, but his mind did not seem to be upon them. His face wore an abstracted air, "illumined," was the word his mother thought of when he looked up at her in answer to her question:

"My son, did I understand you that you had met Miss Rutherford before last evening?"

"Yes, mother, she is an old friend. I knew her in New York, and met her abroad. Her brother was in college with me," and so far had he progressed in his acquaintance with the lady in question that he actually thought as he spoke that his words, "she is an old friend," were true.

It was then her mother's heart started up in fear at that look upon her boy's face. Oh, if he should put his heart in the keeping of one who was not worthy!

"Do you know her character, my boy?" she asked, and if Maurice had not been so abstracted he would have noticed that his mother's face wore an unwonted look of pain, almost agony. "Is she a—Christian?"

"Mother, she——" he hesitated, and then with his peculiarly winning smile put both his hands in hers just as he used to do when he was a little boy giving her sweet confidences, and looking frankly in her eyes finished, "Mother, she needs Christ. Will you help me pray for her?"

There was that in the reply that baffled the mother while it could not be resisted. She kissed him and gave her promise tenderly. She would not ask him further of his relations to their guest. She knew he would tell her if there was anything she should know. She knew she could trust him, and yet her heart was troubled until she took her worry to that never-failing source of comfort, her Saviour. She was a woman who, in an unusual sense, had learned to lay her burden at her Lord's feet and leave it there. Sometimes her friends did not understand this calmness and were wont to think her indifferent or blind to possible dangers; but those who knew her best had learned to believe that it was simple trust which smoothed her brow and kept her young and fair.

She went to Allison at last with the care gone from her face and found her daughter, not in her room, but down in the kitchen flying around with unnecessary haste in preparation for an elaborate meal to make up for her absence from the work in the morning. She seemed cheery, though her mother could see it was a forced emotion, but the wise mother judged it best to accept the cheeriness and not let her daughter know just at present that she was aware of her having remained at home all the morning.

They talked about the dinner and the mother ignored the fact that the dishes were out of the usual order of every-day planning. She entered into the work with as much seeming eagerness as Allison was manifesting and between them they managed to keep up a semblance of sunshine.

"Maurice said he would have the surrey ready right after dinner. He thinks it would be pleasant for you to take Miss Rutherford up the hill drive. The coloring of the woods will be in perfection of beauty now. You would better plan to start right after dinner so that you will have plenty of time. I will see to the dishes."

"Oh, mother!" said Allison in dismay, appearing in the

kitchen door with the butter plate in her hand, "aren't you going too?"

"I can't, dear. You know it is the missionary society day. I have one of the papers to read and it would not do to be absent. Besides, Miss Rutherford has sent some messages to them by me about the box we are packing. I really could not stay away."

Allison turned back to the table upon which she was putting the finishing touches before calling the family to dinner. She could see her brother sitting in the parlor by the window, his fine profile outlined against the window, and she could hear the soft strains of the piano touched by a cultivated hand. Allison could play herself, and had a tender touch all her own which reached hearts. But she knew she could not play like that. She could see the appreciation in her brother's attitude. Her heart rose in rebellion again. Was it jealousy also that was seizing her as its prey? She walked to the dining-room window where she had thought out so many disagreeable problems during the past three days, and leaned her head against the cool pane. As she studied the fretwork of vines and tendrils on the wall outside her chin grew firm with resolve. When she turned away from that window and went silently about her interrupted work she knew in her heart that she did not intend to take that drive in the afternoon, and she also thought she knew a way out of it. Nevertheless she sat at the table and listened to the plans, acquiescing quietly in all they said about the road to take and the hour of starting. It was arranged to give her time for helping with the dinner dishes before she went. She had hoped they would let her off to help her mother, but it became evident that something else would have to be planned.

Promptly at the time agreed upon the carriage drove up to the door and Miss Rutherford was handed in. Allison appeared a moment afterward carrying two books in her hand.

"Well, sister, do you propose to pursue the study of literature this afternoon while the rest of us feast on nature?" asked her brother, as he took the books while she got in. "Library books!" he said, frowning slightly. "Now, Allison, you are not planning to go around there first, are you? It will delay us awfully, for you are morally certain to be longer than you expect, and besides, it is out of the way. Can't you let these go another week?"

"No, the time is up," said Allison with satisfaction.

"Well, what of that? A fine? I'll pay it gladly if you'll give it up."

Allison looked troubled. She had not thought of this. Maurice was apt to carry his point when he was anxious.

"Maurice, really they ought to go back to-day. Mrs. Lynch has been waiting for that blue book and I told her we should be done with it to-day and she promised to be there and get it before any one else snatched it up."

Maurice whistled and reluctantly got into the carriage the while Allison's brow cleared. Having set her will not to go she really wished not to do so.

Arrived at the library she promptly arranged the rest. She had been gone but two or three minutes when Miss Burton, one of the ladies interested in the library, came out to the carriage.

"Dr. Grey, good-afternoon," she said. "Your sister has been so kind as to take my place as librarian this afternoon, as I have quite a severe headache, and she asked me to tell you not to wait for her. She is very good indeed."

As there was nothing to be said to this the carriage started on. Wily Allison knew there could be no contention over the matter if she sent Miss Burton to speak for her, and she set herself to straighten out a muddle in the books with the firm intention of forgetting her troubles if she could. However that was not so easily managed, as she found herself from time to time following the carriage as it wound its way among the hills, and about midway in the afternoon it suddenly occurred to her that if her object had been real love and fear for her brother she would have gone along, for surely the stranger could less easily exercise her wiles upon his unsuspecting heart with a third person present than if they were entirely alone. Poor Allison! She vexed herself with the thought that she had been selfish in staying at home, and made several mistakes in setting down the number of books returned. When the hour for closing came she was weary and glad to walk quietly home.

Meantime, the two who were riding into the glory of the afternoon could not be said to have really missed her. Her brother felt now and then a twinge of pity that she was shut up from the beauties they were enjoying all this long afternoon, but it never once came to his comprehension that his sister was really suffering because she was having so little of his own precious society. He was not an egotistical young man. Besides, his present occupation was pleasant.

They talked of many things. Now and then the young man would speak of his Christian work, or of the God who made the beauties they were looking upon. Once they stopped the carriage on the brow of a lofty hill where two other hills gave way and left an unexpected view of valley, river, and more purple hills in the distance. The clear October sky was perfect, as blue and bright as skies are made, with more of decision in it than comes in June, and with a few tiny, sharp, white scurrying clouds here and there like messengers hurrying about intent upon weighty matters in connection with the coming of the winter season.

They were silent as they looked. Such a view takes words away. Presently the young man said:

"I always think when I come to this spot how much I should like to be just here when Jesus Christ comes back to earth again. I like to wonder how the clouds will look, whether it will be sunset or early in the morning, or will the sky be like this. It seems sometimes, when there is a glorious sunset, as if he must be coming, and the gates of heaven have begun to open for the throng of angels. And the dead in Christ! How wonderful it will all be, with Jesus in their midst!"

The girl by his side looked up into his face. She had come into the front seat that she might better see the view. She could also the more easily watch the changing expressions on her companion's speaking face. His look was rapt now, and as he went on to speak in a few words more of the Jesus whom he loved, Evelyn Rutherford for the first time in her life felt that there really was such a person living now as Jesus Christ. Also for the first time, strange as it may seem, she saw a man who seemed to realize this presence as much as he did that of any fellow-creature. She could see that this was a reality with him, and she wondered and was awed.

They were both silent as the horse turned to wind down the hill again and around by another way home. Evelyn could not think of anything to say that would not seem frivolous, and she was conscious of a distinct wish not to seem frivolous before this man.

"Miss Rutherford, may I be so bold as to make a request of you?" asked the young man, turning his bright, earnest eyes upon her as they neared the foot of the hill. "I have prayed for you so long, will you let me feel that you are praying for yourself? It will be a true joy to me."

It was a long time before there was any answer. She had looked at him at first with a quick, startled gaze and dropped her eyes again. Her fingers twined among the red and gray fringe of the heavy golf cape she wore, and the color crept slowly up over her smooth cheek till it almost reached the shadow of the dark, drooping lashes. Afterward, when he was far away, a vision of that fair face outlined against the dark green cloth of the golf-hood lingered in his mind, though he was not conscious of noting details as he watched for her answer. At last she said huskily: "How could I? I would not know what to say."

The answer was ready. "Will you ask him to make you willing to be his? Are you willing to be made willing? Can you ask him that?"

"Do you mean, will I just say those words, 'Make me willing to belong to—Christ'?" she said with a slow hesitation, like a child uncertainly learning its lesson. It was all so new to her.

"Yes," he said eagerly, "ask Jesus Christ that every day. Will you? And try with all your heart to realize as much as you can that you are talking to a real, living being, and try to want what you are asking?"

The silence was a long one this time, broken occasionally by a little explanatory word from the young man, who fairly held his breath for her answer. He knew she was considering it by the drooped eyelashes and the nervous fingers in the fringe. He prayed in his heart with longing that would not be denied.

They were nearing the village when at last she raised her eyes in answer to his low, "Won't you do it?" spoken for the fifth time with wistful beseeching.

"I will try," she said, in a tone that none of her New York friends would have recognized.

"Thank God!" was the immediate, joyous response.

They neither of them said any more, but the glow on his face told, as from time to time she stole a glance at him, that he was deeply and truly glad. Just why she could not understand. Her promise seemed to her to mean so little, and yet she hesitated about making it because it had seemed to mean so much to him that it troubled and embarrassed her.

They drove up to the door with a quiet gravity in their demeanor. The glow of the setting sun illumined their faces and a glow of something even more beautiful uplifted their hearts.

Allison, as she watched them, decided that it had been very wrong for her to stay at home that afternoon. They had only had more chance to become intimate.

9

An Unexpected Summons

As Maurice Grey unharnessed the horse and closed the stable door he was planning how he might help this soul into a knowledge of Jesus Christ. He thanked God for giving him the opportunity, and manlike planned what he would say and do in the days that were to follow. He hoped it would be possible for him to prolong his visit into ten days or two weeks. He had written the busy physician, whose partner and assistant he was about to become, saying that he would like to do so if he was not immediately needed. He smiled to think how well things were happening, and what a wonderful plan was God's, to allow his children to do such great work for him. There were one or two little books he would like to read aloud to Miss Rutherford if she was willing. Perhaps to-morrow would afford opportunity. Allison would enjoy hearing them too, though if he were alone with Miss Rutherford he might be able to help out with explanations which would fit her case, which perhaps might be embarrassing to her if another person were present. By the way, he must ask his sister to pray for their guest. Allison could be a great help. She was a grand sister for a man to have. She understood and had sympathy.

Poor Allison, at that moment cutting the bread with firmly closed lips and eyes that held the burning tears back by main force! If she could but have known what her brother was thinking in his heart.

Then the young man went in to find on the hall table a telegram just arrived. He tore it open in haste, and with that slight premonition of evil which always comes with those yellow missives. No matter how used we may be to them, or how much we may expect them, there is always that dread possibility of what they may contain.

"I am called abroad on urgent business. Sail to-morrow. Can you come at once? Wire answer."

Thus the telegram read, and the name signed below was that of the great doctor whose partner he was about to become. There was no getting away from that call. It was Duty, stern and plain and spelled with a capital letter. And yet he had thought but a moment before that a higher call had bidden him here to a work for which he was all eagerness. He felt a rebellious stirring in his heart, and then began to wonder if there was not some selfishness in his desire to stay as well as eagerness to do God's will. Supposing he should answer, "I cannot come." What would happen? The world would go on just the same. Doctor Atlee would do something. Ah, but what would become of the cases that none but he and Doctor Atlee understood? What foolishness was he thinking? Of course he must go.

Then he went to the supper table with a grave face to match Allison's. He tried to be cheery and keep the news of his departure to himself until the meal was over, but he soon saw that his mother and the guest had noticed his abstraction. He must explain.

Disappointment and dismay fell upon the little group; the father, because he had planned a good talk with long discussions on various topics with this dear son, who was almost a stranger now; the mother, forgetting her own heart in sorrow for Allison, who she knew would keenly feel her brother's hasty departure; and Allison herself, because she was suddenly overwhelmed with grief at her own conduct, and saw before her her punishment: her brother gone, and the few short hours she might have enjoyed in his society lost because she would not share them with another.

As for the guest, blank desolation settled upon the town of Hillcroft, and she was again in a waste and barren land. Besides, how was she to know how to carry out that remarkable promise which she had but just made?

The fact being accepted, supper was no longer considered to be of importance. The time-table took a prominent position on the table, and a discussion about trains arose and was settled. In the midst of this the traveler discovered that it was growing late and rushed upstairs to make his few hasty preparations. Downstairs they sat about and waited, no one seeming to know what to do. Allison tried to clear off the table, but the hot tears blinded her, and she finally gave up the attempt and went to see if she could not help her brother.

Maurice was just snapping his gripsack together as she tapped on his door and entered. He turned to her with a loving smile.

"Allison dear, I am sorry you did not have the lovely drive this afternoon. It was too bad for you to miss it," he said.

She hastened to offer her assistance, and so kept away from the subject of the drive. She would not now have him guess her true reason for staying at home for anything. To have her dear brother know the foolishness, wickedness, and pride of her heart would be too great a humiliation, so she said:

"Isn't there something I can do to help you?"

"No, Allison, I have everything in, I think, unless—oh yes, I am glad I remembered that. Allison, I wish you would pray for Miss Rutherford—not in any ordinary way you know. Let us claim that promise, sister mine, as we have so many times before, 'If two of you shall agree on earth as touching anything that they shall ask, it shall be done for them.' Now it is time for me to go. Good-bye, dear."

There was a shadow by the door where Allison stood so that he could not see the expression that crossed her face as he stooped to kiss her. Miss Rutherford again! How strangely she had come into everything, even this good-bye to her brother! The tears blinded her so that she stumbled and almost fell as she followed the unsuspecting brother downstairs.

It was all over in such a very few minutes and the household were left standing where he had bade them good-bye, recalling his last words and looking at the place where he had sat and stood a moment before.

One word the young man had had with the guest alone before he left. She stood in the half-lighted parlor looking out upon the moonlit world and feeling a sudden homesickness. He stepped into the room and she turned. Taking her hand he said:

"Miss Rutherford, I cannot tell you how glad I am that I have found you here. You will remember your promise? Perhaps you will also remember now and then that I am praying too? And, Miss Rutherford, my sister Allison lives very near to Jesus. Maybe she might be of help to you. And there are ways in which you can help her if you will."

The others coming in just then there was no chance for her to reply.

She went to her room almost immediately after he left. She felt that the family was depressed by his sudden going away. She was so herself and did not wish them to see it. She bade them good-night in a sweeter way than she had done before; they could not help but notice it. It was as if the winning way she had used with the young man had descended to them. Mrs. Grey pondered what it might mean. Allison, in a softened and reproachful mood, saw but one more reason for blaming herself for her impulsive prejudices.

Evelyn sat down in her room and let her whole acquaintance with the young man just gone sweep over her, culminating in the strange talk they had had that day and the ride and her promise. Why had she made such a promise? She began to see as the day drew toward its end that this promise was going to be a troublesome thing. Perhaps she would forget it. She half hoped she would. And yet—if she should meet him again? Oh, no. She would not like to tell him she had forgotten. She liked being faithful to what she had said to him even though he should never know. He was that kind of a man. One could not help admiring him and one must be true all the way through to him. And where was the fascination? Why should she, so differently brought up, with higher social standing, and believing herself to be worth the interest of any man living, feel in the presence of this man that she was humble as the dust at his feet and he almost a god?

He was like his family. It was a sort of fanaticism, this talk and this unnatural goodness. It was the kind of thing that she had always despised and sneered at. Was it possible that she had at last seen more than this in it? Yes, she admitted to herself, she could but see the effect that religion had on the lives of this one family, and that they seemed to be sweet and natural about their goodness and not overpoweringly egotistical and disagreeable with their oughts and ought-nots, like a few other religionists she had known. There was Allison. How sweetly she had seemed to give up that charming drive. And yet one could easily see that she loved her brother almost to idolizing him. She had seen the look that overspread her face on his arrival, and had been an unseen witness of his parting kiss to her and saw her turn away sobbing when he was gone. It must have been a great disappointment to give up the afternoon all for that fussy, little, dried-up old maid with a headache.

She herself never could have done it. She was sure she did not want to be made into a person who would always have to be thinking of others' comforts and forgetting herself in order to do disagreeable things for other people. What was that he had asked her?

"Are you willing to be made willing to be his?" Then he had known she was not willing, not ready, to give up her wishes and be this other thing that he and Christ—she thought the word reverently, for since the vision she had been given on the hilltop she would never think the name of Christ carelessly again—wished her to be. And he had asked her to pray against herself; to ask to be made willing, to be made to want something she did not want to want. She had promised to try to ask this. She had not realized how much that meant.

How could she ask it? She must ask to be made like— Allison perhaps, or like Mrs. Grey, who cared not for her world, and she did not want to be like them, though she looked at them with wonder and a certain amount of dawning appreciation. They were good and there was no pleasure in goodness. Why should she do this thing in response to a stranger whom she had met but three times, and who was dominated by fanatical views? She could not finish. The power of the stranger over her was so great that she admitted she would do what he had asked in spite of all her feelings.

And then her heart, accustomed always to questioning itself of these things, inquired why there was this power and this fascination, this desire to please a man who might never in this world even know of it? Was she in love with him? She had often asked herself that question about other young men whose friendship and attentions were hers if she chose to take them. Sometimes the answer had been, "I do not know," sometimes, "I like him," or perhaps, "I might care for him," but more often, "No, I do not love him," as these other men passed before her in review. Now as she asked this question of her heart it seemed a profanation. He had not offered her his love. Perhaps he had none left for earthly beings, except his own family of course, aside from the love of saving them, but she felt her heart throb with a strange new joy that he had cared for the saving of her soul. He was not in the least the kind of a man she had expected herself to love when the time came, and it was not a question of love now. It was something infinitely higher and greater, and she supposed better than any earthly love. It was a question of the love of this Christ which was offered her. She impatiently put that other question aside as improper even to think of now. She would not demean herself longer in her own eyes by classing this man with all the other men she knew. Her soul had recognized the true and the good, and for once she would shake off all prejudices and desires and do this one thing he had asked. She would not ask herself if she wished to appear well in his eyes again. Of course she did, but in what measure it did not matter. That she would stand very well with him if he knew her true self she had no hope. His ideal was his sister Allison. That was what he would like her to become. Had he not told her to go to her for an example? Well, there was no use in trying to be such a person, for she never could and did not want to if she could. Besides, her life would not admit of it. When she was back again in New York with Mr. Worthington and her other friends she would forget all about this uncomfortable conscience which seemed to be developing within her, or this strange fancy, but now she must do as she had promised, and the sooner the better, to have it over with. Then she would search her trunk for the very most exciting novel she could find, and read for an hour or two and forget all about the wearisome little town in which she was immured.

She turned the gas out and knelt down by the bay-window seat to pray for the first time in her life, for she had not been taught to pray as a child. It came to her as she knelt that this was the first time she had knelt thus with a real intention to pray. Once a plain-faced woman who had come to be her nurse tried to make her pray, but she stamped her foot and declared she wouldn't, and the woman very soon afterward had been dismissed by the housekeeper because she threatened to tell of something the housekeeper was doing behind the master's back. She had actually been the only bit of religious life that had touched Evelyn's childhood intimately, and Evelyn had not liked her because she sat by the window and cried at night when her little charge was going to sleep. Weeping in a woman always irritated Evelyn. She rarely wept herself unless she was very angry, and then only when every other way of expressing emotion failed.

Two others knelt at the throne of grace in that same house and at that moment, the mother, with tender petitions for the one for whom her boy had requested prayer, but with a drawing away from the girl in spite of herself lest she had come between her boy and his family; Allison, with bitter tears of repentance and reluctant request for the salvation of her sometime enemy. The feeling against Miss Rutherford had been so deeply grounded that it was with the greatest difficulty Allison could overcome it and ask what she was bound to do with any degree of honesty. Even then the supplication was but half-hearted.

The moon, high in the heavens, looked into the bay window and shone upon the bowed head waiting there till she felt that she had performed the ceremony of a prayer to her satisfaction. And out under the moonlighted sky miles away rushed the train, and one young man on that train was lifting up his soul in entreaty that would not be denied.

It was a hard thing, that first prayer. Evelyn Rutherford, Naaman-like in her pride, could not bring her haughty lips to utter those simple words she had been told. She knelt long, trying to compose a more formal petition, but they, unaccustomed, would not come at her bidding, and at last she said humbly, "O Christ, make me willing to be good." Even then, as she hastily arose, it came to her that he had asked her to try to say these words "with all her heart," and she feared that was not possible. However, she had tried, and her conscience was satisfied with the duty discharged. She hastened to relight her gas and search for the novel. Having found it, she settled herself for an hour of relief from the tension under which she had been; but the baron and the lady who were introduced in the first page seemed trifling and frivolous, and their ambitions so worthless beside the view of life she had been gazing upon recently, that she closed the book and went to bed.

Unconsciously her point of view in life had changed with even this short stay in such a household. Had she been put back into her old life at once this would doubtless have faded away like some half-forgotten dream, to be remembered only when life seemed vain and empty. But God had not so appointed.

> *From one stage of our being to the next*
> *We pass unconscious o'er a slender bridge,*
> *The momentary work of unseen hands,*
> *Which crumbles down behind us; looking back,*
> *We see the other shore, the gulf between,*
> *And marveling how we won to where we stand,*
> *Content ourselves to call the builder Chance.*
>
> *We call our sorrows Destiny, but ought*
> *Rather to name our high successes so.*

10

New Reading for Miss Rutherford

The next morning they awoke to find the brilliant weather gone and a gray drizzle settled upon the face of the earth. The day seemed exactly fitted to their moods, for each of the three women in the house had spent a wakeful night. Mrs. Grey, however, had been able to leave her burdens at the foot of the cross in the early morning, and when Evelyn opened her room door to go downstairs, and then went back for something she had forgotten, she heard her moving about across the hall opening windows, throwing back bedding to air where the dampness could not reach it, and singing in the sweet, crooning voice she used so much about her work:

> "Ye fearful saints, fresh courage take!
>   The clouds ye so much dread
> Are big with mercy and will break
>   With blessings on your head.
>
> "His purposes will ripen fast,
>   Unfolding every hour;
> The bud may have a bitter taste,
>   But sweet will be the flower."

Evelyn walked slowly through the hall to catch every clearly spoken word, and as she went down the stairs she heard the closing words:

> "God is his own interpreter,
>   And he will make it plain."

The listener wondered how it would seem to believe those things and live like that. Would she have been different with a mother like this one? No wonder Doctor Grey was such a man as he was. How could he help it living in such an atmosphere?

On Allison's face was a look of fixed purpose. The task her brother had imposed upon her should be performed, as much as in her lay, though she steadily believed that it was useless and she could be of no help to such a girl. Others might, but not she. Her nature had nothing in common with one from the world of fashion. Allison rather prided herself on that fact, though she was unaware of it. Well, three, her mother and elderly friend and brother, all thought she was the one selected of the Lord to convert this girl. She would show them that it could not be done, at least not through her. It may be that it was because of this feeling in Allison's heart that she was not given the highest honor in the leading of this soul to Christ.

The guest herself made the way easier for a change of bearing toward her. In the midst of her night watches had come a remembrance of the words: "There are ways in which you can help her if you will." It soothed her pride, and made it easier for her to accept the thought of being helped by Allison, not that she felt in any immediate need of Allison's help. Her ideas of things were too new and crude to feel any of her own shortcomings. If she were going to do anything in this line she would prefer to study it out by herself, and not be dependent upon one who was younger and not near so worldly-wise. But she was disposed to study Allison with more interest and kindliness than before, if for no other reason than because she was the sister of the man whom she could not but admire. It would be pleasant to know what sort of women were beloved by him. Therefore she set herself to study her young hostess. At least she would discover if there were any way in which she might help her. She would have liked a chance to ask Doctor Grey what he meant by that. How did he imagine his good little sister could ever be helped by her? It must be in the way of the world.

It was in her favor that she came down to breakfast that morning after the young man left. They had supposed in their hearts that she got up early to be there with him, or to show him she was not indolent. But when she appeared that dreary morning in a crimson frock of exquisite fit, with touches here and there that showed no novice had been its designer, they could but admire her, and congratulated themselves that they could think a little better of her. Neither mother nor daughter questioned herself as to whether this willingness to see more good in the visitor was greater than it had been on account of the absence of the young man.

Evelyn talked politics with Mr. Grey during breakfast. Her father was connected quite intimately with some things in New York which interested Mr. Grey deeply, and Evelyn could talk well when she was on her native ground. The views she advanced were doubtless not her own, but those she had heard tossed back and forth across the table at the dinners in her father's house where she had presided. She had paid little heed to them, and if they had not been so oft-repeated week after week, year after year, she would doubtless never have remembered one, but now the well-worn phrases came back to her, and she surprised herself by being able to tell what this and that politician thought about such and such subjects. She had not realized that she knew their views before. Mr. Grey listened and nodded, putting in a keen question now and then, and his wife saw that what the girl said was of no little moment to him. Allison listened also as she came in now and again with plates of buckwheat cakes the like of which the New York girl had never tasted before, though she had eaten in many a place which boasted a famous cook. But somehow famous cooks know not the sweet, old, simple ways of quiet home grandmothers. Allison was trained to be interested in all the questions of the day. She had many a discussion with her father. She often read the papers to him in the evening when his eyes were weary with poring over his books in the office, and she was well-informed on both sides of many questions. She saw that what the guest was saying had a bearing on one of their much-discussed points, and once or twice she stopped and put in an animated word to her father, and he smiled and nodded and said:

"Perhaps you are right, Allison, after all, if these men think so."

Evelyn stopped then to watch this other girl and wonder. There was such a perfect feeling of comradery between her and her father. When the meal was over, instead of going into the parlor to lounge and read, as she had done the first morning, Evelyn asked quite pleasantly, "May I stay here and watch you?" and Allison had consented willingly enough, but she thought it would have been in better taste for her to have offered help, though she would not have accepted it. She did not yet realize how very far apart their two spheres had always been. Evelyn would no more have known how to go about helping than she would have known how to build a house or set a diamond.

That she did not know anything about housework, Allison began to understand as she listened to the simple questions such as a child of six brought up in a plain home might possibly ask about the commonest every-day tasks.

She grew weary after a time and went into the other room. Allison watched her through the open door and saw her go over to the low bookcase. With an impulse to do what she could she followed her, and as the guest idly read the titles of the books she touched the upper shelf.

"These are all wonderful, if you have not read them. My brother and I have kept that shelf for books that we both unqualifiedly like, books that we feel are above the ordinary." She passed her hand lovingly over the backs of the volumes and went back to finish the pudding she was stirring up for dinner. She doubted in her heart whether the guest would care for any of the books on that shelf, and why she had opened her heart thus far she did not know, except for the memory of her brother's last words. It was a little thing, so little that it did not seem worth while for her to lift her heart in a petition that it might be blest, as she often did when trying to help others, her Sunday-school boys for instance. She never gave them a book to read without the earnest heart petition. But little as it was, it was one of the links in the chain of influence that God was preparing for Evelyn Rutherford's soul.

"A Singular Life," read Evelyn, and from some strange attraction took the book down from the shelf. These books, then, were what he considered fine; "above the ordinary," his sister had said. She would read one and see.

Ordinarily the opening pages, being a conversation between a lot of young theologues, would not have been

interesting to her, but it struck her now as unique, utterly out
of the line in which she had ever read, and she went on out of
mere curiosity, becoming after a little interested in the story
and the central character, the man of the singular life who, by
the way, to her fancy seemed in some respects much like
young Doctor Grey.

She laid the book down a little before dinner and looked
wearily out of the window. The life portrayed there was so
different from her own. It was not that it attracted her so
much as it made her discontented with everything. There
was a vague longing to get back into her former self-content.
If she were only in New York. If she did but know whether
Jane Bashford had gone back to the city yet. Jane would be
glad to have her, and the Bashfords were such very old
friends that her father could not object. Besides, Jane would
be likely to invite Mr. Worthington sometimes if she suggested
it. Jane liked dashing people as well as she did.

With the thought of Mr. Worthington, however, came a
vivid flash of contrast between him and the man in whose
company she had spent a part of the last two days. She tried
to imagine him talking as Doctor Grey had done. She knew
that his conversation would have been entirely of the smart
set, their doings and sayings, and as much of a report of what
occurred at the club as he dared to tell her. It was this daring
in him that had fascinated her. It was like spice to a sated
appetite. It was something new and she enjoyed it. Here was
a man who was not afraid to tell things as they were. Of
course, he would not go too far; he knew just where to stop.
Or stay! Did he? In her heart she wavered a little. There had
been times when she had felt it necessary to exercise a little
of her ready hauteur because she instinctively feared what he
might say next; that is, he was not a man one could trust—not
like this other one. But then—and she sighed a weary sigh.
This other lived a "singular life" like the man in the book.
There might be one such in a thousand, but they were not for
her. Why should she be unsettled and unhappy in the place
that belonged to her, because somewhere in the world there
lived a man like that? He would never look at her, would
never likely come within her radius again. He had told her
himself that when he went back to New York it was to hard
work. This he had said when she invited him to call. He had

thanked her, and after a pause, looking at her earnestly had said, "Perhaps I may," and then, "sometime." It was then he had explained that his practice in partnership with the great doctor would be very confining, and that he must not entangle himself with pleasures that would take his mind from his work. She thought of it humbly now. She did not believe he meant to come. She was not altogether sure that when she went back to New York she would care to have him come, but she wished that this day and these thoughts were over, and that this ridiculous compulsory visit was over, and she could get into her normal state again. Why had she made that absurd promise? She began to have a superstitious feeling that it was at the bottom of all her unrest. Then she was called to dinner.

The pudding was delicious, and so were all the viands which preceded it, but the guest did not feel hungry. Allison asked her how she liked the book she had been reading, and she answered listlessly, "Well enough." This answer, to Allison, meant a depraved taste in reading. To brand her favorite book, which she had read and reread and then read again aloud to father and mother and brother, with a "well enough" was more than her spirit could bear. She relapsed at once into her critical state of mind, which did not even pass off when she discovered that Miss Rutherford had gone to her room and taken with her not only "A Singular Life," but also another favorite, "Heather and Snow." She would not care for either of them, Allison felt sure, and she sat down to enjoy herself for a while, and feel that she had performed her duty and it had done no good, as she had prophesied.

Several days of gloomy weather succeeded, during which time Miss Rutherford read not only two but several others of the sacred choice upper row of books. She made no comments upon them, and it cannot be denied that some of them actually bored her and she skimmed them.

Nevertheless she had determined to find out this young man's idea of life and this was one of the ways open to her. Besides, there was nothing else in the world to do. There came daily messages of affection from the plague-stricken house she was supposed to be visiting, and there came no letters of encouragement to return to New York.

A week went by and a distant cousin, to whom she had

written in her desperation, answered that she was sorry, but it seemed absolutely necessary for her to go to Boston for a little while, and she was not sure how long it would be before she would return; while another friend, still in her summer home in Tuxedo, apologized for not being able to invite her as she was having a terrible time with her servants and the house had been full of company and the baby was sick into the bargain. Evelyn curled her lip over the excuses through which she felt sure she could see, and settled herself to stay where she was with as good a grace as possible.

Then one morning a caller came to see Allison. After a few minutes in the parlor that young woman went to her mother with very red cheeks and the expression on her face that her mother knew always meant that she hoped she would say "No," to whatever request she made.

"Mother," she said, speaking in a low, nervous tone, "Ethel Haines has come to ask me to change places with her for to-morrow night—the club meeting, you know. She was to have it there and had arranged the whole programme and everything, but her invalid aunt arrived unexpectedly last night and is so ill to-day they have had to send for a trained nurse. She says they can't have the least bit of noise about the house, and her programme has a good deal of music, and you know the girls could never be still. It is quite impossible for her to have it. She wants to bring everything over here and just borrow our house, and she says she will fix everything for me when my turn comes and I can go over there. I told her I thought it was impossible, it would be too hard for you when Mary is gone. You don't think we could do it, do you?"

There was a note of almost distress in the daughter's voice as she asked this last question that made her mother look at her curiously:

"Why, daughter, I don't see why you cannot do it. It will be very little trouble. Mrs. Munson is coming to sweep the whole house the next morning, and if she brings her things over we shall only have a few cups and plates to wash. Certainly I would accommodate her if I could. It is very hard for Mrs. Haines to have her poor aunt ill so much. Tell her yes. It will help to relieve the monotony for our guest also. She is having a very dull time, I fear, with you busy so much of the time and no one even to talk to but me."

"Oh, mother!" exclaimed Allison in real dismay now, "don't you understand? We can't have it here when she is here. She would criticise and laugh everything to scorn. You have not heard her talk and I have. I undertook to tell her about this club once and mother, what do you think she said? 'Do you dance or are you devoted to cards?' And then she asked if we ever had germans. Can't you see how out of place she would be among us and how she would be a wet blanket on the whole thing?"

The mother looked grave. "Allison, I think you are really very wrong. In the first place, it matters very little what she may think of it at all or whether she laughs or scoffs. I should think this was clearly your duty. In the second place I give Miss Rutherford credit for being more of a lady than to manifest any feeling she may happen to have before a gathering of respectable young people. They may not be such as she is accustomed to be with and their habits may be different, but they live in the same world and speak the same language and have been educated in much the same courtesies. I am sure our guest will be a lady, whatever she may feel in her heart. As for being a wet blanket to the rest of you, if your club has no more spirit than to be quelled by the sight of one poor, lonely stranger from a different class in society I am ashamed of you. For one evening try to amuse her, even though it may be at the expense of a laugh or two. Laughs cannot hurt you when you are in the way of right."

"Mother, I do not like to be laughed at," said Allison, her eyes very bright.

"No, most people don't," said her mother; "but there are occasions when one might even have to pass through the fiery furnace of a laugh and trust the Form of the Fourth to keep the flames from consuming you."

Allison swallowed hard and looked down at the table. Her cheeks had grown redder, if possible. Her eyes looked as if she would like to cry if only she did not have to go back to that girl in the parlor. Mother certainly had a very blunt way of putting things sometimes. There was no getting around the truth when mother chose to speak it.

The daughter turned slowly and walked back to the parlor, to give an invitation most reluctant and ungracious for the usually hospitable Allison Grey.

The arrangements which the caller talked over with her in detail failed to interest her as much as usual and she feared that Ethel thought her not responsive enough, but her mind would wander to her own part in spite of herself and questions kept crowding into her thoughts thick and fast. What would Miss Rutherford think of it all? Would she condescend to come downstairs? Perhaps she would choose to remain in her room. Oh, the relief that would be to this poor, tried soul! But if she did come down would she array herself in that low-necked dress or perhaps another one still worse? Oh, the horror of the thought! And how could it be prevented? She could not tell her and it would likely be resented if she did. She had a right, of course, to wear what she chose.

On the whole, poor Allison's mind was in a tumult that night as she lay and tossed, trying to forget it all and go to sleep.

11

Rebecca Bascomb on Evening Dress

It remained for Rebecca Bascomb to settle the question of full dress in Hillcroft and to set Evelyn Rutherford's mind in a tumult.

It was just after breakfast the next morning and the mother and daughter were hurrying to get the dishes out of the way that they might have all the preparations for the evening complete early in the day. The sun had come out bright and clear. The air was cold and a glowing fire was burning in the corner fireplace in the parlor. At one side of this Evelyn was sitting with a book in her hand. She was not reading, but looking into the fire with a dreamy expression.

Something she read recalled to mind the expression of Doctor Grey's face during that view they had together on the hilltop. She was not always thinking of him. There had been two days when she banished every thought of the new influence which had come into her life, and though she performed her promise, she did it hastily and perfunctorily. She wrote many letters home and began to hope to get away soon. She had even written to her brother, as a last resort, though she was not quite sure where he was. His plans were not always confided to his family. Occasionally, however, the new and startling thought of a Christ—and for her—would come to her piercingly, and with it a clear vision of the face of the young man who had given it to her. She was wondering again about his life and if it was always as beautiful and spotless all through as it had seemed the few times she had seen him, when there came an interruption to her thoughts.

A wide shadow entered the hall doorway. If she had not been absorbed she would have noticed a strange voice in the kitchen and known that Mrs. Grey had asked some one to go into the parlor and sit down a minute while she went to look for a certain skirt pattern desired. Mrs. Grey was not a woman who entered people's kitchen doors uninvited and without knocking, and neither did she care to have prying eyes watching her every movement to report the same as soon as possible to the entire speaking acquaintance of the owner of those same prying eyes. However, there were people in Hillcroft who employed this method of making friendly calls, and Mrs. Grey used discretion in getting them into the parlor as the case demanded.

Rebecca Bascomb wore old, soft congress gaiters and a pair of decrepit "gum shoes," as she designated them, three sizes too large, therefore her step was not heralded.

Evelyn looked up, and she nodded a pleasant good-morning, with a motion half bow and half a ducking courtesy which suited her bulk. She approached Evelyn and eyed her with expectation and enjoyment as one approaches a particularly dainty morsel, rolling her tongue with anticipation.

Evelyn moved her chair back and would have risen to leave the room if she had realized that this stranger had come to stay, but Miss Bascomb said in a voice that Allison used to say was "all meal and oil": "Oh, don't you move. I'll set right here. Mis' Grey has gone to find a pattern for my sister. Are you Maurice Grey's wife?"

She fixed her bright, brown, little eyes on Evelyn's beautiful face and Evelyn, for some reason utterly unknown to her and thoroughly disturbing, was aware that the blood had leaped into her face and mounted even to her brow. She was aware also that the twinkling eyes had observed this with satisfaction and laid it away to put with whatever facts might develop thereafter.

"I beg your pardon," stammered Evelyn, trying to summon her haughty manner and sitting up straight. She would have left the room without answering had it been any other man in the world whose wife she had been taken for, but for some strange reason she did not understand, she felt she must in justice to him set this matter right.

"Be you young Doctor Grey's wife?" came the direct question again, and the little eyes fixed her once more as a pin does a fluttering moth.

"I am Miss Rutherford, of New York," Evelyn answered in her most freezing manner.

"Oh, you don't say! Met him in New York, did you? Well, you're real handsome, anyway. I told my sister when I see you go by with that bright circus sack you wore the other day that I guessed Maurrie had picked up some actor woman, and I knew that would be hard on Mis' Grey, feelin' as she does about bare necks and short sleeves, an' I knew they mostly wore 'em. But, Rutherford, d' you say?" a new intelligence coming into the bright eyes. "Why, now you ain't any relation to Miss Joan Rutherford, be you? I wonder now! If you are, I was mistook. No member of Miss Rutherford's family ever wore anything indecent."

"Miss Rutherford is my aunt. I will wish you good morning," said Evelyn, with a grand sweep of her fine figure, as she left the room at last, to almost come into collision with Allison, who stood wide-eyed and red-cheeked by the hall door.

Allison grasped her hand convulsively and she returned the clasp with her own, as by common consent they fled from the spot swiftly and silently.

"What did she dare to say to you?" questioned Allison excitedly, when they came to a standstill in a safe place, which happened to be Allison's own room, whither she had, without realizing it, drawn Evelyn. "I heard only the last few words, but I know she is capable of saying a great deal. The idea of her daring to speak of that lovely coat of yours in that way. 'Circus sack,' indeed!" And then both girls sat down and burst into peals of laughter.

It was perhaps the best thing that could have happened to them. Evelyn felt almost hysterical from the experience through which she had just passed, and she was not a girl who often cried. Besides, the laughter created a bond of sympathy between them.

"She is a meddlesome busybody!" said Allison, when she could speak. "Mother does not like to have her here, but is fond of her poor old sister. We always treat her well and get her away as soon as possible when she comes over. But she is just dreadful. She would fairly cut your heart out to see your thoughts if she knew how, and there is nothing—absolutely nothing—she does not dare to say."

"But what did she mean about your mother's feeling about bare necks? Doesn't your mother approve of *décolleté* dresses?" Evelyn asked the question curiously, but there was enough of her old tinge of superior scorn in the tone to bring the bright blood into Allison's face and deeply embarrass her.

Evelyn was quick. She had noticed that the family did not array themselves in fine garments for dinner, and she had not done so again; but she had set this down to the quiet home customs of the family and had not dreamed that there was a principle concerned, neither did she suppose that they did not wear evening dress on some occasions.

"It is not the custom to wear evening dress here," began Allison in confusion, and then her bravery came to the front and she looked up with a fine smile of loyalty. "No, my mother does not approve of it, but it seems discourteous to say so to you when you think differently about it. I know that people in society universally dress in that way."

The other girl did not argue the question. It had appeared to her only as an idiosyncrasy of this town. Allison was relieved when she asked quietly:

"Then what are you going to wear to-night at this—what do you call it—club meeting? You must tell me what to wear. I don't want to be dressed out of keeping with the occasion, you know. It might come to the ears of your friend downstairs and shock her."

They both laughed again, and the returning stiffness that threatened passed away.

With the question, "What are you going to wear tonight?" there came a cloud over Allison's face.

"I don't know," she answered, hesitating. "I hoped my new dress would be done in time, but the dressmaker sent word this morning that she had been sick and could not finish it till next week. It is very annoying, for the last time I wore my blue silk waist I spilled some cream down the front, and try as hard as I could I have not been able to get the spot out so but that it shows a little."

"Dear me! That's too bad. Can't you cover it up with lace in some way? Where is it? Let me see it. Perhaps I can suggest some way," said Evelyn, glad to find a little chance to help this other girl, and interested at once, as she always was, in a matter of clothes.

"What a lovely shade!" she exclaimed, as Allison reluctantly brought out a blue waist of good silk plainly made. She knew it would not shine beside Miss Rutherford's elegant and varied wardrobe, and she would rather have kept it to herself, but her real anxiety to cover the spot made her glad of the help.

"That is just the shade of your eyes," said Evelyn, holding up the silk to match them. "Come in my room and let me see if I have not a lace collar that will exactly cover that spot, and I know I have a velvet ribbon just the same color that will make the sweetest knot for your hair, unless you have one."

Allison acknowledged that she had not, and looked with wistfulness at the scientific carelessness of the other girl's arrangement of hair. She longed to ask her how she accomplished such results, but did not feel intimate enough. However, Evelyn was more interested now than she had been since the son of the house departed. She had some pleasant work to do with which she was familiar.

"Oh, let me dress you up and fix your hair, and then we can tell just how it will look. May I?" She said it with so much eagerness that Allison was amazed. This was a new girl, not the Miss Rutherford that had been with them for several days. She felt as if she might sometime get acquainted with this girl. So she submitted.

It was marvelous what a difference the deft touches of the artist gave to Allison's already pretty head. The arrangement of the hair was simplicity itself, with the tiny knot of turquoise blue velvet tucked in among the golden masses, but there was something about it which gave a needed finish to Allison and set off her quiet beauty to perfection. Evelyn would have called this something "style," but the mother, when she looked, called it "artistic." Allison in her heart knew that it was stylish, and she felt a certain satisfaction in seeing it belong to herself. The collar that Evelyn produced from the depths of one of the big trunks was a delicate sheer muslin, embroidered in a fine new-old-fashioned way and edged with the finest of real lace, dainty and unobtrusive. It fitted about the shoulders and over the soiled front in a pretty way, as if it had been made for the purpose.

"But I must not wear your collar," said Allison, surveying the effect with a lingering pleasure.

"I will give it to you, and then it will be yours, not mine, you see," said the irresistible Evelyn. "I am tired of it, anyway. Now you shall tell me what to wear," and Allison had the pleasure of going through the marvelous contents of those trunks, handling pretty materials and gaining many new ideas of originality in dress. It was a pleasure, for Evelyn had money and taste and her clothes were generally a work of art. Allison reveled in the pretty things until she suddenly remembered that it was growing late and there were many things to be done. Raising her eyes from the trunk she saw the other girl looking at her intently.

"You look fine," said Evelyn sincerely, as if she were merely thinking aloud. "If you were in New York and dressed well you would make an impression."

Allison's cheek vied with the scarlet of the dying sage flowers bordering the garden path, and she might have turned and fled, so much was her sensitive nature stirred, had not her mother, coming in search of her just then, seen her through the half-open door and stepping softly in kissed her gently on the cheek.

"What has she done to you, my little girl?" she said, holding her lovingly at arm's length and looking with pleased eyes at the sweet, blushing face. "It is very lovely." Allison, looking into those loving eyes and hearing the gentle praise, was soothed and pleased.

Thus was the perplexing question of dress settled for the evening and the two girls were brought nearer together. Dress has much sin and sorrow to answer for in the world. It is well when now and then it can be used for good.

Pleased with her effort at help, Evelyn grew interested in the evening affair. What were they going to do? Have refreshments? Could she help in setting the table? She always set the tables for any special affairs at home, and was very fond of helping in the arrangement for charity fairs. Perhaps she might relieve them a little. And Allison, charmed with the idea of having things arranged in true New York style, surrendered the dining room into her hands. The result was a thing of beauty. Evelyn even went so far as to rifle her trunk of a bolt of narrow crimson ribbon, and several yards of wide satin ribbon to match. The satin ribbon she fastened in large bows to the four corners of the tablecloth while the four long ends met each other and were fastened in an ingenious way under a branch of red leaves on the gas fixture. Allison had picked the last of the scarlet sage and that was massed in a big glass bowl in the center of the table.

The narrow ribbon adorned the little bundles of white sandwiches which had come in a basket from Ethel Haines, and made cunning little rosettes in the handles of the glass dishes that held the delicate sponge cakes, and there were bright red apples polished till they shone like rubies in a pile at each end of the table, set about with bits of green from an evergreen tree. It was easy to improvise scarlet shades for the tiny lamp and candles Allison possessed, and when the dainty cups were clustered on a white-covered side-table, with the little brass teakettle beside them ready for lighting, the whole was charming.

Yet in spite of all this Allison, as she went from her hairdresser's hand late in the afternoon to finish dressing, thought with trembling of the evening before her and wished it were over. The matter of dress was settled. Evelyn was to wear a white cloth dress with a touch of crimson velvet here and there. Allison thought of the harmony of it with the other decorations with satisfaction, and then smiled to think how she was reckoning Miss Rutherford as one of the decorations.

At the last minute there came a message from Ethel Haines. Her aunt was so very ill that she would not be able to come after all. She enclosed the programme and begged Allison to take charge. She also mentioned that the chief performer of the evening had the mumps and would not be present, so Allison would have to play.

Poor Allison! Her nerves already under a strain gave way. She sat down and let the discouraged tears come.

"I simply cannot play at all, mamma. What shall I do? You know I never play in public, not really fine music, nothing except ballads and things, without practising, and I would not play before Miss Rutherford for the world. She is a very fine performer. Didn't you hear her the other night when Maurice was here? She is wonderful."

Evelyn stood in the door in the soft white dress with crimson touches at her belt and throat, and with her most gracious manner. She felt secretly elated at her success in helping the sister of that young man. She began to think she understood what he had meant and wished he were here to witness how well she was doing it. Moreover, she could but hear what Allison had said, and being proud of her ability to play was naturally pleased. Therefore when Mrs. Grey looked up at her smiling, and said: "Why don't you ask her to play then, dear?" said Allison, her head still buried in her handkerchief, sobbed out: "I wouldn't dare, mother. I am sure she wouldn't do it," she smilingly offered her services to any extent.

Allison looked up ashamed and pleased and troubled all in one. Then she burst out: "But Bert Judkins was to play on his violin and he doesn't know much about it, and will murder things dreadfully, I presume. Some one will have to accompany him and I simply can't do it. He is in my Sunday-school class and I should get so nervous over him I should break down."

"Can't you suppress him?" said Evelyn, frowning.

"No!" said Allison decidedly, a flash coming into her eyes in spite of her misery. "It was a great thing to get him to come. We had to coax him and we hope to get hold of him through his love of music. Some of the girls are going to try to make him feel at home to-night so he will come again, and perhaps begin to come to church."

Evelyn raised her eyebrows. This sort of thing was beyond her, but she was determined that as far as the evening was concerned she would do her best to help.

"Never mind, don't worry," she said kindly. "I'm sure I can blunder through some sort of an accompaniment with him. Come, let us get those candles ready to light and pick the red leaves for the mantel. Are you sure you can find any more?"

"Yes, I know a sheltered spot on the back veranda where they are still bright. I'll go out and get them," and Allison dried her eyes and went away, wondering what spell had befallen this strange girl. If things went on like this she would be really liking her soon.

12

The Club and Bert Judkins

The evening was a strange experience in Evelyn Rutherford's history, because of her first effort to help some one else. She felt extremely virtuous, and wondered what her New York friends would think of her. Then she wondered if that young man who set himself up as her mentor would be satisfied.

Toward the girls, who arrived promptly at five in goodly company, Evelyn maintained a stately distance, like a queen who chooses to grace an occasion but who will not mingle with the throng. From time to time Allison glanced her way with a troubled expression. She had feared Evelyn would hold off in this way and she felt sure the Hillcroft girls would dislike her in consequence. Why Allison should care whether they disliked her or not she was sure she did not know, unless for the sake of her old friend, Evelyn's aunt, who would be grieved thereby. But having presented her she naturally wished to have her liked, and feared that the evening would be filled with embarrassment in consequence of the new element in the midst.

Evelyn sat quietly and watched the exercises. There were papers and brief discussions which were not very animated because a sudden shyness had fallen on the girls. Evelyn decided that they were largely of the class that Allison was trying to help, with a sprinkling of girls of culture like Allison. These for the most part were quiet, unobtrusive creatures, and not particularly attractive. They looked like girls from good homes, and they were tolerably well dressed. The rest were awkward and embarrassed, all but a few, who were bold and talked loud and giggled when they spoke. Evelyn decided that it was a nice thing in Allison to give up her time to elevating these other girls. Perhaps this was what the young doctor had meant, that she might help his sister in her good works, if she would. If that was it she was entirely willing to do what she could, provided the work was all as pleasant as it had been to-day. She should not care to be too familiar with all these girls. This discussion part, with the ten-minute papers on what a young girl should read and how she should read and why she should read, and a number of other heads under the general topic of reading, Evelyn privately voted a bore. She yawned behind her jeweled hand and wished this part were over. The plain-faced girl who was enumerating a list of books for busy readers saw the yawn and hurried so that she choked, and wished she had not promised to write a paper, vowing she never would do so again.

But when the evening came on Evelyn began to be more of a success. Among the first of the boys and young men to arrive was the aforesaid Bert Judkins. He wore a cheap new dark suit and looked well. He had heavy, handsome features and large eyes full of fun. His black hair and red cheeks were set off by a very red tie with a large, prominent glass diamond, which he wore without any apparent effrontery. His hair was nicely plastered in places where its original curls would submit to being subdued, and his hands were clean with a smooth black rim under each finger nail. It was not a part of his up-bringing to finish his toilet by cleaning his nails. He came in with a swagger, his violin in a green flannel bag in his hand. He saluted one or two of the commoner girls with a nonchalant, "Hello, Nan!" "Ev'nin', Nell!" and lounged over to the piano, where he took, as a matter of course, a place of honor for the evening.

Evelyn sat on the piano stool. She had just been introduced to several of the young men, but so far all of them seemed shy and gravitated naturally out of her orbit. In truth they were somewhat afraid of her. The few older young men who had not left the town to go to some city where there was more enterprise, were so busy that they were generally late in attending such gatherings if they came at all.

So Evelyn eyed curiously the lad—for he was but seventeen—who had taken the seat beside her. She imagined from what she had heard and the violin bag in his hand that this was the musician of the evening. She wondered what he was going to attempt and studied him idly. His face was not altogether unattractive. There was a great good-humored conceit and a tremendous love of fun mingled in his face, and the merry eyes were wandering about the room, winking at one and smiling at another, and once he stuck his tongue in his cheek with a comical expression at another. It was evident that nothing ever abashed him. It was only when Allison came his way that a different expression crossed his face. A kind of lighting of reverence and embarrassment changed him into a really handsome fellow. Evelyn saw him look at Allison's hair. Was it possible that a boy like that noticed a change of finery in his Sunday-school teacher? He smiled when Allison came nearer and shifted his eyes to the other side of the room. Evelyn saw that was a sort of diffidence and wondered at it. He had not seemed embarrassed, even by the presence of her, a stranger. There was a gentle kindliness of manner in Allison when she spoke to this boy that Evelyn had not seen in her before, and she perceived that there was a relationship between teacher and scholar that she knew not of.

A sudden interest in the new specimen before her took Evelyn. Maybe she could help here. What if she should try? At least it would be better than sitting and doing nothing. Allison looked doubtfully at Evelyn, wondering whether to risk the experiment of an introduction to the boy. She feared he might not take kindly to the haughtiness Miss Rutherford would be likely to offer him. The hour was drawing near when they would have to play together. She finally risked it and walked away; to her surprise Evelyn turned to the boy all smiles and graciousness. Allison, watching from the other side of the room, was amazed and wondered if this was a side of her nature that Miss Rutherford kept for all members of the male sex. It disgusted her a little and she began to fear that her guest might with her frivolous talk dispel any good seed that might have been sown in his heart.

The two by the piano were getting on well. "Are you to play?" asked Evelyn, "and will you let me see your accompaniments?"

"Why, ain't Miss Norton goin' to be here?" said the boy, looking around the room. "Some of these pieces are pretty hard. Do you think you can play 'em without practisin'?"

"I believe she is ill," said Evelyn, reaching for the sheets of music he held. "I might try them. I think I have seen some of them before."

She was amused at the idea he had of her ability, but she was astonished at the really good music he had chosen, rather disappointed too, because it grated on her to have good music murdered.

The boy leaned over and pointed out one or two places where she must be sure to "hang on" as he expressed it, and he gave her a few other instructions in musical phrases mispronounced which nearly broke down her gravity, but she managed to keep her face straight, as she was almost immediately called upon to open the programme with a piano selection.

She had chosen a brilliant *valse* and took them all by storm with her rendition. Especially did Allison notice the expression on the face of Bert Judkins. He was evidently impressed. He drank in the music and watched the white fingers that moved easily and with such mysterious swiftness among the twinkling harmonies. When the first selection was over it was met by a perfect burst of applause. Hillcroft was not used to such music and it wanted some more. Evelyn good-naturedly complied and jingled off a little medley of nursery melodies, which kept them laughing till the end.

When Evelyn turned back to her companion he leaned toward her and said in a loud whisper: "Say, you've played before a few times, ain't you? I guess you'll do," and he nodded his encouragement and admiration frankly.

There followed a recitation by a young lady who appeared to have been taking elocution lessons very hard, and who ranted and tore about over a few imaginary wrongs she was reciting. Evelyn did not care to listen and she noticed that the boy's face expressed a kind of fascinated horror. When it was done he said to Evelyn, in a kind of low growl, "Aw, she's no good, never was! Too stuck on herself!" and he threw himself back in his chair with a superior air.

It was very strange what a difference a little desire to help had made in Evelyn. At any other time sitting near an ill-bred young fellow she would have curled her lip and wondered how he came to be allowed to breathe the same air with herself; and here she was hoping he would not play too badly, that she might be able to praise him a little. She was indeed pleased to find that he had some idea of the feeling in the music he had selected and that his execution, though crude, was not unpleasant to listen to. She grew interested in helping him by following his eccentric playing and covering any irregularities by her own accompaniment. They scored a great success as the audience testified, and the boy sat down mopping his perspiring brow and saying:

"Well, we did 'em fine that time, didn't we? I never played better in my life. I never had anybody play so good fer the accompaniments before. They always make me get throwed out, some way. I wish you could go along with me every time I play."

She bowed her acknowledgment of his praise and wondered what her friends in New York would say if they could hear that. She fancied her brother Dick would shout over it, and tease her most unmercifully for months. She wondered if Mr. Worthington's black pointed mustache would curl in disdain and he would say, "The impudent little cur," as he had once at a little newsboy who ran against her dress to sell a paper to a hurried gentleman. And then in contrast came the noble, high-bred face of Doctor Grey as he had asked her to help his sister. He would not think she was in poor business, and what harm would it do her for just one night to let this ignorant boy speak his rough compliments. It was not like Evelyn Rutherford to argue thus, but she was being touched by an influence which as yet she knew not. She was praying that she might be willing to belong to Christ, and he was answering her unawares by letting her see himself in the souls of others for whom he lived and died.

The programme, so far as the music was concerned, was a success.

Just before the last selection by Evelyn, Allison read a bit culled from Ralph Connor's "Black Rock." The room was very still when she had finished. Evelyn was astonished at the power Allison had over her audience, at her ability to turn them from laughter to tears, and to imitate perfectly the speech of all the characters. Bert Judkins sat entranced. The story struck home to a world where he lived every day, and the truths contained had made to vibrate a vital chord in his heart. During a tender passage he had dropped some of his music, and in stooping awkwardly to pick it up Evelyn noticed his big, rough hand drawn impatiently across his eyes. When Allison sat down he turned to Evelyn after a moment of quiet and said: "Ain't she a rare one, though? I tell you now, she's good."

Evelyn turned to the piano marveling at the power the teacher had over the scholar, and she played a soft, sweet, mysterious, tender poem of sound that served to deepen the impression made by the reading.

During the hour of pleasant sociability and refreshment that followed before the company broke up Miss Rutherford and Bert Judkins were side by side.

The company were given pencils and cards and asked to go into the hall, where were arranged upon the wall a number of cards, each one representing in picture the name of some book. It was an old device in Hillcroft to make people feel at their ease, but it had never happened to come Evelyn's way, and struck her as quite a new and bright idea. She was quick at guessing, and during the last week in this house happened to have read a good many of the books represented, so that she was able to find out a goodly number, and she made the boy by her side help her. Together they puzzled out the names. He knew only a few books, but those he knew he could guess quicker than she, and when the list was called out they found they had a good many numbers correctly written. By this time Evelyn was interested in spite of herself, in this rough, unfinished boy-man, who was so thoroughly frank and so refreshingly blunt in what he had to say. She came from a world where people hid their true thoughts with pleasant words. This boy said what he thought regardless of others' opinions or the world's. She had always been an admirer of free speech. The boy was worth doing something for. What was it they were wanting to do with him, anyway? Get him to church, Allison had said. And what did they want to do with him when they got him to come to church? Educate him? Elevate him? Or perhaps make him into that mysterious something that Doctor Grey wanted her so much to be. It softened her much as these days went by to think that any one had cared enough for her in any way to think of her every day for a year, and pray for her.

She resolved she would help them with this boy if possible. She could not help to make him over, for that she did not understand, but she might perhaps help to bring him into the place where they thought he might be made over. She recognized that he had the making of a man in him. She had always been able to wheedle boys and young men into doing her bidding. They had often sent her to coax this or that one into some scheme, and she had almost never failed. What if she should try to coax him to go to church next Sunday? What would Allison say if she told her she had asked him and he had consented? She resolved again to try.

To this end she led him to the dining room and seated herself, as had been planned beforehand, at the little tea table to pour tea. She retained her vassal, however, and found he was not at all a bad hand to serve cups of tea to the company. But presently there came a lull in tea pouring. All were served and satisfied, and they could sit and chat. She had treated the boy much as she would have treated a young man in her own social set, had given him little compliments on the way he helped her, and made him feel she liked to have him by her side. Only when Allison came that way she felt she had a rival in his admiration.

But after all it was he who opened the way for her to carry out her purpose. It was while he was devouring sponge cakes, a whole one at a bite, a large plateful within reach, and he not troubled by any feeling of bashfulness about taking all he wished. Allison had just passed by them into the other room. She hardly knew whether she was glad or sorry of this sudden devotion of her scholar to her guest. It certainly kept Miss Rutherford from curbing the spirits of the other guests, and kept Bert away from several mill girls who had been invited to-night as an experiment, also to be helped, who would not be helpful to the young man in question. But what were they talking about? Horse races? Dancing? What possible theme could they have in common? Well, she would be likely to hear of it next Sunday some time during the lesson. Bert would be sure to say, "She told me so and so." Allison sighed and went back to her mill girls and a shy boy who could not be induced to talk with any one else, and tried not to worry.

At that moment Bert swallowed a huge bite and washed it down with the entire contents of the tiny teacup, passing it for more. Then he leaned over the little table and said:

"Say, she," nodding his head in the direction Allison had just gone, "has been tryin' this long time to get me to come to one of their young folks' meetin's at the church Sunday night. She's tried every way coaxin' pretty near, an' I won't give in because I used to go there and they put me out fer whisperin', and I said I'd never go in there again. That was five years ago, and I ain't went since. But now she's got a new dodge. She wants me to take my violin next Sunday night and play for them. She's got the pieces picked out she wants me to play an' all. She's go'in' to lead the meetin' herself. She's been at me again to-night, but I ain't give in yet. But I'll tell you what I'll do. I do hate to disappoint her, she seems to want it so much, an' if you'll go along an' play my accompaniments I'll do it. I will now."

With which magnanimous offer he leaned proudly back in his chair and swallowed the new cupful at one gulp and began on another cake.

Evelyn was too much taken aback to answer at first. The conceit, the impudence, of the young rascal was swallowed up in her amusement. What would her friends think to hear her submitting to such talk? But how strange that he should open the way to what she had decided to try to get him to do.

If it were not for the absurd condition she would bind the bargain at once, but of course she could not do that. Go and play for this untutored boy at a public meeting and in a church! She never did such a thing in her life. It would not be dignified. And yet, why should she not? There was no one here whom she knew or for whom she cared a whit. No one would tell the story. She might as well enjoy this adventure to the end; there was little enough in this town to enjoy, surely. And this was harmless, only a joke. She felt sure Allison would be pleased.

Just at that moment Mrs. Grey passed through the room and smiled as she saw the two together with a lighting up of her face that reminded one of her son. Evelyn's decision was taken. She turned to the boy and said:

"All right, I will go. But you must bring me your music beforehand to practice."

The company broke up soon after that, and the boy swaggered off between two of the mill girls who laughed and talked so loud you could hear them down the street, and yelled, "Oh, Bert, ain't you too funny!" again and again.

Then Allison, after watching them go down the walk, turned silently and bent her pretty head on her hands and sighed. She was tired and discouraged and did not know how to trust what she had done to her heavenly Father's keeping, and above all did not know how to trust this strange, unwelcome worker who had been forced upon her.

Evelyn on the contrary went to her room well satisfied with her day's work. It was not so stupid after all to be good, if this was being good. She prayed her prayer with more vim and less humility that night, and was perhaps not so near to the kingdom as when she had not expected to be noted for what she had done.

13

Allison's Meeting

"Did you say that you were anxious to get that boy to go to church?" asked the guest, as the two girls sat together the next afternoon over a bit of fancy work. Miss Rutherford had offered to show Allison how to make such a sofa pillow as she was embroidering and Allison had been glad to accept. It was not every day she had a chance like that. The conversation, however, so far had been confined to the pillow and the stitch and the way to hold the needle. Now Allison was mastering the difficult operation and the teacher felt at liberty to talk of other things. She had been waiting all day to get the right chance to display her triumph.

"Do you mean Bert Judkins?" asked Allison with quick apprehension, she scarcely knew why. "Yes, I said so. Why, did he talk about it to you?" Her interest in fancy work was for the moment abated. She feared that her work and her prayers were to be of no avail. Bert had been very shy of doing anything he was asked lately. He had even stayed away from Sunday-school several times. Now, doubtless, he had been laughing over her anxiety with this stranger. There was a real pain in her eyes as she looked at Miss Rutherford for an answer.

"Won't you tell me why in the world you care?" asked Evelyn interestedly, not ready to answer Allison's other question yet.

Allison shrank from replying to this. She felt keenly that the other girl could not understand her motives, and would know no better after she was told. But she had asked and there must be an answer. It was her duty to witness for her Lord before this one as well as before Bert Judkins, though she wished in her heart that it were the rude boy instead of the girl of the world.

"Because I want him to be a Christian."

It seemed to be the only thing to be said but Allison felt it would be like Greek to her questioner.

"Yes, he is a good deal of a heathen," laughed Evelyn; "but tell me why you care? Why don't you just let him alone as he is? What makes you take so much trouble for him, just a young, ignorant boy? I'll admit he is bright and funny sometimes, but he is awfully impudent and ill-bred. I know you can't enjoy him always. What is it that makes you take so much trouble? In other words, why are you such a good girl?"

Allison's face grew rosy under this and she scarcely knew how to answer. Had she been heart and soul enlisted in helping this stranger who had come within her gates, as others wished and hoped she would be, she would have welcomed this talk with joy and hastened with eagerness to explain her love to her Saviour and through him to all for whom he died. But so thoroughly had she fixed it in her mind that Evelyn Rutherford was beyond the pale of her influence in any possible way that she merely felt now an impulse to guard all sacred things from her polluting gaze. As the blood receded she made answer in almost cold tones:

"My Saviour died for him. If he is worth that he is worth any effort of the Saviour's followers."

Evelyn looked at her curiously. It was the same language her brother had used more feelingly. She saw that Allison was shy about talking the matter over.

"And what do you expect to do with him after you have got him to church?" asked Evelyn, after a moment's silence.

"He will hear of Christ, and will little by little begin to realize his love, and will"—she hesitated for a word—"be willing to be Christlike, I hope. And he will learn—he knows already, that we are praying for him." Allison spoke softly with her eyes on her work. It was necessary to explain all this, though she had not the least hope it would be understood.

But to Evelyn the words came with memory's reflections. How strange that she should use those words, almost the same that her brother had used in speaking to her. There seemed to be a language spoken among these strange people that was different from that of the world. She had never heard of the shibboleth, but she recognized it now without the knowledge and her heart warmed to the thought in a way that surprised herself. Then there were others going about praying for people in the same way in which he had prayed for her. She was not the only one to have this unique experience. Were there many? Allison had said "we" are praying. Did that mean all those other girls? Their plain faces and commonplace attire suddenly took on a new interest in the mind of the girl who had ignored them.

To Allison's surprise she presently answered in a thoughtful tone: "Yes, I see." Then she added with a laugh, "Well, you have your wish. He is coming."

"Coming?" said Allison, dropping her work. "How do you know? Did he say he would?"

"Yes," said Evelyn with a sudden resolve to say no more yet. Callers came just then and took Allison to the parlor and when she returned Evelyn had gone to her room.

Evelyn managed to be at the door when Bert arrived the next noon with the music as he had promised, and as it happened, Allison had gone to the store on an errand for her mother, so that there was no question of why he had come. The guest with a guilty feeling went to the piano and began to play. The music was all unfamiliar to her except now and then a strain that she seemed to have heard in church; but Allison wondered much on her return to hear the several familiar tunes played over and over again. Once she opened the parlor door and peeped in, but Evelyn seemed to be looking over the church hymn book; doubtless it was curiosity which led her to try them.

The sounds ceased altogether soon and Allison heard her going upstairs. Troubled thoughts were going on in her turbulent young heart. A new difficulty had arisen. They would always arise with a foreign element in the house. There was a question of what to do now, or rather Allison said there was no question, though she knew in her heart there was. She had deliberately determined not to put it before her mother at all. She was fearful of what her mother might say, and in this case her impetuous will was determined.

It was just this. She was appointed to lead the young people's prayer meeting the next evening. It was now Saturday afternoon and she had not yet been able to fix her mind on the theme and prepare. Why? Partly because she felt that her heart was not right before God, and partly because she was troubled by the presence of this stranger. Of course she would not ask Miss Rutherford to accompany her to the meeting; it would not be necessary, nor a thing to be desired in any way. Equally of course, Miss Rutherford would not accept were she to be asked. Miss Rutherford would curl her haughty lip at a prayer meeting wherein the young and unlearned and the *girls* took part. Allison could talk and pray and lead a meeting well before her own circle of acquaintances and she had done it so much that it had ceased to be the terrible cross to her that it was to some, but to do anything in public before this other girl in whose presence her spirit seemed to be a groveling creature, she could not and would not. She had reasoned this out many times till her brain was weary and that night she put the whole matter into a deliberate resolve that she would have no more to do with it, and turned her attention to her preparation. Nevertheless she could not get away from the feeling that she was sneaking off to her meeting and leaving behind a duty undone. She thought she felt a little as Jonah did when he was told to go to Nineveh, only she would not admit that she had been told.

Miss Rutherford attended church in the morning with the family, and enchanted the eyes of the feminine portion of the audience with the hat she wore, though her entire costume, according to New York custom for church-goers, was plain in the extreme. It was the very elegant plainness that turned many eyes in her direction, and marked her a distinguished stranger.

Rebecca Bascomb had done her work thoroughly, and very few present did not know that she was "Miss Joan Rutherford's niece, the daugher of her only brother," and a few added touches that Miss Bascomb affixed according to the gullibility of her audience. There were a few, a choice few, who were given as a delicate morsel an account of her visit at the Greys' the other day.

In the afternoon Allison went to Sunday-school. She had eased her conscience greatly by asking Evelyn if she would care to attend, promising to take her into the young ladies' Bible class if she would, and went away to her work with a lighter heart. If she would not go to Sunday-school naturally she would not expect to be invited to go again that day.

But the afternoon was not all brightness. Allison's boys seemed to have arranged to take a day off from good behavior and fall back into their old ways before she took the class. Especially was Bert Judkins trying. He whispered during prayer time and whistled during the singing, and smiled at Allison seraphically whenever she turned reproving or pleading eyes his way. He growled in low bass whispers something about one of the girls in a classroom across the main aisle, till the others giggled, right in the midst of the most solemn part of the lesson. Allison had put much work into the preparation of that lesson and had hoped it would reach the hearts of two or three of her class in particular. Behold, those were the very boys who seemed most possessed not to listen. When Bert Judkins, during the first hymn that followed the lesson, leaned forward and said he had to go, he had an engagement, with a twinkle that made the other boys nudge each other and giggle, Allison drooped her head on her hand in despair, and if she had been alone would have cried.

Bert, however, did not go. He sat back in his seat and looked at her furtively, noting the sad droop of her mouth, and the discouraged turn of her head, and reflected upon his own behavior. He had not meant to be so trying. He was half ashamed that he had decided to please his teacher that evening, and rather puffed up about it on the whole. He was obliged to equalize matters somehow, and hence his spirits during the class. He had known that it would annoy her to have him leave the class before the closing exercises were concluded. It was a part of the code of honor of the school not to run out during prayer and singing and remarks. He had felt that he must do something of this sort in order to hold his own among the boys and in part atone for the part he intended taking in the evening meeting.

But now as he saw her greatly troubled look and knew that she was really anxious over him his face grew thoughtful and the influence that had made him yield and go to the meeting kept him quiet during the remainder of the session. He touched his hat respectfully as he passed her at the classroom door, and did not tumble out over the feet of the other boys as he often had done before, and his teacher, ever watchful, thought he had not altogether forgotten his promise to her that he "would think about" what she had said to him concerning Christ.

However, she sighed deeply as she went home, and wished that it was not her night to lead the meeting. She did not feel in the spirit of it. She had a lurking bitterness toward Miss Rutherford for having in her opinion been the cause of Bert Judkins' behavior in Sunday-school. Just how she did not attempt to tell herself, but her influence was probably to blame in some way.

Just what she would have thought had she known that Miss Rutherford had been faithfully practising hymns ever since she left the house for Sunday-school, and only ceased as she heard the gate click and knew that Allison had returned, it is hard to tell. She was glad when she came in to find the parlor and library deserted, and to hear footsteps above in the guest's room, which told her she would have a little time alone. She went to her own room presently and tried to absorb her mind in the topic for the evening. When that failed to cheer her she knelt beside her bed, but while she was praying for help and strength her mind kept recurring to the thought that perhaps she should invite Miss Rutherford to go with her. She arose by and by and deliberately put her mind to making out her programme for the meeting and selecting her hymns. It was drawing near to the hour and her work must be done. She reasoned with herself that she was growing morbid over the whole thing and that after this meeting was well out of the way she would try to make an opportunity to say something to Miss Rutherford about religion. She must do it, hard as it seemed to her, and useless as she was sure it was, or her conscience would drive her distracted. Why had all her friends so mistakenly selected her as the one to do this work? Why, but because they had failed themselves? The thought was almost bitterly spoken to herself as she went to the glass to smooth her hair. Glancing at her watch she saw to her relief that it really was time to be off. Now in a few minutes she would have put all possibility of doing that disagreeable thing that conscience kept suggesting, behind her.

She hurried down, declining her mother's offer of some tea, saying she must be there early to find some one to play and arrange about the hymns.

"Perhaps Miss Rutherford would go if you asked her," suggested Mrs. Grey.

There it was again! Mother and conscience! Allison turned with an impatient frown.

"Oh, mother! She would not go, and I could not lead, if she did. I really must hurry. Good-bye. Are you coming to church to-night? There goes the first bell," and Allison was off down the front path before her mother could say more.

It was perhaps five minutes after this that Mrs. Grey heard her guest's door open and the soft swish of descending skirts. The sounds halted several times, and at last Miss Rutherford peeped cautiously into the room, dressed to go out.

"Is she really gone?" she asked merrily, coming in and sitting down to button her dainty gloves.

"Who? Allison? Did you intend going with her? Why, that is too bad——" began Mrs. Grey, with a troubled expression.

"Oh, no, indeed, I was not going with her. I have been avoiding her all the afternoon lest she should ask me. You see I'm in league with that absurd boy of hers, and we were going to give her a little surprise. He and I are going to play for her to-night, and she doesn't know it yet. It is all right for me to do it, is it not, Mrs. Grey? I never did such a thing before in my life, but he said he would go to church and play as she had asked him if I would go with him and play the accompaniments. It's really very funny, and I don't know how I came to say 'yes,' but I did. And then I thought it would be rather interesting to surprise her. There he comes now. Is it surely all right for me to go? Is it very public? Will many be there?"

"It is all right, dear, and I am very glad you are trying to help that boy too. Allison will be so glad. She has put a good deal of work and prayer on him."

Mrs. Grey put out her hand with that inviting motion she had and Evelyn before she realized what she was going to do stooped gracefully and kissed her hostess on the forehead.

Then she went to the door to meet her young escort, who was resplendent in a new necktie and well-plastered hair.

But Evelyn, as she walked beside him in the twilight, was marveling why she had given that kiss. Whence had come that impulse? Were there depths in her nature which she knew not of, which had never been sounded as yet? And what was it that was stirring her so unexpectedly among these strange people?

They walked demurely into the chapel, those two who had planned the surprise. The room was fast filling up but no one had come yet who could play. Allison sat doubtfully regarding the piano stool at her left, and wondering if she must take up her cross and play too, as well as lead. There were none of her boys there. Bert must have been joking when he told Miss Rutherford he was coming. She had hoped one or two others would come, but she had not seen them hovering around the gate when she came in, as they would have been sure to, she thought, if they were coming. Her heart felt heavy and discouraged. She did not raise her eyes to see who was coming down the aisle toward the front seats; she was intent on finding a hymn that she could play for an opening without giving much thought to her music. She wanted to be able to think what to do next. It was very embarrassing to have to play and lead at the same time. If only some one would come! She bent her head over her Bible in a little desperate prayer that Mamie Atkins or some one who could play just a little even would be sent quickly. Then she raised her eyes to behold suddenly before her, sitting as composedly as if they were accustomed to that seat on every Sabbath evening, Miss Rutherford and Bert Judkins! And Miss Rutherford was taking off her gloves! Could it be possible? And the young lady was smiling, a really merry smile. Was this the Miss Rutherford who could be so cold and haughty?

Suddenly Allison's cheek grew crimson. She remembered her goading conscience and her undone duty, the invitation ungiven, and the intention ungracious. And here had been help and a degree of sympathy, and God had been trying to show it to her through her conscience, and she would not hear nor answer the call to duty. She looked at Bert, saw his expression of sheepish delight in pleasing her, flashed him a happy smile of thanks and then another at Miss Rutherford. Allison was one who forgave royally when she saw she ought to do so. She came at once to the young woman's side:

"How good of you to come," she said in a low tone. "And I never even asked you if you would like to. Will you forgive me?" Then to Bert: "Oh, Bert, I am so glad!" and the boy looked down at his violin and felt fully repaid in his heart for all the embarrassment among his kind that this had occasioned, and resolved to do it again if it made her as glad as that.

14

"Yours Dismally, Dick"

The evening was to Evelyn a remarkable experience. In the first place had come her surprise at Allison's "Will you forgive me?" When had any one ever asked her forgiveness before? She could see that Allison was really in earnest, and about so trivial a thing too, as a neglect to invite her to go to church. It gave her a little inkling of the place that meeting held in Allison's heart. It also showed her that Allison regarded her for some reason as outside the sacred, privileged circle who might enter here.

She and Bert did their part well. The piano and violin together sounded a grand keynote for the singing, and the many fresh, untrained voices took up the music and sang with a will. At first Evelyn felt almost inclined to stop playing and turn around to watch and listen. It seemed her playing was not needed. The music swept on in high, sweet melody, even though the voices were some of them harsh and most of them more or less crude. There was in the singing a quality of true praise that rose above all little discords as if the sound of angel voices mingled in the air above their heads. Evelyn almost fancied there was a wonderful hidden instrument above somewhere like an Æolian harp, and in spite of herself raised her head to look when the song was over. She had never played for a large company to sing before and was astonished at the result. And how suddenly they hushed as they took their seats again. Allison was standing by the little table up in front talking, with her head bowed. Why, she was praying! Actually, a girl—a woman—praying before others! Evelyn felt the blood tingle in her own veins at the very idea. How dreadful it must be to do that! How could she? But her voice was sweet and clear: "Father in heaven, forgive us for our mistakes and our foolish willfulness, and undo any harm we may have done, and help us to show others that we love thee."

There it was again—that same loyalty to the One, Christ Jesus. The brother had talked that way too. She began to perceive the possibility of the wideness and the sweetness of such a tie.

Of the reading, songs, and prayers which followed, and the part taken actively and eagerly by many of the young people, Evelyn had very indistinct ideas afterward. It was a series of surprises. It was as new to her, nay, more novel, than to the wide-awake, interested boy by her side. He had been there before, though five years ago. He knew well who took part. To Evelyn it was like being set down in another world.

She and Bert Judkins played, when Allison gave them a sign, and though they had not practised together, the result was very sweet. Evelyn entered into the music; especially did she do so when, at the close of a series of exceedingly brief prayers, Allison motioned to them to play "Just as I am, without one plea." They had known she would call for it soon and were seated, ready. Very softly the unexpected strains floated out, like far-away, heavenly music. Allison rejoiced in her heart that Evelyn knew when to play softly, and had in some way succeeded in toning down Bert and his violin, which loved to soar loudly. Perhaps Bert too, was softened by the hour and the spirit of the meeting. The tender music filled the room and every head remained bowed. Just where the last note lingered tremblingly, Allison's sweet voice, tremulous with suppressed feeling, took the key and started them softly singing:

> *Just as I am, thy love unknown,*
> *Hath broken every barrier down;*
> *Now to be thine, yea, thine alone,*
> *O Lamb of God, I come!*

Evelyn was not familiar with the words of this hymn; it was not an old household, church-time, childhood memory. More quickly to her lips would rise the phrases of the latest opera. But she had practised this tune over and over, for the melody had caught her as being very tender, and though she had not realized it, the words had been before her and fixed themselves in her mind. Now, as she listened to them, voiced in what seemed a sweet and earnest prayer, she realized that the words had become her own property. "Thy love unknown, thy love unknown," kept going over in her mind during the remainder of the evening. Yes, that was the love Doctor Grey had told her about. She began to feel that there was an unrecognized relation between herself and Christ. Would that love unknown some day break down every barrier and bring her to him? It was the first time the possibility of such a happening really had come to her and it startled her. She tried to put it aside to study this curious gathering, but it would keep recurring to her from time to time.

When the meeting was out and Allison stood a moment talking to the pastor, who had come in toward the close, Evelyn turned to Bert: "Now, I want you to stay to church," she told him with an air of command which evidently pleased that young gentleman. He smiled a knowing smile and twinkled his eyes in a mischievous way.

"All right. I'm in fer the whole business," he remarked jauntily. "Got the rest of the gang outside waiting fer me to come fer 'em. I made 'em all come and we're goin' to occupy a front seat. Guess she'll get enough of us fer once," and he looked toward his teacher with that mingling of reverence and impudence which can only be possible on the face of a boy of that age and class.

Sure enough! The opening hymn was but being read when in filed twelve boys led by Bert Judkins, who had disencumbered himself of his violin. Down the long side aisle they came, embarrassed and grinning and almost falling over one another's feet in the long transit, but into a side seat near the front they all finally got themselves noisily seated, drawing the attention of many an astonished pillar of the church.

Allison had quickly bowed her head when she first saw them, and when a moment later she raised it, there were tears in her eyes, mingled with the pleasure in her face she could not conceal. They each in turn stole furtive glances back to their teacher and received her answering welcome smile and thereafter sat like twelve statues, listening respectfully, save during the singing, in which they joined with fervor.

Evelyn looked and wondered and pondered. What did it all mean, this new world into which she had come? It was not without interest to her. She felt that she had some part in it. She even caught the spirit and exulted the least little bit when all those boys came in. Anyway, it was less dull than any church service she had ever attended before. One service a day was as much as she ever forced herself to attend, and even that was often merely a Sabbath evening "sacred" concert.

Later that evening Allison stole timidly to Miss Rutherford's door and knocked. Evelyn, in pretty negligée of soft pink cashmere, opened the door and invited her in with a look of surprise.

Allison's golden-hued hair was all down about her shoulders in shining wealth of waves, and Evelyn sat watching the delicate face in its lovely setting that looked like the halo of some saint.

"I couldn't sleep," said Allison, "till I had come and told you how wicked I have been. I did not want to invite you to go to the meeting with me lest you would laugh at me. And now you have been so good as to come without asking and influenced my boys, at least one of them, to come, and I want to thank you."

"You absurd child," said Evelyn, laughing; "you needn't trouble your conscience about that. It was quite a lark. I was richly repaid when I saw your face as those great hulking boys stumbled into church. Now go to bed and don't worry any more."

"But there is something else," said Allison, hesitating and twisting a long lock of bright hair around her finger. "I want to ask you if you are a Christian?" The ready crimson mantled her face as she said it, but she looked bravely up at Evelyn. That young lady laughed.

"No," she answered gayly; "I'm a heathen. Bert and I are about alike. You'll have to think of some way to get hold of me." Then another swift impulse seized her for which she could not account and she stooped and kissed the pure white forehead and said in a voice of smothered feeling: "You are a dear little girl, and I wish I were half as good as you, Allison."

Her duty done, the worn-out little Christian slipped back to her bed, marveling much at this strange girl who had so many different sides to her nature. And she had called her "Allison" with something tender in the accent and had said she wished she were good. There must be more in her after all than one would think. Perhaps there was in most people. There were her rough, uncouth boys. It was easy for her to see the good hid beneath their unpolished exterior; but when it came to a girl of the world like Miss Rutherford, Allison had felt there was little good there to look for. She had been mistaken surely. She was wrong. Her brother was right, as he always used to be when they were children and any question came up for discussion. He always took the mild, charitable side and his sister the impulsive, prejudiced, critical. Well, at least she had done her duty at last. The other girl had admitted that she was not a Christian, and now it became her duty to pray for her; yes, and to work for her too, if there was any way in which she could work. Why was it that it was not so easy to try to influence her as it was that class of boys? She must examine into this. Of course it was God's work just as much. And it was apparent from what Miss Rutherford—could she ever call her Evelyn?—had said that she had been wrong too, in supposing she had no influence with her.

She fell asleep at last, weary with turning the problem over in her mind. To-morrow she would try to do better.

"'To-morrow,' whispereth weakness, and to-morrow findeth

him the weaker. 'To-morrow,' promiseth conscience; and behold, no to-day for a fulfillment."

Allison found those lines not long after and remembered and searched out some others she had known a long time and printed them together on a card which she placed on her wall for her reminder in the duties that should come to her in future:

> *To-morrow, oh 'twill never be*
>   *If we should live a thousand years!*
> *Our time is all to-day, to-day,*
>   *The same, though changed; and while it flies,*
> *With still small voice the moments say,*
>   *"To-day, to-day, be wise, be wise."*

The morning dawned bright and clear, and the early mail brought a letter for Evelyn. She took it up to her room to read. It bore a Philadelphia postmark, and was written in a cramped hand, as if the writer were in an uncomfortable position. It read as follows:

Dear Sister:

Your letter with its plaint has just reached me. I had forgotten the outlandish name of the place where Aunt Joan resides or I would have sent for you a week ago. I am in a worse fix than you even. In short, I'm laid up in a dismal hotel room with a broken leg. I slipped on a miserable little piece of orange peel and fell down three small stone steps right here in the hotel. I never knew before that legs broke so easily, and I didn't believe them when they told me it was broken, except for the abominable pain that made me faint dead away several times. If I had had my senses about me I would have been sent straight to the hospital, but they had me up in my room and the bones set before I knew what I was about, and here I am with a man to look after me. I have sent for John, but I am not sure I can reach him, as he went off to some back country place to visit his mother. If you have a mind to come on and stay here at the hotel I'll do my level best at chaperoning you as well as I can from my bed. It would be a relief at least to me to see a familiar face once a day. I have not sent a word to any of our acquaintances here, for the simple reason that I feel too simple at my accident to have them know about it. If I had been thrown from a horse or hurt in rescuing a young lady from a burning building there would be a halo of glory about me, and I could afford to hold *soireés* for my friends and be admired and pitied; but a man who can't stand up on a level landing and avoid a single square inch of orange peel is too insignificant even for pity.

Of course, if your quarantine is raised and you have found some one to flirt with and don't want to come, do as you please. But I thought this might be a little better than smallpox. I shall doubtless get on my feet some day if I live long enough, or don't get desperate and shoot myself. In the meantime this is the best I can do for you, and I guess daddy will excuse you for coming to nurse your broken-up brother. If he doesn't, I'll shoulder all blame.

Yours dismally,
Dick

Evelyn read this letter with mingled emotions. Ordinarily this invitation would have been anything but attractive to her. She was not a born nurse; she did not like to be with sick people; there had never been any deep, tender feeling between her brother and herself; and she had not many friends in Philadelphia. Nevertheless, Hillcroft was destitute of occupation for her unless she undertook the reformation of Bert Judkins, or his like, for which she did not feel particularly qualified. The waiting here was likely to be long and tedious if she had to stay till her aunt was out of quarantine, and she felt nervous about going to her even after everything was pronounced safe. Undoubtedly her father would be satisfied if Dick chose to send for her, and the change would be a real relief. Meantime, underneath all these questions which she weighed deliberately, there was an undertone of desire, or perhaps it was only willingness, to do something for some one else which would be accounted good in herself.

In other words, she had watched the unselfish lives of those around her long enough to wish to work out a little salvation for herself. And so, without much thought, and certainly not "with fear and trembling," but with a full degree of assurance of success, she set out to work salvation for herself. She would be good to Dick, poor fellow! It was hard for him to be shut up there when he had expected to go off hunting in a few days. There had always been a certain degree of fondness between them, but never the deep affection—at least not suspected by themselves—that there was between Allison Grey and her brother. Evelyn wondered now, as she hurried downstairs to make known her decision to her hostess, if there ever could be cultivated such a tie between herself and Dick as existed between Doctor Grey and his sister. She felt a faint yearning for something of the sort. It would be nice to have one's brother care as much as that.

To do her justice, she was not anxious to shine virtuously before any human beings. She wished only to feel satisfied in her own heart that she had been doing some good to some one else, and—yes, before that other One, Christ. She would like to feel less small when she knelt to make that daily petition. It occurred to her on the way downstairs that it would be much pleasanter if Dick had fallen down in New York instead of Philadelphia. Perhaps he might have sent for his friend Doctor Grey. She would like to meet him again, though perhaps it was just as well, after all, not to, for she desired above all things to get away from the unrest with which the strange new thoughts had filled her.

Mrs. Grey fully agreed with her guest that she ought to go to her brother, and a message was sent by the doctor over the telephone to the quarantined aunt, who also cheerfully acquiesced in the arrangement.

Evelyn packed her trunks hurriedly as she discovered that she could leave by the noon train and make connections with the Philadelphia sleeper. There was no time to talk; everything was confusion and hurry. Almost before they were aware, their guest was gone and Allison was unhitching the pony from the post across the road and driving away from the station. She drove slowly and sighed several times. She could not tell whether she was glad or sorry that Miss Rutherford was gone. She felt that her attitude during her stay had been a mistake, and that she had let many opportunities for witnessing for Christ go by unheeded. She would be glad to live that part of her life over and do better, but on the whole it was a relief to her to have the dear home nest to themselves once more. Miss Rutherford was a person from too different a world to ever be congenial. Life with her had been at too high tension to be comfortable. Allison was glad to come in sight of the loved home and know that her round of pleasant duties would be again uninterrupted. Miss Rutherford had said, "You must come to New York and see me some time. I should love to show you New York." It had been spoken very cordially, but Allison meant never to go. She shuddered at the thought. What questions of right and wrong she would have to meet, what constant challenging of her views! How little her tastes would blend with the probable Rutherford home life! What agonies of social etiquette all new to her would she have to face! Never! Never!

Does our heavenly Father sometimes smile at our fierce assertion of what we will and will not do, seeing in his loving kindness that this is the very thing we need most, and forthwith brings it to us, that we may bear and learn and then give him glory when we understand?

15

On a Mission to Dick

Evelyn was seated in the parlor car with her belongings about her, the neat farms and pleasant homes once more whirling past her, and Hillcroft a thing of history. She could not help remembering the journey thither and comparing her anticipation with the actual facts. How different it had been from what she had planned! She had not even seen her Aunt Joan. She found to her surprise a lingering disappointment about that now. She had lived for nearly three weeks where Miss Joan Rutherford was a loved and honored member of society. She had learned to respect her from what she had heard of her, if she did not love her yet, and now that she was actually speeding away from Hillcroft, she began to think how disappointed her father would be when he learned she had been there without even seeing his dear sister. For she knew that his sister was dear to him, even though he was a man who seldom spoke of his personal feelings. He always answered her letters promptly and insisted upon his children doing the same, much to their dislike; she could remember that one of the few times when he had punished her most severely was because she had spoken disrespectfully of this aunt. For the first time in her life it occurred to her that her father led a lonely life. It had seemed his natural part and she had never thought he needed anything else. She loved him, of course, and supposed he loved her, but they never exhibited this love in any way. What a difference it would make in their home if there were such ways as they had at the Greys'. Would her father care to have her meet him when he came home at night and kiss him? Could she do it? What if she should try? She began to realize that it was not all her father's fault that their home life was cold and each one went his separate way. Could it be that her father was lonely and would like his daughter to be affectionate and companionable? It must have been hard to have his young wife die and leave him with two children to bring up. He had his business, true, and perhaps all his thought and feeling had been absorbed into that. Still, she could remember times when he would drop his paper across his knee and sit back in his chair with a sad expression and his eyes shaded. Was he recalling his early life and dreams then? How strange that she had never thought of her father in this way before! Perhaps she might be a little good, like Allison, if she attempted to make things a trifle pleasanter for her father and brother. Suppose she should sometime be changed into such a girl as Allison. It couldn't be done, of course, but suppose it could. What would they all think of her, her father and brother and the servants? What would Jane think? And what would Mr. Worthington think? Yes, and what would Doctor Grey think? Ah, but he would never know, and why should she take all this trouble, anyway? Oh, dear! Life was a dismal thing at best. She was anxious to get back once more into the whirl of things and forget all this fanaticism. It was actually getting into her brain. She wished she had something to read. True, there was in her bag a tiny volume Allison had given her when she left her at the train, but she could see at a glance that it was more of this uncomfortable religion which she hoped she was leaving behind in Hillcroft. She wanted something better. She rang for the porter and asked him to summon the news agent with some books from which she could select one. He came whistling in from the door behind her chair, slamming it after him, and at the porter's sign dumped his pile of books in the aisle by her chair, while he selected a few for her scrutiny.

"Did you want a love story, ma'am, or some real blood and thunder? This here book is——" He stopped with an exclamation. "Hello! Is this you? You ain't goin' home so soon, are you?"

She raised her eyes with freezing dignity to the saucy, handsome ones above her and beheld Bert Judkins.

"I'm taking this feller's route while he's sick. I could get it permanent if I was to try, 'cause he's tired of it, but she"—he paused and nodded back toward Hillcroft—"she's awful set against it. She says I'll have to run Sunday, and I s'pose I will. But a feller's got to live, though she won't allow that. She says you've only got to do right and starve if you ain't got looked after. There ain't any 'got' about living. Course, if that's the way you look at it, she's 'bout right, an' if I decide to do what she wants, I sha'n't try fer this. Say, has she roped you into this thing too, or are you one of 'em? I didn't think you was quite their kind, but you're a jolly player."

He piled his books at her feet and seated himself familiarly in the chair next to hers, which happened to be vacant.

It was a trifle amusing and also embarrassing. Bert Judkins in the parlor of her hostess as an amateur violinist, among people who knew him and for whom she did not care, and Bert Judkins as newsagent on a parlor car filled with elegant strangers was two different beings. However, they were all strangers to her, and she glanced about and decided it did not matter in the least. She could, of course, order him off or send for the porter, but she had tasted of the joy of helping on a good cause, and to her credit, be it said, it did not occur to her to go back upon her one-time *protégé* in this way.

He did not stay long. His business called him away soon, but he managed to get in a good deal of talk and a few troublesome questions.

"Did you say she'd roped you in?" he asked again, without the least consciousness of being impudent. Evelyn colored and understood. Was this boy even going to keep it up? She turned him off again and again. But he was keen enough to understand that she knew from the way he changed his conversation. It was as if he felt a responsibility upon him to do or say something that his teacher would have done were she in his place. He was awkward at it, but he was never shy.

"I say," he said, when he had for the fifth time turned off his question by picking up a book and examining it, "mebbe you'd make another partnership affair of it. I don't know as I'm just ready to say I'd do what she wants yet myself, but mebbe bime-by I'd say yes, if you would. Something like we did Sunday night, you know."

"Well, you let me know when you are ready," said Evelyn quickly, glad to have a chance to get out of the thing and at the same time say nothing to hinder Allison's work.

"I will, that's a bargain," said he with a brisk business-like air, "and I guess I'm about made up not to go on the railroad 'count o' Sunday travel, anyway not till I'm sure about the whole shootin' match."

With which elegant and reverent expression he whirled himself and his books into the next car and left Evelyn in a state bordering on hysterics. It was silly, of course, to mind what the uncouth boy had said, but again and again his sharp questions came back, making her think of other questions as searching, but asked in quiet, cultured tones. How was it that this thing seemed to pursue her as she went? Well, that boy would leave at Pittsburgh and then she would deliberately settle herself to forget it all.

Bert was very busy during the remainder of the way to Pittsburgh. He did not have time for talk. He paid her little delicate attentions that any gentleman might have done, perhaps, and she knew it was for Allison's sake. He came in with a book he had found among the stock, "The Sky Pilot," which he told her was "a dandy" and "she" was "awful fond of," and another time he quietly laid a box of Huyler's best chocolates in her lap. She showed her appreciation of these attentions by a quiet smile and would not offend him by offering to pay for what she knew he gave for love of his teacher, though she resolved to make it up to him when she should be where she could select some good music for him, which she would send through Allison.

Just before the train rushed into Pittsburgh he halted by her seat, pencil and note-book in hand.

"Where did you say you lived in New York?" he demanded. "Sixty-fourth Street? What number? I might be there some day and then I'll call and see you. Good-bye. Hope you have a good journey. Sorry you can't play for me some more. Mebbe you'll come back again some day. Ta ta," and with a familiar wave of his hand he swung himself out the door much to her relief, as other passengers were gathering about preparatory to leaving the car and looking curiously at the ill-assorted couple.

He appeared to her again as she was trying to find a place where a decent supper could be obtained, and pushed into her hands another volume. "It's 'Black Rock,'" he explained. "The other one. I knew you'd want to read it too. I got it off the agent in the station. There goes my return whistle," and off he went this time without the parting sentence which she had been dreading.

What had she done? Given him her New York address! What if he should suddenly appear there some day with his familiar "ta ta" and his strange mixing of subjects and pointed personal questions? He certainly would create a sensation. Nevertheless, as she settled herself in the sleeper two hours later she had to admit to herself that Bert Judkins had enlivened her lonely journey for her that afternoon and that she had him to thank for the two fascinating books into which she had dipped enough to know that they contained food for future thought. Gwen's Cañon was to be to her a study. She did not understand it now. The cañon in her own life which would come some day, as yet seemed so impossible that she could but stand outside the story of this other girl and wonder.

Finally the experiences of the day and, to a certain extent, of the past three weeks, faded somewhat and she began to look forward to to-morrow and its possibilities. As she thought of her gay brother lying in a gloomy hotel room she felt a pity for him new to her. Her own position as nurse was strongly influenced by the atmosphere in which she had been moving lately. A month ago she would have been going to Philadelphia more for her own sake than her brother's. Now the feeling of help for him was strong upon her and grew as she sped nearer to him. Something like love glowed in her heart. Of course it was love. She had always loved her brother, in a way, but she did not remember to have ever realized it before, except the time they thought he was drowned, for a few hours, when he was a little fellow. And yet he was a lovable fellow, handsome and bright and scholarly. His tastes were much like hers, but they had been separated during late years. She had been away to school and he to college, and afterward they each had their friends and engagements and came and went without much reference to each other, a fashion the Rutherfords had. Evelyn began to see that this had been her fault largely, for it is the woman of a home who keeps the home the center of the life of the family. A man does not know how to do it. She resolved at least to make some little changes in the way she had been doing. There was no reason why she should not have more of her brother's society. It might be very convenient, and she certainly envied Allison the love of such a brother. It would at least give her something to do. Yes, she would try to be more sisterly to poor Dick and see how it worked. Of course she would not do anything outlandish, but this was the spirit of what Doctor Grey had wanted her to do, she recognized that, the spirit of Christianity. At least it was the spirit he and his family showed and she would try on a bit of it and see how it fitted. With this reflection and the hurried prayer which was fast becoming a habit, she fell asleep.

Philadelphia looked almost as dismal as Pittsburgh in the early morning light. The air was full of a fine cold mist and the streets were wet and sticky. She took a cab and drove to the hotel at which her brother was staying. She sent up to find out how he was and word came down from the nurse that he was awake and very restless. Then she went up at once.

She had not sent word she was coming, nor sent up her name by the porter, so her entrance was an entire surprise.

Mr. Richard Rutherford had lain awake nearly all night. He was suffering somewhat, but his main trouble seemed to be nervousness, the nurse explained, as he met Evelyn at the door. He had declared he would not lie there any longer, and demanded to be allowed to turn over to move or do something forbidden, until the nurse was well-nigh out of patience. He stood at the door, heavy-eyed, telling the story in a half-complaining tone to Evelyn and the patient called him in no pleasant voice from within. Something in her brother's intonation roused all the womanliness and motherliness and loveliness in the girl. She saw in a flash how some woman was needed, their mother if she had lived, perhaps—if she had been such a woman as Mrs. Grey. What peace and comfort Mrs. Grey would bring into that forlorn room in a little while! She saw as in a vision how she might try it herself; that this was meant for her to do, that it would be a good and right thing to do; and she seemed to know at once that it would be difficult because of her unaccustomedness and because of her ease-loving nature. Then without more ado she resolved to do it, at least for a few minutes or hours, till this need should pass. She would be Mrs. Grey, or Allison, as far as she knew how. She put the nurse aside without ceremony and entered. Going softly to the bedside where her brother lay, white and suffering and impatient, she stooped over and kissed him gently on the forehead. She reflected afterward that she was getting into a great habit of kissing people, and it was rather nice after all, much as she used to despise it. It touched her to see her brother's look of pleased surprise as she kissed him and said:

"You poor dear! I am so sorry for you!" Her words were from her heart too, which surprised her even more. She had never had much to draw out her sympathy and knew not that her soul contained any.

"Oh, Evelyn, is that you?" he said, eagerly grasping her hand. "Nobody ever looked so good before. I've been in this wretched spot for ages it seems to me. Last night was a purgatory. That nurse is a fool!"

Evelyn meantime was swiftly taking off wraps and hat and noting with observing eye what was needed. How could she the most quickly make him comfortable? His forehead was hot when she kissed him. His eager response to her greeting touched her more than she cared to show. She laid hands upon a clean towel and dipped it unceremoniously into the ice pitcher and went over to him to bathe his face and hands.

"Oh, how good that feels!" he said, closing his eyes and submitting to her gentle passes on face and hands. "Why didn't that fellow think of it when I felt as if my head was on fire. He is as stupid as a boiled owl."

The nurse meanwhile had taken advantage of the presence of the lady to slip into the hall and tell his grievances to a sympathetic chambermaid, who was answering calls from early risers and hovering near a linen closet.

Evelyn wiped her brother's face and hands gently and straightened the bedclothes. She found his hair brush and brushed his hair. Then after ringing for a maid and a bill of fare she ordered up a dainty breakfast, and strange to say she did not select expensive dainties such as she had been used to do, but chose rather some of the plain, homely things which she remembered as tasting so good at Hillcroft. They would not be so good as Allison's, of course, but perhaps their very homeliness might coax Dick to taste them.

He watched her as she moved about, setting a chair at just the right angle here, opening a blind and arranging a curtain there. The room looked like a different place since she had come into it. He had always known that his sister was beautiful; but he had never noticed that tender, lovely expression of womanliness that she wore this gray morning. Had it always been there and he too blind to see it, or had some new influence come into her life? He felt his heart quicken with a new feeling toward her.

When the breakfast came up she sent the heavy-eyed nurse to get something to eat while she remained and fed her brother herself and ate her breakfast there with him from the same tray. The Evelyn he thought he knew would have taken her breakfast before she came up to see him at all and then have left things to the hired nurse. This Evelyn seemed to know beforehand what he wanted. When the breakfast was over she darkened the room and soothed him to sleep by gentle passes of her hand across his forehead, utterly refusing to talk until he should have had a good long rest. She had seen Allison put her father to sleep in this way more than once when he came home in the evening with a hard headache after an unusually trying day. It was marvelous how much her three weeks' visit had taught her. There was not a turn she had to take now but something Mrs. Grey or Allison had done guided her in her untried way. It was strange they should influence her so, she thought. She forgot that they were almost the only people she had ever watched about homely work-a-day life. She sat for a while in the darkened room while her brother slept and thought about it all, and wondered what she should do next, and if she would be able to carry out her new character till Dick was well. Then she shut her lips a good deal as Allison had done and resolved that she would; after that she set herself to see what she could do to make the room more homelike.

When Richard Rutherford awoke after a long, refreshing sleep he thought that he had been moved to another place. The sun had come out and the curtains were drawn back to let a flood of it across the room. This had been done as he showed signs of waking. There was a glowing fire in the hitherto cold, black grate, and his sister in a crimson dress sat in a little rocking-chair by it with her feet on the fender. A large bright screen kept the light from hurting his eyes and the delicate perfume of Jacqueminot roses floated through the air from a large bowlful on a little stand near the bed, which also contained several new books and the morning paper.

16

Miss Rutherford Plays Nurse

The transforming of that stiff angular dreary hotel room into a homelike spot was not a difficult thing for Evelyn Rutherford to accomplish. She was a girl who generally achieved what she set about. The reason she did not often do nice things was that she did not rouse herself from her own pleasure or ease to take the trouble. Now, however, it pleased her whim to leave no stone unturned to make this first attempt at goodness a success. Perhaps the very energy she put into this and the strange vagaries into which her fancy led her were only the ways in which she eased the pains of a newly aroused conscience which she knew not how to soothe to sleep again, or at least she had at hand none of her old means of doing so.

It is not difficult to do nice things with plenty of money and taste at command. She had known at a glance what was needed, and sent a messenger boy out to one of the great stores near by with a written order for a few articles to be delivered on approval. After the boy had started down the hall a new thought came to her and she recalled him and added an order for a few plainly framed good pictures, within a certain price, to be sent, from which she could make a selection. Perhaps it was these as much as anything else which gave the "at home" air to the room when Richard Rutherford awoke, though he did not at first notice them. His sister had selected them by fancy rather than knowledge, for she was not an art student and did not judge pictures by their worth, only by the way they spoke to her. She had chosen from the lot sent over to her some horses' heads and dogs by Rosa Bonheur, a pretty etching, and Hoffman's child head of Christ. It was a curious collection. She knew that her brother was fond of horses and dogs. The Hoffman she had seen at the Greys' and been struck by the wonderful expression of the face, and a fancied likeness in the eyes to Doctor Grey. That it was supposed to represent the boy Christ Jesus, strange to say, she did not know until after she had bought it. She had this hung on the wall opposite the foot of the bed, and when her brother began to notice the pictures this was the first one his eyes rested upon.

He lay quietly looking about him for a moment when he first awoke. There was a restful, homelike quiet pervading the room. His sister had her head turned away from him and seemed to be thinking. The nurse was nowhere to be seen.

The door opened softly and the doctor stepped in. The patient looked up with a smile.

"Why, you look more cheerful to-day. And what's happened to the place? It bears the touches of a woman's hand." He glanced about, and then seeing Evelyn, who had arisen in surprise and was standing by the mantel, a half-suppressed "Ah!" escaped him.

Evelyn wondered if it was her imagination that detected a note of pride in her brother's voice as he said: "My sister, Doctor MacFarlan, come all the way from Ohio to coddle me." At least, whether it were fancy or truth, it went far toward strengthening Evelyn's purpose in her new way. Ways of carrying out her plan crowded into her mind thick and fast. She actually began to plan for self-sacrifice, a thing she had always detested. It made her feel more virtuous when she had done something to please her brother to know that it had cost her an effort, or the surrender of something which made life pleasanter.

When the doctor was gone and the nurse had made his patient as comfortable as was possible, Evelyn ordered dinner. This time the table was set by the bedside in regular order, the roses in the center and everything as dainty as if she were serving a luncheon at home. This became the established way of taking their meals. Evelyn did not attempt to go down to the dining room at all, but stayed with her brother after she found that it seemed pleasanter to him. It is true this did not require much sacrifice on her part, as she was alone and would not enjoy dining by herself, but she liked to think she was doing a good deal by this little act. Indeed, in the days that followed she began to feel that she could almost compete with Allison herself for deeds of valor and sanctity. She intended to make up for it by a gay season in New York when this siege was over, but in the meantime why not cover herself with glory and still her conscience? So she wrought diligently, even arising at night once or twice to bathe her brother's aching head and read aloud to him when she heard from her adjoining room his restless moans and knew he could not sleep.

She gained for all this devotion a tender acknowledgment once, "Oh, you are a good sister!" This went farther into her heart than all her self-praise had done and brought her nearer to her brother. Nevertheless there were days when he was cross and hard to manage and soothe. And in these days she would have found it easy to return to her former habitual haughtiness and left him entirely alone, were it not for her growing interest in her experiment.

All this time her little daily prayer was uttered with a growing complacency and a tendency to forget its import, to merely continue the habit as a sort of talisman to keep her right in the eyes of a man whom she respected and honored.

It was the afternoon of her arrival that they had their talk about the Greys.

"I don't remember to have seen that Hoffman before," said the young man, looking earnestly at the picture hanging on the wall in front of him. "Where did it come from? Nor in fact any of these other pictures," looking around curiously. "I have not been moved, have I? This surely is the same room, for I have counted the cracks in the ceiling enough times to have them indelibly impressed on my memory, and that surely is the same little imp glaring at me from the wall paper. I cannot be mistaken. How did you manage it, Evelyn? Are you a magician, to wave a wand and bring forth beauties everywhere?"

Evelyn smiled. It was pleasant to have her efforts noticed.

"Oh, I sent over to W——'s for some pictures and chose a few I thought you would like. What did you call that head you were looking at? A Hoffman? Who is it supposed to be? They had it in Hillcroft, and Allison was very fond of it. It seems a remarkable face. I was glad they sent it over, for I always liked it."

"Why, Evelyn, don't you know that picture? It is from the famous painting of the child Christ in the temple, by Hoffman," said the brother, who was more of a devotee of art than his sister and knew pictures and their artists, by name at least.

Evelyn started and actually flushed, she knew not why. Was this then the Christ picture? Was that why it had appealed so to her? And the likeness to Doctor Grey. Had she not heard in that young people's meeting in Hillcroft something said about the followers of Christ growing into his image, or likeness? whether from the Bible or elsewhere she knew not. Was this, then, the explanation? Of course the picture was but a figment of the artist's imagination, anyway, for no one knew how the real Christ looked, but still she could not understand the ideal. And this ideal Christ-expression was the same she had noted in his follower on that hilltop as he looked off and saw in fancy the opening heavens and his coming Lord.

Evelyn turned away from the picture with a sigh almost of impatience. Was this thing then to pursue her everywhere? Could she get away from it in no way? Here she had deliberately chosen this picture and now she could no more look at it in comfort. How annoying that she should not have known! Of course she had supposed it was some religious character or some saint, but not the Christ himself.

"No, I did not know what it was supposed to represent," said Evelyn slowly. "Perhaps you would rather have some other picture hanging there where you have to look at it all the time. We can exchange any of these."

"No, leave it," he said, looking at it thoughtfully. "It is a fine face and I like to study it. There is such buoyancy of youth and entire hopefulness in the face. It rests one. Somehow I shall not dare complain so much with that cheerful countenance over there. Who is this Allison you speak of? That is a peculiar name. I don't remember ever to have heard it before. Does it belong to man, woman, or child?"

Evelyn laughed. "Allison Grey is a very beautiful girl, Dick. You would simply rave over her, and say she ought to be painted and 'sculped' and have poetry written to her, and all those things your artist friends do. She lives in Hillcroft, and it was in her home I was staying, much against my will. Oh, no, it was not uncomfortable. I assure you I was treated most delightfully, and now that it is past I look back upon the experience as something rich. I don't know but I was rather sorry to come away after all. I never was in a place where people seemed to think so much of one another and of their home, before. Allison is Dr. Maurice Grey's sister. You remember him, do you not?"

"Grey? Why, surely. You don't say! How peculiar! I remember now, he did live out West somewhere, but I never bothered my head to learn where. Odd to think he lived in the same town with our revered aunt and we never knew it. The world isn't so large after all, is it? Grey was a good fellow.

We would have been close chums if he had not been so overwhelmingly busy all the time. When he was not buried in his books he was out slumming or off at a prayer meeting. He tried to get me into all those things, but somehow I didn't incline that way. I sometimes think it might have been a good thing for me if I had stuck to him and his schemes. He wasn't any of your molly-coddles, either. He was captain of the baseball team at one time and a first-rate runner and good at all outdoor sports. And he had a voice like a whole orchestra, from the bass drum up. Did you ever hear him sing? No, of course you didn't. My, but he can sing! He was head of the glee club, but gave it up because he had so little time. He was one of the men that make you think there is something in life worth while besides just the pleasure you can get out of it. You like to have him around. You feel safe when he is by. You know nothing very bad can happen to him. Though I don't know but he makes you feel uncomfortable too; he is doing so tremendously well with his own life that you feel mean to look at your own. I have often wondered what kind of a home the fellow had. He used to speak of his mother and sister, and father too, with real affection; but he was one who would feel affection for a cat that belonged to him, so you could not judge by that. Besides, he is so unusual that there can't be many like him. His family are doubtless quite commonplace. How did you find them?"

"Anything but commonplace," answered Evelyn quickly. "They are the most extraordinary people I ever met. They do absolutely nothing to please themselves, so far as I could find out, without first inquiring whether it will help or hinder some one else. I felt smaller and smaller the longer I stayed. Not that they obtruded their goodness, oh, dear me, no! They were sweetness itself, but I could not help seeing how differently they looked at everything. Still, they seemed very happy."

She stopped, musing, and looked at the picture.

"Tell me all about it," said her brother, looking interested. "Humanity is always interesting. I like to get hold of a new type. What kind of a house do they live in, and what do they do from morning to night? Begin at the beginning and tell what they did the first thing in the morning and what they had for breakfast. I'm sick of all the people I've met lately; perhaps these will be a change. I suppose you found a good many pretty funny things, didn't you?"

Evelyn hesitated. She suddenly found that there were some things she did not care to tell; also it grated on her just the least little bit to seem to make fun of the people who had been so kind to her. Dick doubtless would think some things very queer and they had seemed so to her when they occurred, but now that she had come to tell them for some one else to laugh over she shrank from it, she knew not why. Moreover, the thing that had impressed Evelyn more than any other habit of the Grey household had been the family worship, held before breakfast every morning. At first she had not known about it, because she came down late; but afterward, when she began to get down earlier, she found that they came together to ask God's blessing upon the day. Whenever the family were all gathered at the evening hour for retiring they also knelt in prayer together. This had been so utterly new and embarrassing together to Evelyn that she did not like to speak of it. She felt afraid of betraying her own emotion in her voice if she should attempt to do so. How could she help remembering the strange, creepy sensation that came over her when she first heard Mr. Grey's kind voice as if he were talking to a friend, say:

"And bring to the stranger who has come into our home for a little while a rich blessing. May she be a help to us, and may we in no way hinder her."

But her brother was urging her impatiently: "Go on, Evelyn. What time did you get up at Hillcroft?"

Thus urged Evelyn began:

"We had what they called prayers the first thing in the morning, and at night before retiring they had them again."

She paused, expecting her brother to rail out against a perpetual prayer meeting. He was looking dreamily at the picture and he only answered:

"Ah! that accounts for it!" then he turned to his sister, suddenly remembering that she had been for a time a part of this strange household. "I suppose it was rather hard on you, wasn't it?"

Why she should resent this she did not know, but she did. Nevertheless she went on to describe the white house with green blinds, wide porches, and pretty lawns; the village, and what people she had met; and above all, the life of commonplace, every-day work and kindliness. She did not use many words nor express any opinions herself, but she gave a very true picture of Hillcroft.

"It sounds pleasant," said the young man with his eyes closed. "I think I shall visit Aunt Joan myself some day. It would be interesting to walk about that quiet little town and meet Miss Rebecca Bascomb. Do you think the star-eyed goddess with the gold hair would condescend to flirt with a fellow for a few days?"

"Dick!" said Evelyn, almost sharply. "Don't! You don't know her. She would no more flirt than she would commit murder."

"Really! That sounds interesting! A young woman who will not flirt! I shall surely visit Aunt Joan some day. Such a curiosity as a young woman who will not flirt ought certainly to be brought to New York. If you are right, which I very much doubt, there is still some hope of the human race," and he laughed as he saw the color mounting swiftly into his sister's face.

"Dick!" she said in a vexed tone.

"I beg your pardon, my beloved sister, but isn't it true? Come, confess. By the way, what has become of Hal Worthington, upon whom I last saw you exercising that art? Have you dropped him for another victim, or only loaned him to Jane while you were away. I hear she has quite taken him up."

Evelyn's eyes grew dark with irritation, but it was not her way to break into angry exclamation.

"I know nothing about Mr. Worthington," she said freezingly, "and if you talk in this way I shall certainly leave you to the tender mercies of your nurse."

"A truce! A truce, sister! I beg your pardon humbly. I cannot afford to quarrel with you now. Tell me about Hillcroft. But, indeed, you have relieved my mind. Let Hal Worthington alone, he isn't worth your notice."

"You men always are hard upon one another," said Evelyn coldly. "There's nothing the matter with Mr. Worthington."

"Just as you women are on one another," responded the brother, laughing. "But there's everything the matter with

Worthington, Evelyn, believe me. I hope you won't have anything more to do with him."

"Indeed!" said Evelyn politely. "I'm obliged to you for your advice, but it's wholly unnecessary. I assure you I choose my friends where I please, and consider myself fully able to tell a *man* when I see him."

Richard Rutherford frowned and was about to speak angrily again, and perhaps tell his sister some truths which she might as well have heard then as later, and the whole of Evelyn's scheme was well-nigh on the verge of shipwreck when the doctor, with his light tap on the door, entered and put a stop to the talk.

Evelyn retired to her room to smooth her ruffled feelings. She was more annoyed than she cared to have her brother know. Two natures were striving within her for the mastery. The one was typified by her intimacy with Mr. Worthington, the other by her chance meeting with that other man, Doctor Grey. Each was antagonistic to the other. Since she had been at Hillcroft she had begun to feel out of harmony with Mr. Worthington. If her brother had said nothing about him she would not have felt inclined to renew her friendship with him, but she hated above all things to be managed and advised and treated as if she were a child. Therefore she resolved to show her brother when she got home that she could take care of herself. In her private heart, however, she laid aside the warning and concluded that it was all well for her not to go with this gay young man any more.

During the days that followed she told her brother many things about the Grey family, and Allison was mentioned more than once. Bert also came up for a description and the young man laughed loud and long over his sister's discomfiture in the Pullman car. He also showed surprise and hearty approval as she told of her adventure—for so she accounted it—in playing at a prayer meeting. He declared he should like to meet Bert and forthwith demanded to have "The Sky Pilot" and "Black Rock" read aloud to him. After these were finished Evelyn bethought herself of the upper row in the library at Hillcroft and sallied forth to the book store, returning with a number of them.

The young man seemed interested in these books. They were in a new line for him. They were studies of human character and as such he recognized their worth and beauty and was not a little touched with their pathos. He laughed till he cried over Abe, the stage driver, and Bronco Bill, and he turned his head aside to wipe away the tears over little Gwen and the coming into port of the Pilot. When they came to "Snow and Heather" and read of Steenie's "Bonnie Man" he lay with thoughtful eyes on the picture of the boy Christ before him.

It was while they read "A Singular Life" one day that Richard broke in upon the reading:

"He joined the student volunteers when he was in college I remember. Did you ever hear about it? I wonder if he outgrew it or what was the matter that he gave it up. He was very enthusiastic."

"Of whom, pray, are you speaking? Emanuel Bayard in this story? And what may a student volunteer be, I should like to inquire?" said the reader, pausing and closing the book with her finger in the place.

"Why, I was speaking of Maurice Grey. Someway Bayard reminds me of him. He was much such a fellow. And a student volunteer—why, Evelyn, you are certainly very ignorant. It was a movement that swept through the colleges; I don't know but it's going on yet. A great many students joined it, promising to go to foreign fields as missionaries if possible. I know Grey was one, for he tried his best to get me interested."

"Really! How strange! What would he want to go as a missionary for? It would be bad enough to be a missionary at home. I can't imagine any one getting to that point of sacrifice. Not one so well educated and cultured as Doctor Grey. I suppose he has given it up as one of the follies of his boyhood. Of course he did not expect to succeed in his profession as he has, at that time."

Then she went back to her reading, her mind keeping up an undertone of thought of which Doctor Grey was the center, typified by the hero of the story she read.

17

Mr. Worthington's Repulse

In the meantime Dr. Maurice Grey had not been idle. His new practice took every atom of time the day contained and sometimes much of the night. To fill the absence of a man so great required unceasing labor and energy. His life carried him into many homes where were distress and sorrow in one form or another. Constantly he was appealed to, to do the impossible. He sometimes longed for the power of some of the old disciples to work miracles, till he remembered that he who was managing all the affairs of the world knew and loved each one of these sufferers more than he possibly could, and was working his best in each life. But all that was in his power to do to help he certainly did. He was indefatigable day and night. Neither did he slight the poor and lowly. He kept up well the reputation Doctor Atlee had always had of being no respecter of persons in his work of healing. His coming brought many a ray of sunshine into darkened homes.

But with all his hurry and burden of other lives upon him he did not forget to pray. He kept up his college habit of praying for certain individuals; but among them all there was one name which he never forgot, which stood at the head of his list, and for which he prayed with all the earnestness his earnest soul could feel, and that name was Evelyn Rutherford. Just what his feeling toward her was he had not asked himself. It was enough that he wanted her to belong to Christ, wanted it with his whole soul. He would put his energy into that thought. He had no time for any other. What did it matter? God would work out any plan in his life he

126

chose, if he but waited and did his duty, whether of sorrow or of joy. If either were meant for him he hoped he would be given the right spirit in which to meet it.

He heard from home that Miss Rutherford had left them suddenly to attend upon her brother in Philadelphia. He was disappointed that she should have gone from there so soon. He had hoped much from her contact with Allison, both for herself and for his sister. Allison was too quiet and shy, and needed contact with a girl who was used to mingling with the world. Allison was consecrated, and must make an impression upon one who knew not Jesus Christ. He wondered why it had been planned to separate these two who had been so wonderfully, almost miraculously, brought together. Then he wondered if we should have all our wonders explained when we got on the other side, and he left the matter there.

He called at the Rutherford house one day to inquire how his old friend was getting on, for he thought they would have word, but he found the house closed and not a servant about. His card was among many others which Evelyn found as soon as she returned. It was crumpled and dusty, and she knew it must have lain under the door some time.

It was well on into December before the Rutherfords finally returned to their home on Sixty-fourth Street. The broken bone had not behaved well, and Evelyn's work had been much more trying than she had anticipated. Nevertheless, it was with a certain satisfaction that she reviewed the weeks she had spent in Philadelphia. They had not been altogether unpleasant. She had discovered that reading aloud was a very pleasant way of enjoying a book and getting a great deal more out of it than one could possibly get alone. She had discovered that there were lots of books in the world that she had never read which were vastly more interesting to her than the class of society novels she had been accustomed to devour. Of course she had a mind above these other books or this would not have been the case. She had discovered—and this was a very important revelation—that her brother was good company. Each had developed an unsuspected affection for the other, and the time had passed much more rapidly than either had hoped. It was therefore with a loving solicitude that she saw him hobble into the house on his crutch, and hastened to prepare a couch for him and make him comfortable on their return to New York. He would come before he was at all strong enough.

The father, coming upon them unexpectedly the day before they had thought he could arrive, was pleased to see Evelyn bending over her brother to settle the pillows comfortably. Something in her attitude reminded him of her mother as a girl, and he stopped an instant on the threshold to look before he spoke. He was gratified beyond expression to have his daughter put her arms about his neck and kiss him as if she were really glad he was come home once more. He could not remember so spontaneous a greeting since the days when she was a tiny child. He was not a father whose way was to show affection, but he had a well of it hidden in his heart, and though his blunt, plain-spoken words were often against him, he loved these two children of his deeply.

He cherished that kiss in his heart, though his only outward response beyond a smile was:

"We made faster time over than we expected, and got in an hour ago. I came right up from the steamer."

Evelyn was so satisfied with her experiment in Philadelphia that she set about establishing a new order of things in New York. She took the management of the servants more into her own hands, and finally dismissed entirely the housekeeper, who had been with them for several years, and had grown fat and lazy in her position and lax in her duties. She wrote to Allison for the recipes of one or two things she had eaten at their house and knew her father would enjoy, and once she essayed to go into the kitchen and attempt some waffles herself. Sorry-looking affairs they were, and worse tasting; and a much bedraggled young woman it was, with burned fingers and aching back, who finally, with the aid of a trusted maid—it was the cook's afternoon out—carefully removed all signs of her experiment, resolving the while mentally to conquer waffles some day if it took a year to learn.

But her attempts were not all in the culinary line. She turned her attention to the library, and made it as attractive as her skill could; and then she would coax her father in to sit with her sometimes when he came home weary with his business, and ask him questions about politics and things in which she knew he was interested and for which she had primed herself by reading the morning papers. He was surprised and pleased with this attention, and would sometimes come into the music room when she was playing and lie down on the couch to listen, staying an hour or two if she played so long.

She marveled to herself that little things that could be so easily done could have such an effect on the home life. They seemed to be more of a family now than they had ever been, though she felt that there was something lacking, and that something she knew from the Hillcroft picture she had looked upon, was a mother. However, she was doing the best she could, and she plumed herself mightily upon her success, insomuch that she felt she was now quite able to compete with Allison in goodness.

And then one day on coming home from a round of much-neglected calls, she found Doctor Grey's card again, and suddenly remembered her promise. Yes, she had kept it, but for some reason her conscience did not entirely approve of her. She had said the words over every night, but she had been so engaged in working out salvation that she had forgotten that she was to ask it with her whole heart and try to desire it. The words had become so familiar that for the moment she could not tell their import. That is the way we do with things most sacred when we are otherwise occupied. It is the devil's one weapon against vows and promises and mighty words of warning or invitation. We hear the Bible till we let its meaning slip by us on oiled wheels of familiarity. We forget the relationships we bear to one another and their sweet and wonderful meanings by the very intimacy that the tie brings with it. And so Evelyn Rutherford suddenly realized that she had forgotten that she was to ask to be made willing "to be good," as she phrased it, in the very act of trying to get to herself that righteousness another way. Not that she reasoned it out in this way. Oh, no; she was too little familiar with such thoughts to reason. She simply was ill at ease again, and when she knelt that night to say the prayer the words would not come so easily, and the angel had to stand quite near to listen that he might carry up the incense of that feeble little orison to the throne.

The next morning was Sunday and she arose very early and underwent not a little inconvenience that she might attend the church service. It seemed to her that this might ease her restless spirit. As she did not belong to any church in particular and the family went where they chose when it pleased them to go at all, she idly chose a church where the pastor had lately become noted for his unusual sermons and where she knew the music was fine. Not feeling in the mood for meeting acquaintances she took a seat in the gallery, where she could look down upon the audience and where she was comparatively hidden. The opening music over, she settled back in her seat half-repenting that she had come, and began to search out one and another whom she knew in the audience. She wondered what they came to church for, and why Miss Spalding wore such hideous hats and did her hair in such a wretched fashion, and forgot entirely to note the text or the opening words of the sermon, which were usually exceedingly fine. So the papers said, about the preaching of the eminent young divine. Then suddenly the whole scene was changed for her.

The vestibule door swung silently on its hinges and some one stepped noiselessly into a seat just below the curve of the gallery and took a seat where she could see him, and behold, it was Dr. Grey!

His reverent attitude at once brought it sharply to her mind that this church was a sacred place; the worshiper below felt it to be such. She saw from the instant rapt attention he gave to the minister that he intended to make the most of the service. And now, behold, she heard the sermon herself, and heard it as through the ears of the quiet listener seated below her. The thoughts of the preacher were reflected in unmistakable lines on the speaking face, and all the way through to the end Evelyn felt as if she were being preached at, and by one who cared for her salvation. By the droop of Dr. Grey's head in prayer she recognized that the sermon had passed into petition and then she felt herself prayed for. Suddenly she was seized with a longing to hear him pray for her. Had he kept it up yet? He had said he would, and she believed he was a man who always remembered such things. What did he say when he called her name before the throne? What name did he speak? How ran the words?

The closing hymn was announced and she suddenly recollected in confusion that she had not bowed her head nor even closed her eyes during prayer. She was glad that few could see her where she sat. Then she began to dread the close of service and to half fear, half long, to meet and talk with Dr. Grey. Would he ask her if she had kept her promise? Would he say anything about that dreadful sermon that seemed to have cut straight into her life and showed how barren it was? Then the question was settled in an unexpected way. The man downstairs seemed suddenly to become aware of the outside world once more. He took out his watch and with a hurried motion put on his overcoat and slipped out of the church. Ah, yes, he was a busy man. He had work in the world to attend to, something worth while. In a gleam of revelation she saw how useless her life thus far had been and went home more miserable than she had been for a long time.

Mr. Worthington dropped in that afternoon. She had not been cordial to him of late, but she hailed him as a respite from herself and for an hour was as gay and reckless as she ever had been before she went to Hillcroft. She laughed and chatted and used her fine eyes to good effect. Then suddenly her father and brother entered from the street, and the glance that each cast into the room as they passed by without coming in, reminded Evelyn of what they thought of her visitor. A vision of a fine, serious face in reverent, attentive attitude in the tinted shadows of the dimly lighted sanctuary came between her and the reckless face of the man with whom she was talking. All her brilliancy left her, and she declined coldly an invitation to an unusually fine musical performance and took the violets he had brought her, from her belt where she had fastened them, throwing them carelessly on the table. She seemed out of harmony with him all at once and shuddered at a joke he ventured to perpetrate. What would Dr. Grey say could he see her in such company? She mentally reviewed the conversation of the afternoon. It did not bear even her own scrutiny. She was ashamed and began to plan how she might rid herself of him. It was not an easy task seeing she had so far lowered herself as to encourage his attention. Was it true, as her brother had said, that she was a flirt? She would not like to have that other man know it. She would not have liked him to see her this afternoon.

Mr. Worthington was too keen not to feel the depression

of the atmosphere and soon took himself away wondering what had come over Miss Rutherford so suddenly. He was as near to being in love as he had ever been in his life, and he was in great need of some girl's money if he would save the reputation under which he had been masquerading. Perhaps he had better be a little more guarded in his speech, though she had seemed at one time to be dashing enough and not afraid of anything. Well, there was no accounting for women. But this one was worth cultivating a little further and going slow for, if that was what she wanted. She appeared to welcome him heartily enough till her father and brother arrived. Probably that was the matter; they had taken a dislike. He had always considered her brother entirely too nice about some things. However *he* could pose as a moral hero if need be. And he whistled an air from the opera as he went his way toward Jane Bashford's, where he was sure to find five o'clock tea and a welcome.

18

A Hospital for China

Although the busy doctor found little time for social duties he nevertheless made two more attempts to call on the Rutherfords, but on both occasions found none of the family at home. It was doubtless due to his being obliged to choose his time whenever there came opportunity, and to his lack of knowledge concerning the social engagements that would be likely to take the members of the family from home. As a college student when he had been in town occasionally he had informed himself about these matters, but now all was different. He must go when he could. Duty was ever present to watch over his movements.

The second time he turned away from the door quite disappointed. He had seen Miss Rutherford passing a house where he was visiting a patient only the day before. She had been in a carriage and leaned out to smile and bow to a lady on the sidewalk. Of course she did not see him. He had just stepped to the window to examine the thermometer for the patient's temperature, as the room was so darkened he could not be sure he was right, and looking up had seen her. The sight of her face awakened his strong desire to meet and talk with her again.

When, at a late hour that evening, he was able to return to his own inner sanctum and commune with himself, he sat for a time thinking with his weary eyes closed, and then abruptly arose, and going to a closet, searched out a large, wooden box, among several that had not been unpacked since he came to New York. He sent his office boy for the hatchet and opened it, and there were revealed myriads of photographs. They were relics of his college days, and had not been unpacked since he took them down from his walls when he left. He searched among them for some time in vain. Now and again he would stop and look thoughtfully at a face as old memories were brought up, but for the most part he went rapidly over them as if hunting for some certain one. At last near the very bottom he found the object of his search. It was a handsome photograph, somewhat faded and soiled by dust, showing a beautiful girl, with fine, dark eyes, and masses of black hair about her shoulders, standing by a boy with eyes like her own. They were apparently about fourteen and sixteen years of age.

He unceremoniously bundled the rest of the pictures into the box and tumbled it back into the closet, to be set to rights at another time. Then he seated himself and proceeded to study that picture.

He could remember so well the day when it came into his possession. It was the day they were all packing to leave college. He had gone over to Dick Rutherford's room a moment, for Dick was leaving that day, and had all his boxes nailed up, and his room entirely dismantled. He had wandered about the room and sat down on the window ledge while he talked, and noticing this picture slipped down face to the wall behind the bedstead, he had reached down, pulled it out, and showed it to Dick. He could see Dick's face now as he waved it aside.

"Never mind that old thing. Throw it in the waste basket, leave it on the floor. I haven't another crack of room where I could get in even a microbe, and everything is locked. I'm mortally afraid they will burst before I get home now. There's plenty more pictures at home, and besides that's only my sister and myself when we were kids."

"But you don't want to leave your sister's picture about for any one to get hold of, Rutherford," he had reminded him.

"Oh, well, I'll trust it to your safe keeping, then," he had said with a laugh as he went out.

Maurice Grey had not been sure to-night that he had kept that picture, but a dim memory of putting it in his box which stood in his room ready to be nailed up, caused him to go in search of it. Now, after looking at it a long time he carefully cut out the girl's picture, and placed it in a little oval velvet frame that had been given him with some baby-patient's picture, and stood it on his bureau. There he surveyed it with a curious satisfaction. No one could possibly know who it was, he thought, and no one would ever notice it. The original of the picture would scarcely be likely to find it out. After that he went to call again with the same disappointing result.

As he came down the steps of the house on Sixty-fourth Street he recollected a missionary conference which was going on at that time, and decided to spend his leisure hour there. It was long since he had been able to indulge in one of these meetings, and he was deeply interested in them. He had never quite given up his desire to go to a foreign field, although his opportunities in his own land had seemed to open up in such a way as to indicate his duty at home. Missionaries were by no means so hard to find as they were at the time he had eagerly pledged himself to go if opportunity offered.

He smothered his disappointment about the call as best he could, told himself it was just as well, that he was getting to long for the things of this world too much, especially when they were things he never could have, and went to the meeting.

The meeting was more than usually moving. The Spirit of the Master who said, "Go ye into all the world and preach the gospel to every creature," seemed to be there in very truth. There were present several returned missionaries who knew how to speak to the friends at home and stir their hearts to the love of Jesus, as well as to those who had never heard of him. The climax was reached when a missionary from China told in simple language of his work and of the needs of the region where he was stationed. He spoke of cases that had come to them for treatment, begging to be taken in and cured, but they had no room in the mission for this; that they needed a hospital in that region fully equipped with a good man at the head, and that there was no money for that. The man made the story live, until his audience saw before them the poor, suffering creatures. The listeners were roused to a tremendous pitch of excitement. There were men gathered there who represented a large amount of money. Some of them had been brought by consecrated friends to hear this very man speak. A few of them gathered in a group at the close of the address and talked, and their talk was not without a firm foundation. They were willing, these men, to put their hands in their pockets and help along the work, if that hospital could be established and put in running order before another year.

"How are you, doctor?" said one, as Maurice Grey pressed forward to get a word with the speaker. "We've about decided to have that hospital. I wish we could put you at the head of it. You would be just the man."

"I wish you would," was the unexpected response, fully confirmed by the eager face and eyes full of deep feeling. "Oh, I should like it above all things."

"Do you really mean it?" said the man, wheeling about and looking him in the face. "You, with your prospects and your position, would you leave it all to go to China and nurse those poor old women? Why, man alive, you'll be able in a few years, if you keep on as you've started here, to support two or three hospitals yourself."

"I would count it the highest possible honor to go," said Maurice Grey solemnly.

"Well, then, if that's so we certainly ought to furnish the funds for your work," said the old gentleman, wheeling back to the others who stood silently listening.

And it did not all end in talk.

Evelyn Rutherford, upon returning from a play which she considered extremely lacking in interest, and during which she had been annoyed more than once by the obtrusive attentions of Mr. Worthington, who took it upon himself to monopolize the seat next to her in the box, was conscious of deep disappointment to find by the cards left on her dressing table that she had again missed Doctor Grey.

She frowned at herself in the glass and wondered if it was ever to be so with them, always missing each other. Why did she care, anyway? He only called from politeness, of course. But still she would have liked to be at home, just to see if he still continued to seem to her so much of a man. She was growing cynical about men. She had decided that there were very few good ones, always excepting her father and brother, for they were growing nearer to her in these days.

It occurred to her just as she was about to retire that she might make a way to meet Doctor Grey again if she chose. She wondered it had not come to her before. What more natural than that he should be invited to dine with them when she had spent several weeks in his father's home? It must have even seemed strange to him that no attention had been paid him at all. A quick crimson dyed her cheek, for now that the thought had occurred to her it seemed inexcusable that it had not been carried into effect before. It is true she had sent Mrs. Grey and Allison both exquisite presents at Christmas time, but kindness such as she recognized theirs to have been could not be repaid by a few paltry gifts. What did they think of her that she had extended no invitation to the son who lived so near to her! Perhaps, however, she was more troubled about what the son himself would think than about his family.

She hastily scanned the leaves of her engagement book to see what day was unoccupied, and then sat down at her desk and wrote a note of invitation. She would wait till she could consult her father and brother in the morning before sending it, for she wished to be sure they would be at home that night; but her conscience felt easier with the note already written.

As it happened, both her father and brother had engagements on the evening selected, and it became necessary to wait until the next week and write another note, so that it was nearly two weeks after his useless call that Maurice Grey stood once more upon the brownstone steps and waited for the butler to open the door.

Evelyn, mindful of Miss Rebecca Bascomb's warning, had selected a dinner dress that was cut rather high, and filled in the neck with something soft, transparent, and white. The dress was black and very becoming. She studied herself in her mirror more critically than she had done in many a day. On the whole she was dissatisfied. Neither face nor dress looked as she thought his ideal woman would look. But why should she care? she asked herself as she turned away with a sigh.

She had hoped to have a moment or two with him before the others came in, but he was late himself, instead of her father and brother, as she had planned. He apologized; he came from a very sick patient whom he dared not leave sooner. He had almost feared it was too late to come at all, but he had presumed to come in spite of the hour, as his social pleasures were so few.

They went out to dinner at once. Evelyn presided like a queen, so thought the guest. He watched her as if it were a pleasure. Long afterward he could close his eyes and see her white hands moving among the cups and mixing the salad dressing, and recall the stately bend of her head as she answered the servant in a low tone.

The young doctor was almost immediately engaged in conversation by Mr. Rutherford and his old friend Dick, but his eyes feasted themselves upon the beautiful woman who presided at the table. She said little herself. She could but be conscious of his eyes, and her own drooped in consequence. She wondered for what he was searching her so. Did he expect to see her life written on her face? Was he studying her to see if she had kept her promise? Looking up at that instant she met his gaze and smiled. It was a simple little thing to do, but her color heightened after it. There had been no outward reason for that smile, but in her heart she knew it had come to answer his question about the promise. Did he also know it? For he smiled back, a glad, happy smile, like a boy just out of school and enjoying his freedom to the full. She cherished that smile for many a day thereafter. She had never seen him in this bright, gay mood before; he joked with Dick and they told many stories of their college days, in which all were interested. In fact, the guest proved himself so fascinating that Mr. Rutherford strolled into the drawing room with the young people, later in the evening, to enjoy the conversation. It is needless to say he never did that for the sake of joining the group which contained Mr. Worthington.

Evelyn sat a little apart from the three men, but deeply interested in what they were saying, and watching them intently, thinking how well they seemed to get on together, and wondering at it, seeing that they represented homes so different. She hardly knew why this pleased her so much.

She did not thrust herself into the conversation; but they included her often and Doctor Grey would turn his eyes to hers as if seeking a sympathy he felt sure of finding there. It was an evening such as Evelyn had never passed, a vision into the might-have-been which it had never even entered into her heart to conceive before. She felt happier than she had felt since she was a child, and she did not try to question why she felt so; she simply accepted it as one accepts things in blessed dreams.

Then into this pleasant room, where for the time being pure happiness reigned alone, there entered the serpent in the shape of Mr. Worthington.

It is needless to say that he had not one thing in common with the hour or the company. Mr. Rutherford and his son arose and stiffly bowed good-evening to the caller, Dick looking extremely annoyed at the interruption. Doctor Grey was introduced and a shadow crossed the brightnees of his face as he quickly looked the stranger over, placed him, and then cast a questioning glance at Evelyn. She wondered if he had seen her with Mr. Worthington.

The caller essayed to draw Evelyn into a *tête-à-tête*, but she did not respond. She answered him in a tone calculated to make the conversation general, and remained where she had been sitting before he came in. He drew his black brows together in a frown as he took in the situation and reflected that he had come at an unfortunate time, though, perhaps, it was as well to make his favorable impression upon father and brother now as at any time. Then he set himself to listen and join in the conversation as soon as an opportunity should offer.

The doctor had been telling a story that seemed to interest them all when the caller had been announced, and he was now finishing it. Evelyn wished he would talk on all night so that there need be no opportunity for the other guest to speak, for she felt unhappy and humiliated by his presence. She resolved that she would have nothing more to do with him hereafter. How could she, when she saw these two together?

"Oh, Maurice, that is too good," said young Mr. Rutherford, laughing at the conclusion of the story. "I tell you, we must manage to see more of one another. Can't you plan your time next winter so that we can have at least one evening a week together somewhere? I tell you, you will kill yourself, if you go on at this rate. Come, say you will. You could have done a vast amount of good to me if you had held up on some of your slum work in college and put in a little time with me." Richard Rutherford looked at his friend with the winning smile that always had brought to him friends when he chose, and it was met by one full of response, but with a tinge of gravity.

"Dick, I should like it better than I can tell you, but——" here the smile faded entirely and his face grew grave and almost sad—— "but I do not expect to be in New York next winter."

"Not in New York next winter, man! Why, what do you mean?" asked Dick, astonished, and Evelyn gave the slightest perceptible start which she hoped was unobserved. She did not know that her father from looking moodily at the young man by her side, had turned sadly toward her, wondering if his pretty daughter was going to throw herself away on that worthless creature, and seeing her slight motion, had speculated behind the hand that partly shielded his face what it might mean.

"I expect to sail for China in September," said the young man quietly, a great reverence in tone and voice as if he were going under high commission.

"For China? Have you a foreign commission? Are you going as an ambassador? What! You have not joined the army?"

"Yes, I have a commission," he answered, smiling with that pleasant way he had of talking his religion to his friends that reminded Evelyn of the day upon the hilltop; "but it is from a higher tribunal than the government of the United States. My commission is an old, old one, and in a sense I joined the army long ago, but I suppose you have forgotten it. I am sent as an ambassador of Jesus Christ. I go out as a medical missionary this fall."

During the silence and almost consternation that followed this statement, young Worthington, with inexplicable bad taste, saw his opportunity.

"Are you going to take your wife with you or have her sent out by Adams Express Company, selected by the people at home who pay the bills? I hear that is quite a fad among missionaries now, to have their wives chosen and sent over to them when they get ready. It must be a great convenience to those who find it hard to choose for themselves. I heard of a fellow the other day who advertised for one, but when she came he found she had but one eye. You'd better keep a sharp watch on them if you intend to try that way. You might get left."

If the young man expected to raise a laugh he was mistaken. The faces of both the Rutherford gentlemen expressed the extreme dislike and superiority one might feel for an impudent little cur that has snapped at one's feet.

The eyes of the young doctor flashed with a righteous fire of indignation. Evelyn thought she had never seen him look so handsome. She did not know he could be so roused. She involuntarily drew her chair sharply away from Mr. Worthington.

Then spoke Maurice Grey: "The man who will so dishonor a woman as to marry her when he bears her no love is, to my mind, not only unworthy of being a missionary of Jesus Christ, but also hardly worthy the name of man, surely not gentleman."

"You are married, then, or about to be?" persisted the young man, determined to carry off the situation in spite of the atmosphere which he could not help but see was hostile in the extreme.

"No, Mr. Worthington; a man would require a brave heart, indeed, to ask any woman he loved to share the hardships and dangers of a missionary's life. One would need to be sure that she also felt the call to go before daring to ask a woman to share such a life with him."

"Oh, the hardships and dangers are things of the past," sneered the young man. "Missionaries nowadays live like princes, with all that they need paid for and companies of servants to do their bidding. They really have very little to do."

"Pray, when were you a missionary, Mr. Worthington?" inquired Evelyn, in her most cutting tone. "You must have been on the spot to be so well informed."

Doctor Grey looked up in surprise. He had never heard this Evelyn. The icy tones did not belong to his ideal, nevertheless they did him good at this juncture.

Mr. Rutherford, Sr., relieved the situation by ignoring Mr. Worthington entirely, and, leaning forward, asked in earnest tones: "But what does Doctor Atlee say to this? I understood that you and he were partners, and my son told me this morning that he heard Doctor Atlee call you his better half. Does he know of this most extraordinary and self-sacrificing move on your part?"

A strange, sweet light overspread the face of Maurice Grey: "Yes, he knows, and I am going with his blessing. It is hard to give up the association with him. He is a grand man. Did you know it was his early dream to go as a missionary himself? Yes, and he gave it up to take care of his invalid mother, who was suddenly thrown upon his care. She is still living and still an invalid, and he is devoted to her. He says he wants me to go in his place. He has been wonderful. He is giving a large sum to the new hospital I am to have in charge."

Then did Dick Rutherford begin a fire of questions about China and the work, and Maurice Grey answered with some of the stories the returned missionary had told which had roused his sleeping desire to go, until they all were stirred.

Finding that it was of no use to try to turn the conversation to his own level, or to secure Miss Rutherford's attention,

Mr. Worthington again essayed to take part in the conversation.

"If all that is true, I should think you would not care to marry," he said in his lazy tone. "One could scarcely find any attractive woman who would care to relegate herself into barbarism." He desired to erase, if possible, the impression he had created by his last blunder, but he was on entirely foreign ground himself.

Evelyn's great dark eyes fairly flashed at him as she said in a low tone: "The woman who will not go to the ends of the earth for the man she loves is not worthy to be called a woman."

Maurice Grey turned his fine eyes upon her with that pleasant light of sympathy in them. Dick Rutherford looked at his sister with complacency. He was glad to hear such a sentiment from her lips, but he scowled at the young man who had called it forth and resolved to find some way to keep his sister from him.

The evening closed abruptly by the sudden recollection of Doctor Grey that it was time he looked in at the hospital to see how a man was doing who had that afternoon undergone an operation.

"Now, Evelyn, *that* is a *man*," said her father as he turned from bidding their guest good-bye, "and that other fellow is a—a contemptible puppy!"

19

Farewell to Doctor Grey

The days that followed were full of a suppressed excitement for Evelyn. She marveled daily over the spirit of sacrifice that could make the rising young doctor with such life and prospects before him deliberately go to that far-off land to do what any common doctor might do. It was again that same old problem that she had puzzled over at Hillcroft, what strange power was the motive? She began to feel a certain desire, faint, but still perceptible even to herself, to feel that power in her own life. She put more real earnestness into her prayer by fits and starts now. Sometimes she fancied she really meant it.

She was glad she had thought of inviting Doctor Grey to dinner. She watched daily to see if he would call. She remained at home a great deal afternoons, and often in the evenings pleaded some excuse for foregoing a social engagement. She longed to have a talk with him, just to ask him one or two questions, and—yes, just to have him tell her once more he was praying for her, if he was. It somehow had grown to be a comfort to her when she was unhappy to think of that good man praying for her. Good? Oh yes, she was doubly sure of that, now that he was giving up all for his Christ.

Her brother met him several times in these days, for he talked of it when he came home. Twice he had gone to his office and been taken out by him among his patients. He told of some of the homes. He described a few of the desolate places among the poor where they had gone after answering calls to names well known in the social circle. He told how he had taken his clean handkerchief and wet it in a cooling lotion to place on an old man's aching brow, and how he had helped to wash a dirty little suffering child because there was no one else by who knew how. Mr. Rutherford senior seemed interested and questioned, always finishing with:

"Well, he's a man. I wish there were more such among our friends."

To all this Evelyn listened, now and then asking a question, but for the most part silently.

And still the days went by and the doctor did not call as he had promised.

It was late in the spring when he came at last and warm enough to have the windows open. There were faint hints of spring in the odors of the air, even in New York.

When his card was brought up, Evelyn secretly rejoiced

that neither her father nor brother was at home that evening and she could have the caller to herself. There were so many things she would like to ask him if only she could muster the courage.

Marie stood waiting orders.

"Tell John as you go down, Marie, not to admit any other callers this evening. I shall not be receiving," said Evelyn.

"Yes, ma'am," said Marie, and tripped away.

But John was not in the kitchen where she had expected to find him and her lover was waiting in the moonlight at the back door, so she slipped out for just a few minutes till John should return. She could run in if she heard the bell ring. Alas, for Marie's good intentions. The moonlight and the lover were absorbing, and the bell would need to ring very loud indeed to reach the pretty ears filled with such sweet words as the lover knew how to say.

The two people in the parlor had scarcely said the few preliminary words of welcome, and each was just taking in the pleasure of the anticipated hour together, when Evelyn heard the front door open and then John's accustomed voice announced, "Mr. Worthington," and without waiting for further ceremony, and quite as if he were on intimate terms in that house, the visitor entered.

Evelyn arose, her face flushed with embarrassment. "Why, John, I am not—didn't Marie tell you?" she began, and then she saw the young man and there was nothing further to be said, she bit her lip and gave him a cold bow. It could not be said to be a welcome. Her heart grew cold within her. What should she do? What could she do? If she had but had the wit to say plainly when he first entered that she was engaged—but no, that would not do, and he would misunderstand. If only he had not seen Doctor Grey! But there was no remedy for it now. Her ready wit and easy grace almost deserted her.

Maurice Grey saw her discomfiture and pondered what it might mean. He confessed his own disappointment, but told himself it was no more than he should have expected and perhaps it was better so, and he sighed to himself.

There was a pause during which the three considered how to proceed, and then Evelyn recovered herself somewhat.

"I was just asking Doctor Grey about his sister and

mother when you came in. I visited them in the fall, you know," and she turned to Maurice and went on with her questions.

"I have been wishing I had Allison here with me for a while," she went on. "I tried to make her promise to come when I left there. Is she still as busy as ever? I have heard from her but once."

Mr. Worthington gloomily chewed his mustache and pondered. He had not been calling frequently at the Rutherford house lately and the few times that he had ventured he had found Miss Rutherford out, or otherwise engaged. He did not care for this pious fellow, who seemed to be monopolizing the conversation, but his experience at their last meeting had been anything but successful so far as his participation in the conversation was concerned, so he refrained from another attempt.

There were a great many things she would have liked to talk about, but Evelyn shrank from touching on any of them before this listener. For instance, there was their foreign meeting. Doctor Grey did mention it, a few minutes later, with a rare smile, and Mr. Worthington looked on curiously and wondered who this fellow was, anyway, who seemed to have been abroad with the family.

General conversation did not succeed. At last Evelyn bethought herself of her brother's words and an inspiration came to her.

"Doctor Grey," she said, "my brother tells me you can sing. He has talked so much about it that I do want to hear you. Won't you come into the music room and sing for us?"

"If it will please you," said Maurice Grey quietly and as if it were a matter of little moment; "but then I may ask you to play?"

Now Mr. Worthington was a singer of gay songs, with a voice of no little worth in his own estimation, and he followed them to the music room in no very fine frame of mind, determined to show this conceited fellow how little he knew about music. But, instead, he sat and listened as the magnificent voice rolled forth. He knew he could not sing like that, and he knew that Miss Rutherford knew it. Therefore when in the second selection he was asked to take the tenor he refused to sing at all and so put his voice into such comparison, pleading huskiness, suddenly developed, as his reason for declining.

The two at the piano had it quite their own way now for a time, while he sat in the shadow of the great piano lamp and listened, inwardly fuming. They even sang one or two duets, making Mr. Worthington half regret that he had said he was hoarse, and Miss Rutherford called for another and another favorite, which the singer willingly and gladly sang. Every word was written clearly in her heart for the future, though she knew it not. The echoes of "Calvary," which he found among the pile of music, kept ringing on in her soul for days.

> Rest, rest to the weary, peace, peace to the soul;
> Though life may be dreary, earth is not thy goal.
> Oh, lay down thy burden! Oh, come unto me!
> I will not forsake thee, I will not forsake thee,
>   though all else should flee!

"And now," said he, sitting down and throwing his head back in the easy-chair in a listening attitude, "you are to play. I want all those things you played at Hillcroft."

And Evelyn forgot completely that other one in the shadowed corner of the couch and played to one listener only. She played as Mr. Worthington had never heard her play before, and he had heard good music enough to be somewhat of a judge.

"Oh, that is rarely sweet!" said Maurice Grey, as though he had been drinking at some delicious fountain. "And now can you play *'Auf Wiedersehen'*?"

Without replying and without waiting for the notes her fingers sought among the chords for the keynote, and the soft sweet strains of the old loved tune stole through the room.

Doctor Grey was very still when it was over. Mr. Worthington was about to attempt some method of breaking up this musicale, but was not sure how to begin. He did not seem to be in things at all. He felt like knocking the lamp over, or kicking the other fellow downstairs, or something desperate. But he found there was no need. At last he had sat him out.

"And now," said Maurice Grey, with an apology for

looking at his watch, "it is my duty to say good-bye. Or shall it be 'Auf Wiedersehen'? I cannot tell you how I have enjoyed this evening. I shall carry the memory of it with me for many a long day. I leave to-night on the midnight train for home, and in a week I start for the Pacific Coast, where I am to embark for China. Matters have been hastened a good deal. It seemed best that I should be on the ground and oversee the new hospital building, and so I am going at once."

She followed him into the hall. Something in her manner kept Mr. Worthington in the parlor after having shaken hands with the man whose whole body he would well have enjoyed shaking. Evelyn felt as if she were stunned by this sudden announcement. She did not know what to say. He was going, and none of the things she meant to ask and none of the—something, was it comfort?—she had hoped to get from him spoken. He took her hand a moment as he lingered at the door and said in his low, appealing voice:

"Have you remembered the promise?"

And she answered as low, "Yes," with her eyes down.

She looked up in time to see the light of joy in his eyes and then down again as she felt the tightening of his clasp on her hand when he said in tones almost triumphant:

"I knew it. I knew you would. And, may I know, is it being answered yet? Do you feel—are you any more willing to be—His?" His voice was yearning, anxious, as if he could not bear to go away without this answer.

Almost immediately she felt that it was so and answered in a slow hesitation: "I think so." The confession meant much to her and revealed much of her own heart to herself. Then she looked up in spite of her embarrassment to see the light of joy in his face for she seemed to know it was there and to realize that the sight of it would soon be but a memory which she must fasten now or lose perhaps forever.

Then he was gone, but not until she knew how glad he was.

She waited an instant before she went back to the drawing room. Mr. Worthington was studying a book of fine engravings. She stood in the doorway for an instant surveying him with a fine scorn until as he looked up she said in her most cold and haughty tones: "I must ask you to excuse me. I am not feeling well," and swept from the room and up the stairs.

She did not stop at her own room, but went on up the next flight of stairs and the next, still wearing her magnificent air of pride until she climbed up into the cold dark attic, where trunks and old furniture were stored, and where were dust and utter darkness and silence.

There, after closing the door behind her, she sank down upon the dusty, bare floor, regardless of her soft white robes, and, burying her face in her lap as she might have done when a little girl, she sobbed and cried aloud. No one could possibly hear her up here. The servants' rooms were far removed, and besides they were all downstairs. She could scream, if she chose, and no one would know. Never in her life had she wept so bitterly. Her whole being was broken utterly. "Oh, I love him!" she said to herself, though not aloud, for it was a secret too dear and sacred to be trusted even to darkness and dust.

"I love him better than my soul, and he has gone, gone, gone, forever probably! He does not love me. At least not in that way. But I am glad, glad that he cares for my soul. Oh, what shall I do?"

Over and over again her heart cried this pitiful wail. The proud girl had reached the depths of humiliation. She wished she could die; no, could be utterly exterminated, and yet, no, that was unworthy of one to whom it had been granted to love a man like that. She must not. But oh, what should she do? And then his own voice seemed to float out of the shadows in a whisper to her heart:

Rest, rest to the weary, peace, peace to the soul;
Though life may be dreary, earth is not thy goal.
O lay down thy burden, O come unto me.
I will not forsake thee, I will not forsake thee,
  though all else should flee.

Gradually the words soothed her turbulent soul. She began to realize that it was late and Marie would soon be returning. She must get to her room and be in the shelter of the dark before she came. No one must know this secret of hers. And so she got herself down without being seen, and wished, as she slipped from the cover of the darkness above that she had a mother to whom she could go, who would put loving arms around her and comfort her. She felt sure that Allison's mother would do that, and that Allison would not be afraid to go to her mother with such a secret.

And so she lay down with her aching, lonely heart, while once more a train flew through the night bearing one from her who prayed for her every waking moment.

20

Bert Judkins Makes a Call

It was late in the autumn before Mr. Worthington ventured to call again upon Miss Rutherford. In the meantime he cultivated Miss Bashford. Evelyn had introduced him to Jane. Jane had approved of her friend's admiration of him during the first of their acquaintance. She managed to help it along by invitations and in one way and another. Evelyn had often met him at her friend's home. Jane rather enjoyed inviting any one who was tabooed by the exclusive people. She liked a little dash of spice in her life. The two girls had decided at the outset that there was no real harm in a young man just because he had been wild. Just what the terms "wild" and "fast" conveyed to these two is somewhat uncertain. They had been quite young, and enjoyed the company of one who was master of the delicate art of flattery; and they had come to think him unusually brilliant and wealthy. As a matter of fact he scarcely owned the clothes on his back, and lived from day to day by gambling.

To Evelyn, who was two years the senior of Jane, this

was all in the past. If she had been confronted at this juncture with the things she had said and thought about this young man less than a year ago, she would have said, "How could I?" But Jane was still living under the same illusions, and now that Evelyn had somewhat withdrawn, she was having a great deal more of that young man's society than was good for her.

Evelyn Rutherford felt as though she had passed through years of experience during the last few months. She seemed to be another person. She had seen very little of Jane lately, and had almost forgotten their common interests in the absorption of her own sorrow. She had spent the summer months in travel with her brother, but had come home feeling like the preacher of old, that all was "vanity and vexation of spirit."

But Mr. Harold Worthington was not one to easily give up a prize he had come to consider his own. There was something the matter evidently. He did not understand it, therefore he went to Miss Rutherford's friend, with whom he had whiled away the time in a mild flirtation. She surely would understand. He told Jane that Miss Rutherford was offended about something, and asked her intercession and advice. Jane gladly undertook the office of peacemaker.

There were some private theatricals for a charity in process of development. Miss Rutherford had been assigned a prominent part, and had declined to take it, or in fact to have anything to do with the affair. They would go and argue the matter out with her. Jane had heard some remarks about her ability which she felt sure would touch her friend's vanity. She thought she knew how to reach her and bring her to reason. They would go that very evening. It suited Jane very well to carry out any scheme of Mr. Worthington's. She was not so sure she cared to have Evelyn change her attitude altogether, but it was pleasant at least to be made a confidante. So they went.

Jane was wily enough to send only her own card to Evelyn, and to tell John she wished to see her but a few minutes. In case John or the maid mentioned the presence of her companion, Evelyn would suppose she had stopped on her way to some other place.

Evelyn sighed as she received the card. She felt almost

like declining to see any one that night. If it had been any one but Jane she thought she would have done so, but Jane was so old a friend. However, she did not feel at all in the mood for Jane's light chatter, and wondered how she ever cared for it. How little would she care to confide to this girl all that was now in her heart!

Over and over again she had turned the last few words Doctor Grey had spoken to her, as one will turn the last sentence of the dear dead over and over until every word becomes a precious dagger with which to stab the heart that loves, and until every wish the words convey becomes a treasured command to be obeyed at all costs.

She knew that the man who had gone out from her life probably wanted for her above all things that she should belong to Jesus Christ in some peculiar sense which she did not understand. That he wanted this for her was not enough. She wished it for herself. It was with her as it is with one who grows to love the Lord Jesus with all his heart, whatever the Christ would have him do, that is joy indeed. And so through this sad love of hers the answer to her prayer had come, and she was willing to be made Christ's.

The young missionary, starting out to foreign lands in the service of his Master, knew not that he was leaving behind one whom he might have helped to the light, who was almost as ignorant of the way to find Christ as if she had been born in China, and who would have to grope along in the darkness and stumble many times ere she at last reached the foot of the cross. But he did not dream of this. Such ignorance in our dear civilized land is hard to be understood by those who have grown accustomed to think that everybody who is civilized is not a heathen.

And so Evelyn braced herself for going down to her friend, expecting to be bored with gossip of their petty world which had come to seem to her so small and insignificant. Strange how one can change in less than a year and not know it!

She felt indignant at Jane as well as at Mr. Worthington for the intrusion. She knew that he understood her last dismissal, and he had no right to force himself into her privacy in this way. She barely greeted him civilly, and was not herself even to Jane. This action on her part was calculated to make Jane more of a partisan for Mr. Worthington than ever, and she warmed up to her subject and made a most winning little speech in behalf of the theatricals, telling how disappointed Mr. Worthington was that she would not act, as he was to have had a part near to her, and did not like the proposed substitute.

But to all of this eloquent appeal Evelyn merely answered: "I really cannot do it, Jane. I don't feel in the least like it, and I don't care for some of the participants. I have not been feeling well. You must excuse me."

"But," said Jane, nothing daunted, "it will do you good, and get you out of yourself. I heard you were moping. You'll have nervous prostration if you keep on. It's just the dull weather that ails you. Come, you simply must. This will probably be one of the best things of the season. It is early, I know, but we are counting on enough being in town to make it a success. The Bartleys are coming up from the country early, and so are the Lexingtons, just especially for this performance."

Then Evelyn heard the opening of the outer door, and a strident voice, that somehow was familiar and awakened memories which set her heart beating faster, she knew not why, inquired:

"Does Miss Rutherford live here?"

Perhaps even the loud voice would not have been heard so clearly had not Evelyn's ears been quickened by a desire to have some interruption to this conversation which merely wearied her. She could not place it instantly, but it somehow spoke to her of freedom and interest and things in her life which awakened the sense of pleasure. There seemed to be a quiet parley between the stately John and the caller, whose voice perhaps held a dash of impudence in the tone, and then the dignified butler, with a deprecating air, appeared at the door:

"Miss Rutherford," he began in a distressed tone, "there's a young—ah—person at the door who insists—"

"Just tell any one she's very much engaged, John. She can't possibly be spared now. I have come to see her on very important business!" broke in Jane impatiently, with an apologetic laugh.

"Perhaps your business is just as important as mine, but

'll bet a two-dollar dog you ain't come so far to transact it," broke in the strident voice, with the impudence strongly marked, from behind John's liveried shoulder. "How d'ye do, Miss Rutherford. I told this gentleman here you'd want to see me, but he didn't seem to recognize his friends," this with a wink at the much scandalized John. "A mighty hard time I've had to find your place, but I got here, I did. Didn't I say I would?"

There had been no time for any one to speak, but Evelyn had arisen and come forward with her hand outstretched, exclaiming: "Why, Bert, where did you come from?"

"Oh, I just dropped down," went on the irrepressible youth sliding into a small gilt chair covered in pale pink satin and tilting it back on its hind legs. Then he suddenly rose and clapped his hands to either overcoat pocket.

"Oh, here! Got somethin' for you." He threw down on a small flower-stand a large bunch of sweet English violets and tossed a box of bonbons beside them. "'Sweets to the sweet,' is the saying is," he went on, "and here," handing her a crumpled envelope, "here's *her* letter."

Evelyn took the envelope eagerly, but just at this point Mr. Worthington decided it was time for him to act.

"Miss Rutherford," he said, with his most superior and English manner, and abhorrence in his every feature, "would you like this—person removed?"

Then suddenly Evelyn remembered that what she had once dreaded had come to pass. Two at least of her New York friends had heard Bert Judkins talk to her. She realized at once that she did not care now, and wondered why it was. She felt an irresistible desire to laugh and another almost as sudden and astonishing desire to tell the whole thing to Doctor Grey. How was it she felt so sure that Doctor Grey would enjoy an account of the scene?

It took no time for all this to flash through her mind. She did not give way to any of her feelings, but was studying the address on her letter with a perfectly collected manner, while with much the same assurance the irrepressible Bert was studying his opponent. He had not seemed to see him before, and he felt sure he could look him out of countenance, but he preferred to take neutral ground till he saw how the land lay. His glance was somewhat disconcerting to the city young man, however. Evelyn did not seem to notice him at all. She looked at Jane with a pleasant smile, quite as if she were doing an accustomed thing, and said: "Jane, dear, please excuse me a moment. I must see what message this letter has from Hillcroft. Bert, will you come up to the library with me? My brother is there and he wants very much to know you."

She led the way and Bert followed, having first turned on his heel toward Mr. Worthington with a smile accompanied by a very amusing grimace.

"By-bye," he said, blowing an imaginary kiss, and disappeared up the stairs, three steps at a time, and then had to wait for Evelyn to mount the last one.

It may be that Miss Rutherford would have severely deprecated this action on the part of Bert had she seen it—he took good care that she should not—but she was in a state of mind to sympathize with him in spite of his manners.

She was glad to find that her brother was in the library.

"Richard," she said, "this is Bert Judkins, of Hillcroft. You remember him, do you not? I want you to entertain him till I get rid of some callers."

She waited a moment to glance over the note from Allison, and then seeing that it was of a nature that made her heart throb with longing, she put it back in the envelope for further perusal when she should be alone. She came back to the drawing room as coolly as if nothing had happened, and said as she took her seat once more:

"He is an odd boy, a *protégé* of a friend of mine in Hillcroft, where I visited last fall. He is quite a musical genius in his way."

"I think he is a rude, bad boy," said Jane crossly, for her companion was in a hopelessly bad humor. "I think he ought to be arrested."

"He really does not mean to be rude. It is just his way," laughed Evelyn; and then she was dignity itself and no one cared to say any more about the matter.

The callers did not stay long. They saw it was of no use. Evelyn would not take part in the theatricals and she would not talk about them. The topics she continually started were not in their line and so it came about that the hostess was soon free to go upstairs, giving strict command to John that she should not be called down to see any one else that evening.

As she entered the library her brother was laughing loud and long, with his head thrown back against the big leather chair.

Bert sat in another chair, which he occupied with every bit the air of ownership the other gentleman wore, topped off by a well-pleased smile at himself for the impression he was making. He had but that moment completed a detailed account of the encounter downstairs, with the anti-climax which Evelyn had not seen. It must be confessed that Mr. Richard Rutherford enjoyed it. If Bert Judkins' teacher had been present she would have been tried in her soul that he should show no better breeding than this. Allison was trying to elevate Bert in manners as well as morals, but she found it still harder to do.

It became necessary to almost send the guest home when a reasonable hour had arrived, as he was not yet proficient in the art of early leave-taking, but Evelyn could see that her brother had enjoyed hearing his talk. It was something new and fresh to him and Bert's ideas were sometimes quite original.

"Now look here," said Mr. Rutherford, as the guest at last got as far as the hall door toward departure, "you want to have a good time while you're in New York. I suppose you'll go sight-seeing all day."

"You bet!" said Bert. "Got a list as long as from here to China of things I must see and places I must go. *She* made it out."

Mr. Rutherford had been fumbling in his pocketbook. He brought out two tickets. "Here, take these theatre tickets," he said graciously. "You'll find some one else to go along, I dare say, and I shall not be using them, as I have another engagement. It's a good play."

Bert took the tickets and studied them carefully a moment and then handed them back. "Much obliged," he said in a matter-of-fact tone, "but I don't want 'em."

The donor was a little taken aback at this lack of gratitude and said stiffly: "You don't care for the theatre, then?"

"Who said I didn't?" was the belligerent response. "I used to go every night I got a chance when I was back in

Chicago. No, but *she* don't like 'em, an' I promised her 'fore come that I wouldn't go near one of 'em. When I make a promise to a lady I generally like to keep it, you know."

"Indeed!" said the astonished young man. "And who is the lady to whom you have made such an extraordinary promise, may I ask?"

"Why, don't you know her? Miss Grey, Miss Allison Grey. She's my Sunday-school teacher."

"You don't say so!" ejaculated Richard Rutherford, still bewildered, and then he bethought himself of another ticket which he searched for and brought to light.

"Let me see, didn't I hear that you were fond of music and somewhat of a musician yourself?" he said.

"I rather guess you did," said the boy, with no apparent embarrassment.

"Well, here is a ticket to one of the Thomas concerts. It's the great Thomas Orchestra, you know, as fine music as you can find in the world."

With shining eyes Bert clutched the ticket. "Now you're shouting!" he said, tossing his hat into the air and catching it to express himself more fully. "Gee whizz! Won't I tell 'em about that when I get home, though?"

Bert came again just before he left New York. He had enjoyed his stay immensely. He gave a few characteristic descriptions to Evelyn of the things he had seen. Suddenly he turned to her and said: "Say, who was that sucker you had here the other night?"

"Sucker!" said Evelyn. "What in the world do you mean, Bert? You seem to have a great many new words in your vocabulary. I wonder Miss Grey doesn't put a stop to your slang."

"H'm!" said Bert, twirling his hat thoughtfully. "Well, she does try pretty often, but it ain't much use. It kind of comes natural, you see. Why, I mean that cad who undertook to run me out the other evening. He ain't a particular friend of yours, is he? 'Cause I saw him last night down on the Bowery drunk as a fish. He ain't your kind. You better keep him out o' here."

Evelyn's cheeks grew hot in spite of herself. She did not like to think of her past friendly relations with the man in question, but she assured Bert he was no friend of hers now.

"Well, I'm mighty glad," he said with a relieved sigh. "And say, I got something else to tell you before I go. 'Bout that partnership of ours. You said I was to tell you when I was ready to make it a go, and I've about made up my mind I'll try it if you'll say the word. I'd like mighty well to tell Miss Allison you were coming too. It would sort of make up for me being so long about it if I brung you along."

How strangely were the different influences of her life closing around her, even this one which she had not counted an influence at all, this boy whom she had essayed to help; and was he perhaps to help her instead?

She looked at him thoughtfully and then gave him a bright smile and said: "I'll do my best, Bert."

"It's a go, then," said Bert solemnly, taking her hand in good-bye as if he were registering a vow, and perhaps he was.

21

Allison's Invitation to New York

Evelyn dismissed her maid for the night and sat down in her room to read her letter. It was not a long one, but it contained many things that set her heart throbbing wildly. There was mention of Allison's brother and of how much the church and Sunday-school were interested in his work in China; even her Sunday-school class had pledged each a dollar a year from their meagre earnings to endow a bed in the new hospital, this last started by the indefatigable Bert. Allison spoke of taking the same drive with her brother when he was at home that he had taken with Evelyn the year before, and described the scenery vividly, so that Evelyn closed her eyes and could almost feel that she was there again with that man beside her who could tell her so much. Oh, if he were here but for a little minute, how she would question him! She would find out what it was he wanted her to do, and how to go about it. Why had she never done so? Why had she not made opportunity? The letter went on to say that they had spoken of Miss Rutherford during their drive, and that Allison's brother had told her how kind Miss Rutherford had been, making bright spots of friendship in his desert of hard work. The tears rushed to Evelyn's eyes as she read this. How little it had been; barely one invitation to dinner and a call or two.

Allison closed by saying she wrote this at Bert's request, as she felt he would be more welcome carrying a message from her, though she feared Evelyn might not be particularly overjoyed with the visit.

Evelyn leaned wearily back in her chair at last and let the tears course slowly down her cheeks. She was not used to crying, but she seemed to be unnerved and not like herself. She had tried to tell herself all summer that she must get over this strange infatuation for a man whom she would probably never see again and who did not care for her. But somehow she did not want to get over it; it comforted and strengthened her to feel that she cared for him. A new desire had been roused in her heart to find out just what it was he had wanted her to do and just how to do it. All summer she had prayed, though the words of her prayer had changed. They were no longer "make me willing," but "show me the way." The first had been answered. She had come to believe in the miracle of prayer. Nothing could have been farther from her mind when she first began to pray than that she would ever be willing to give up her life of gayety and "be good," as she phrased it, but now there was no attraction in the world for her. Everything she had formerly enjoyed was distasteful to her. She could even understand how Allison was happy in her home and her work. Oh, if there were but a home and work for her, perhaps she too could be happy, yes, even with that great longing in her heart for a love that was not hers.

What if she should try the Bible? Was it as great a talisman as prayer? If she but had some one to help her. And then a thought came that moved her to prompt action.

Allison was just the one she needed. She would write and invite her at once.

She went to her desk and wrote:

Dear Allison:

Your letter reached me to-night and showed me exactly what I want and need. It is you. Will you come to me? I want you for two or three months, if your mother can spare you. Now, please don't plead that your work will keep you. One heathen is as good as another, and I think perhaps there is room for your work here in New York.

Don't wait to fix up a lot of clothes. I am being very quiet this winter. Somehow I don't care to go out as much as I used to do. And I have hosts of things that we can fix up beautifully for you, should any occasion offer when you need more than you have to have in Hillcroft. Marie, my maid, is skillful at sewing and fitting, and time hangs heavy on her hands just now, so if there is anything you need, get it here and let her make it. I really cannot wait for you to come, now that I have set my heart upon it.

We had a most unique visit from Bert. I am glad he came. I will tell you about it when you get here. Now, please don't say there is anything to hinder your coming, and do write by return mail to tell us when to meet you.

Your sincere friend,
Evelyn M. Rutherford.

The letter written, Evelyn felt happier. She sealed it and then went into the library, where she was surprised to find a light still burning and her brother with a newspaper across his knees but his eyes shaded by his hand. He did not stir as she came in, and she thought he might be asleep. She searched silently in the bookcase for some minutes, and then mounted a chair to reach to the top shelf. In doing so she caught her foot in her skirt and almost lost her balance. A slight exclamation of dismay and the fall of a book she had been reaching for just above her head brought her brother to her rescue.

"What are you doing up there, Evelyn?" he asked, helping her down and putting the book back in its place.

She hesitated a minute, half annoyed, and then spoke the truth:

"I was looking to see if there wasn't a little old Bible up there that I used to have when I was in school. I want to see one for a minute, and there doesn't seem to be one in the house. It is odd, when you come to think of it, but I can't remember that we ever had one."

"I have one. I'll get it for you," he said, not seeming to notice her look of surprise, and presently he returned from his room with a handsomely bound Bible, apparently new.

"Thank you," said Evelyn as calmly as her brother had spoken, but she went to her room with not a little curiosity.

Evelyn sat down with the book in her hand and turned to the fly-leaf. Written in a clear, bold hand were these words: "A parting gift to my dear friend, Richard L. Rutherford, with the hope that he will sometimes read it, and that it may grow as dear to him as to his friend, Maurice Hamilton Grey."

The date was in the last week before Doctor Grey left for the West.

Evelyn's heart stood still. It was almost like having another view of him to read these words. This, then, was how Richard came to have a Bible; and he too had been thought of and probably prayed for. She drew a long breath and wondered if her brother felt any longing for the things that had been growing more and more interesting to her. The Bible did not look as if it had had hard usage, but neither did it look as if it had never been opened before. As Evelyn sat back and turned the leaves it opened of itself to a place that had been marked, and she read:

"Then Jesus beholding him loved him, and said unto him, One thing thou lackest."

She read back a little way and thought how well that described her brother. Did the one who marked it think so too? Oh, that she could find a verse marked for herself! She put her face down into the cool pages and closed her eyes and tried to pray, but no words would come, and the prayer went up to the throne a great longing unphrased, and the Father who knoweth all knew the interpretation and the answer thereof.

When that invitation reached Allison she was laying out an elaborate plan of work for the winter. There were plans for her class, for the mill girls, for the young people's meeting, and for their club. She was the center of a great many things in the little village, and truly it seemed to herself that she could not well be spared. In fact, when she first read the letter she did not entertain the thought of going to New York for a moment. But gradually during her walk home from the post office her brother's words came to her: "Allison, Miss Rutherford told me that she was going to ask you to visit her some time. If she ever does, I hope you will go. It will do you and her both good. Go to please me, sister mine, if for nothing else."

Now, going to China is not quite like going to heaven, but Allison regarded her brother's request much as if he had left this world forever, and when the memory of his request came to her she stopped suddenly in her walk and looked down at the letter in her hand in dismay. When Maurice had said that she had hoped in her heart that Miss Rutherford only said it in kindness and had forgotten it by this time. Indeed, she had never expected to be invited.

She opened the letter again, and walking slowly read it through once more, almost stumbling over a root in the walk and causing Miss Rebecca Bascomb to wonder if she had a lover somewhere who wrote letters to her that she couldn't wait to get home to read.

It was a troubled face that she presented to her mother a few minutes thereafter as she threw the letter into Mrs. Grey's lap. The spirit of the writer had entered into her soul. She had read the real desire to have her in her second perusal, and stern duty was beginning to plead on both sides. It was not in Allison to want to go. New York meant to her the world of fashion. Her life had been sweet and guarded and hitherto somewhat narrowing in its tendency, in spite of the efforts at broadening that father, mother, and brother had tried to give. It was for this reason that Maurice Grey had long ago told Evelyn Rutherford she could help Allison if she would. He longed to have his sister see other ways of doing, view the world from another standpoint, and draw her own conclusions.

The mother recognized this side of the question—which Allison would not admit in the matter at all—even before she noticed the real appeal in the letter.

Allison retired to the sofa in gloom. She did not want to go. She did not believe she ought to do so. She did not care to go among other people and see new sights. It was enough to stay in her dear home with father and mother and work for those all about her. Were not these many young people who recognized her leadership of more value than the one girl in the city who probably would tire of her in a few days?

She said something like this to her mother, who reminded her what the Lord said about leaving ninety and nine and going after one lost sheep. It may be that her son had given her some hint of the state of Evelyn's heart, or it may be she only guessed it from the letter and from her boy's very tender way of asking mother still to pray for her.

Poor Allison saw nothing but giants in the way whenever she thought of the proposed visit. There, for instance, was the inevitable question of clothes, which has troubled every woman since Eve made her apron. It was all well enough for Evelyn to talk about going off without getting ready. Perhaps she, who had quantities of clothes made by the best skilled tailors, could do that, but Allison well knew that her own new dark blue broadcloth made in Hillcroft would look quite out of style put down in New York. Did she not remember her first sight of the gray broadcloth lined with turquoise silk? She had an eye for fit and finish even though she were not the possessor of it. It was not that her clothes were not plenty good enough for anything in Hillcroft. Indeed, Miss Bascomb had sometimes remarked that the Greys dressed their daughter entirely too well. It would foster vanity in her, she declared. She was dressed as well as any of the girls in Hillcroft, better than many; but, for instance, take that same blue broadcloth. It was made by the family dressmaker, the best the town afforded, and she had cut the left side gore of the skirt upside down. Now everybody knows how quickly the nap of broadcloth will turn itself back if made up the wrong way of the cloth, and to Allison her dress was marred. The goods had all been used, and they had tried in vain to get more of the same. It had been bought some months before and it could not be matched. Miss Betts said she cut it "in the ev'nin'," and she didn't believe that it would "ever be noticed in the world." Allison knew that Evelyn would see it at once. Moreover, the skirt was not the shape she had told Miss Betts to make it. Oh, it would be a great trial to go on a mission to New York. She would much, much rather go to China. And there would be theatres and dancing and cards, and, perhaps,—who knew?—wine offered her to drink, and she would have to decline or seem rude, and to tell all her sacred reasons why, and then be laughed at. Why had Evelyn Rutherford ever come to Hillcroft, and why had Maurice ever said that about her going to New York?

They were all against her, even Miss Joan Rutherford, to whom Evelyn had bethought herself to write. She came over the next morning with shining eyes to say how glad she was that her dear Allison was going to visit in her brother's home, taking it for granted that of course she was going. She stayed only a few minutes and she slipped a tiny chamois bag into Allison's hand as she went out, saying:

"There, dear, you'll be needing some spending money while you are away and I'd love to have you spend that for me on yourself. You're part my girl, you know."

When Allison opened the bag she found five ten-dollar gold pieces gleaming there. After that the going seemed inevitable. Not that Miss Rutherford alone could have turned the scale, but father and mother urged her strongly also.

"It will do her good," said her mother while she yet shrank from having her daughter leave her. "She needs to get out of herself and to have wider views of life. There is no telling for what God is preparing her and she must be ready to fill any place. She needs to see a little of cultured society."

The question of dress did not worry the mother. A breadth or two upside down was not such a serious thing at her time of life as it was to Allison.

"There is that black silk that has been lying in the trunk for two years waiting for a time when it was needed to be made up. You can take it as it is, and here is grandmother's real lace shawl. Take Miss Rutherford at her word and let her maid fix it up for you. She will only enjoy it. Don't you remember how she entered into fixing your old blue silk waist? You must have a new cloth dress of some sort, and that you can get in New York, ready-made, perhaps. Your father and I will attend to that. Keep your gold pieces for something you see when you get there."

And so Allison in fear and trembling bade good-bye to her class and her home and the dear protecting arms of mother, and started on her first trip into the world alone. Although she was twenty-one years old she had been so sheltered that in some things she was little more than a child.

When she had been on the train about half an hour the thought came to her that Evelyn would probably want to make her dress low-necked, at which she became so indignant and altogether frightened that if it had been possible she would have turned back home and declared that the visit was impossible. But trains do not stop on fancy, and she sped on her way.

Her letter accepting the invitation had reached Evelyn one evening when the family was at dinner. A smile of real pleasure lit up her face as she read it.

"Dick," she said, laying down the letter beside her plate, "Allison Grey is coming to make me a visit. I invited her last week and her answer has just come. She will be here Thursday evening."

"You don't say!" said her brother, looking up with interest from a legal document that had come in the mail. "I shall be glad to make her acquaintance. I have been quite curious to see her ever since your friend Bert was here. A girl that can influence a fellow of his make-up to keep away from a New York theatre when he has free tickets is quite a curiosity."

"Of whom are you speaking?" asked the father, laying down his paper and giving his attention once more to his soup.

"Allison Grey. She is Doctor Grey's sister, father, from Hillcroft. She is Aunt Joan's idol. You will like her, I am sure."

"Well, now, that will be quite a novelty. Anybody belonging to Doctor Grey and your Aunt Joan will certainly be welcome. I have often wished we could see some sensible young people around. When does she come?"

"Thursday evening," said Evelyn, again referring to the letter; "and, Dick, you'll certainly have to go with me to meet her. She will be lost in New York, for she never traveled alone before, and it is Marie's day out, so I can't take her."

"With pleasure," said the young man, smiling.

Evelyn took a childish pleasure in preparing for Allison's visit. She had not thought she could ever be so glad about anything as she was over the coming of this girl, who, after all, was but a mere stranger. She put the room next to her own in dainty array for her reception. It might be that the true, homey look would be lacking, but Allison should have everything that money could buy to make that room beautiful for her.

The soft velvet carpet in blue and white gave back no sound. The heavy brass bed, with its draperies of costly lace over pale blue, and its blue silk eider-down quilt thrown across the foot; the elegant little dressing table, with its appointment of silver brushes, all spoke of a life of ease and elegance. Above the mantle she hung Hoffman's child picture of the Christ.

When at last Allison stepped, bewildered, from the train and looked about her at the crowds of people and the myriads of twinkling lights she wished she were at home. Then almost instantly her bag was taken from her by some one and a young man said in a pleasant voice:

"Miss Grey, I am Dick Rutherford. Welcome to New York! My sister is over here out of the crowd. Will you step this way?" and she followed him through what seemed to her a dense mass of humanity to where Evelyn stood.

It was all so different from the way they had met in Hillcroft. Evelyn had learned to be gentle and kind. Allison thought she had grown more beautiful, only paler, and wondered at the way she treated her. She took her in her arms and kissed her, actually, right in New York! No, not in New York yet, for there was that dreadful ferry to cross. She had been thinking of it with fear ever since it began to grow dark. How good it was of them to meet her on this side.

Then they led her to the ferryboat and Mr. Rutherford made a way for them to pass to the front that they might watch the lights of the great city coming nearer and nearer. It was like a fairy dream to Allison. Never having seen anything like it before, she could not help thinking her thoughts aloud, and she said almost under her breath:

"Oh, it doesn't look like a wicked place. It seems as if it were heaven we were coming to!"

Some one had crowded between Allison and Evelyn so that she did not hear, but her brother caught the low-spoken words, and his face grew grave at once as he watched the delicate profile against the darkness of the night. He realized that here was a pure, sweet soul.

"It is by no means heaven," he said, with almost a sigh, and Allison, becoming conscious of what she had said, blushed and looked up at him shyly. She was not much used to young men, not men like this one, excepting her brother.

It was all like a beautiful dream after that. They found the carriage waiting at the end of the ferry, and at the house Evelyn led her to that lovely room and helped her to take off her things herself. There was not even a sign of the dreaded maid. Somehow Evelyn seemed to have developed a way of making one feel at ease, or was it because the reality was so much less to be dreaded than the anticipation? Allison found she could laugh and talk quite naturally even when she was made to sit down in Evelyn's room with a substantial and inviting repast before her on a little table drawn before the fire, and afterward Evelyn made her tell all about her beloved Sunday-school class. Perhaps this more than anything else helped to still the homesick feeling. All the time they were talking Evelyn was studying the outlines of the other girl's face, drinking in every line and expression, and noting everything that could remind her of one who was to her as though he had been dead.

22

Allison Finds a Mission

When Evelyn said good-night, before she closed the communicating door between the rooms, she kissed Allison on each cheek. "That is one for your father and one for your mother," she said, smiling. "I know you will miss those kisses. I wish I had such a mother as yours, Allison."

Allison was just ready to turn out her light when Evelyn knocked at the door once more and said gently: "May I come in a minute?"

She was in her white night dress, with the soft cloud of blue-black hair behind her. Allison, looking at her, wondered how she had ever thought her haughty and cold.

"Allison, will you pray for me?" she said half shyly. It was not like Evelyn to be shy, but it suited her well. "I know you can pray," she added, "because you did in that meeting. I want you to pray with me now."

There was a sweet wistfulness in her eyes as she looked up at her guest, and Allison, trembling, awed at the new duty which had been so unexpectedly thrust upon her, yet knelt down hand in hand with the girl she had dreaded—and sometimes feared—and prayed in tender, trembling tones for her. It was harder, this prayer, than any she had ever offered before.

And when she finally lay down to rest, she stayed awake to marvel. She was beginning to know already that it was right that she should have come. She thought over all the happenings since she came into the house; she remembered the young man's earnest face and his tone as he answered her, and liked it and wondered what the elder Mr. Rutherford was like. Then the face of father and mother drifted before her, and of her brother, so far away. She resolved to write him soon of her visit; he would be pleased. And her thoughts were lost in dreams. The next thing she knew she heard the busy rumble of the hard-at-work, wide-awake city, and awoke to find it broad daylight. She was surprised, indeed, to find it nearly nine o'clock when she looked at her watch under her pillow, and hastened to dress.

Evelyn came to her presently and told her not to hurry, that breakfast would be sent up to them presently.

Allison smiled to herself to think she had done the very same thing on her first morning that she had so despised Evelyn for doing a year ago, slept beyond the breakfast hour. Was she beginning to learn already the lessons that had been set for her on this visit?

It was all so pleasant and dreamlike, this life that Evelyn lived. Allison began to half wish it belonged to her. The deft, white-capped waitress, slipping in and out with the dishes, the grace and ease and daintiness of everything—how much her mother would enjoy it!

After breakfast, Evelyn said: "Now, what about clothes? I am responsible for bringing you off in such a hurry, you know. What is to be made, and what is to be altered, and what is to be bought? I shall just enjoy helping you. Let us get anything of that sort off our minds and then we can be free to do what we please. You will not need to dress much, however, Allison. Is there anything to be done?"

Then Allison, in her own frank way, moved by the genial manner of her hostess, confided the story of the blue broadcloth and its left gore, and went on to tell of the black silk and the lace shawl and a few other details of her toilet, asking timidly if Evelyn thought the lace shawl could be used in any way. Somehow, in the light of New York, grandmother's real lace shawl did not appear so very splendid after all.

They went to unpack the trunk, and Allison's courage rose when Evelyn unqualifiedly admired the lace shawl and declared it would drape beautifully. Marie was called upon the scene and Allison stood meekly watching her quick fingers as she took measurements like one who understood her business. Her pretty face dimpled into smiles at Evelyn's playful charge to make the dress as pretty as if it were for a princess, and she promised to do her best.

They whiled away the morning and most of the afternoon in this and other talk, Allison luxuriating now and then between times in the latest magazines that lay about in profusion; and then the time came to dress for dinner—that dreaded hour! Allison had not yet seen Mr. Rutherford. At luncheon she and Evelyn had been alone. She dreaded the ceremony of the evening meal, with the colored butler and the handsome young man looking at her. She dreaded the question of dress again, and began to wish once more she were at home. Why was it that a Christian could feel so miserable and out of harmony with life just because her environments had changed? It was all wrong. There must be something the matter with herself. Meanwhile, what should she put on? She stood helplessly before her trunk when Evelyn came in. Now, there was among her clothes a certain little cream-colored china silk, a relic of the summer, plainly made, and little thought of by Allison. She had not thought of wearing it.

"Put that on," said Evelyn; "I know you will look sweet in it, and where is that lovely old yellow lace scarf of your mother's you showed me? It will be charming. Here, let me fix you, dear—and a knot of black velvet in your hair."

Allison was amazed at the effect of the arrangement and the few touches. The white china silk no longer asserted itself for what it was, but served as a background for the long, rich scarf knotted fichu-style about her shoulders and hanging far down in front. The band of black velvet about her neck and the touch of it in her gold hair completed the picture. She did not know half how lovely she was herself.

But some one else saw it as she shyly came into the dining room a little later. Richard Rutherford drew his breath in quickly, as he was wont to do before an exquisite painting or a lovely bit of statuary, when he came forward to greet her. He held in his hand a bunch of magnificent roses.

"These look as if they belonged to you, Miss Grey," he said, as he separated a half-dozen heavy-headed white buds from those he held and handed them to her, their rich, dark green leaves showing off their lovely petals to perfection.

"Here, Evelyn, these are for you," and he gave the pink ones to his sister.

Allison buried her face in the flowers in delight and then fastened them in the knot of the lace at her breast, where they gave the last touch of art needed. She sat down to the table feeling that she was at a grand party. Yes, she was unsophisticated or she could never have enjoyed it so intensely nor dreaded it so deeply. For after all it was quite easy. She looked up to find Mr. Rutherford's kind, keen eyes upon her inquiringly. They were eyes like her dear Miss Joan's, only with a sadness in them and a lack of that light of peace. But they were pleasant, and she could see by his expression that he was pleased by what he saw.

Strange to say, during that first dinner, which had been regarded by her with so much apprehension, it was Allison who did most of the talking, and she directed her conversation to Mr. Rutherford, senior. Afterward she blushed to herself to remember it, and wondered if she had seemed very forward saying so much; but at the time it had all been so natural. Mr. Rutherford had asked a question about Hillcroft, and Allison had been led on by a word from him now and then until she had described vividly the old stone house where Miss Joan Rutherford lived, the garden where she worked and which she loved, the country round about, and, above all, the dear lady herself. Mr. Rutherford's heart warmed as she went on and his eyes lit with pleasure. Here, at last, was a girl who knew how to appreciate real worth, even if it was in an old woman.

Evelyn watched her with surprise. Here was another Allison. She had seen her in her quiet home; she had seen her doing kind acts; she had seen her among the young girls and with the wild, rough boys of her Sunday-school class; yes, and she had seen her leading a public meeting: but she had never heard her talk at length before, and did not know how well she could appear when she forgot herself and let the color come into her cheeks and enthusiasm light up her dark blue eyes that shone and scintillated with her various expressions. And her language was most poetic. How well her father liked it! Why had she never thought to describe Hillcroft and what she knew of Aunt Joan's house to him. He was listening as eagerly as if he were hungry for the tale.

The young man watched her with a growing interest which changed little by little from the mere curiosity he would give to a new species of the human kind, to a look of genuine admiration. It was true, as Evelyn had said, that she was beautiful, and yet with the quiet beauty of the Puritan maiden. There was a shy droop to the dark eyelashes that made one long to see the flitting light in the clear eyes. And how well the simple white gown suited her! Richard did not know if it was costly or not, he merely knew it suited her.

On the whole, Evelyn Rutherford was pleased with the impression her guest was making. She had not known that she cared about this, but now she saw that she did. She was particularly pleased that Dick should like her, for then he would not be bored by going about with them. She knew her fastidious brother would not have liked a dowdy-looking girl, nor enjoyed an awkward, stupid one. Allison was neither of these, for while she fancied herself awkward in the extreme and dreaded each new course lest she should commit some error of form with fork or spoon, she was, in fact, quite generally free from self-consciousness, which is the source of all embarrassment and awkwardness.

"What have you young ladies on hand for to-morrow?" asked the young man as they arose from the table. "There is a fine collection of paintings on exhibition and to-morrow is the private view. I have secured tickets in case you care to go. You won't see many pictures because of the crowd, as it is the private view, but Miss Grey may enjoy seeing the people who think themselves worth looking at. Then we can go another time for a good look at the pictures when every one is free to come and very few are there. I wonder why it is that everything in this world that is to be had for the asking is discounted by the majority."

Allison looked her delight at hearing of the pictures but felt dubious about the fashionable people. She was not sure she had anything that would do to wear to such an assemblage.

The evening passed very pleasantly in talk and music, Allison urging her hostess to play, and declining to do so herself, saying she was no musician and only played a little for her own pleasure.

Time passed without count. Allison was astonished to remember on waking the third morning of her stay that it was

Sunday. A homesick feeling stole over her. They would all be going to the dear home church soon, and then would come the afternoon school. How would her boys get on with the man she had secured to teach them? She felt slightly troubled about it, but he had been the only available person and they had promised to keep things up during her absence for her sake. With a sigh she knelt to pray, giving them into the care of the Father who knew better than did she how to plan for their good.

The family breakfast was very late, but Evelyn had come down fully dressed for church, as had Allison, so that they had but to get wraps and gloves and start. And when they appeared with these on they found the two gentlemen waiting below to accompany them. To Allison this seemed perfectly natural, but to Evelyn it was an intense surprise. She could not remember that her father had attended church since she was a little girl. As for Richard he never went, at least not to his sister's knowledge. She had been going herself regularly but a very short time.

The great church, with its quiet, restful colors, and rich tones in costly stained windows, in woodwork, walls, and carpet, its deep-toned solemn organ that rolled through the hushed air like the earnest of the judgment day, all impressed Allison deeply. It was wonderful! grand! holy! It touched her sense of the poetic and traditional. All pictures, in her imagination, of the temples of old, were like this. It was different, so different from the bright little crowded church at Hillcroft with but two precious stained-glass windows and the rest clear white, through which the full boisterous sunlight could come at will, and with almost a buzz of kindly greeting from neighbors coming in before the service began. Nevertheless she missed something that made her feel lonely. What was it? Only homesickness? She felt it more when the first hymn began. How very few people were joining in the morning praise! It startled her, so that she almost stopped singing for a moment, frightened at hearing her own voice so plainly, and then Richard Rutherford with whom she was sharing her book took up the strain in his fine tenor voice and she took heart to sing softly once more. But why was it? Did the people not know the tune? At Hillcroft that music would ring out with deep volume, and even old Mrs. Banks, who had no voice above a quaver, would open her mouth wide, and one could tell by her eyes that she was truly praising in her heart if not in strict musical accord.

When the sermon began the "dim religious light" of the sanctuary in such harmonious accord with her ideas of all things holy, proved its restful power by putting her almost to sleep. The sweet, well-modulated tones of the preacher rather lulled her spirit to repose. She found to her distress that little by little the pulpit seemed to be moving slowly away from her and a delicious sense of losing consciousness was stealing through her being. She roused herself as best she could but still that droning kept going in her ears, and the desire to droop came over her eyelids, and she was glad indeed when the organ sounded forth again in the closing hymn.

As they walked home together along Fifth Avenue Richard Rutherford, who was by Allison's side asked:

"How did you like the sermon?"

Allison was slightly embarrassed. "It was sweet and—and all that he said was true," she began, then looking up into his laughing eyes she colored slightly: "I'm afraid I did not hear it closely, Mr. Rutherford. The truth was, the quiet place made me intolerably sleepy. I am ashamed, and I am afraid I did not get much help for the week out of it."

"Is that the way you judge of a sermon, Miss Grey, by its helpfulness to you?"

"Why, yes, don't you?" she asked innocently, looking up at him.

"Indeed, I fear I never have thought of a sermon in that light with regard to myself at all," he said gravely.

Allison could not quite make up her mind what he meant by that, so she asked a question: "Why don't the people sing? I thought the first must be a new tune, but the second and third were no better. Half of them were not trying, some not even looking at their books."

"Why should they?" he asked in an amused tone. "They pay a good salary to the four individuals up in the choir loft to do it for them. Most of them feel that the exertion would be too much, and many that the professional singers can make better music, in which latter fact I suppose they are correct.

The majority of people are very poor singers when you come down to it."

Allison opened her great blue eyes wide in surprise.

"But praising is a part of worship," she said. "I thought a choir was to lead the people. To hire one's praise would be doing as the heathen do when they pay the priest for saying prayers for them."

"Indeed! It hadn't appealed to me in that light before, but now you speak of it there is a sort of similarity between them. By the way, Miss Grey, you have a way of bringing out startling contrasts, just as your brother does. He has made me feel anything but comfortable a number of times. However, as I am not a member of that congregation I cannot be supposed to be hit this time; but, upon my word, it seems to me that it would be much better to have the praising business done up by some one who knew how than to have the church filled with discord."

"Do you know Browning's 'The Boy and the Angel'?" answered Allison thoughtfully. "Do you remember how when Theocrite left off singing 'Praise God' at evening, morning, noon, and night, and went to be the pope in Rome, while the angel Gabriel came and took his place, working at his trade and singing as Theocrite had done:

> God said, 'A praise is in mine ear;
> There is no doubt in it, no fear:
>
> 'So sing old worlds, and so
> New worlds that from my footstool go.
>
> 'Clearer loves sound other ways;
> I miss my little human praise.'

And when Gabriel came and sent Theocrite back to his cell, he told him that when his weak voice of praise stopped in that cell, 'Creation's chorus stopped.'"

He watched her understandingly, his eyes showing his appreciation as she spoke.

"Yes, I remember," he said, "and your point is well taken; but after all that is merely a fancy of Mr. Robert Browning's. You don't really suppose that God prefers to have Mr. Brown and Mrs. Jones and Mrs. Schuyler and Miss

Morrison, who can't sing a note except out of tune, praise him in church in preference to those four wonderfully trained voices, do you?"

"Certainly I do," said Allison earnestly. "Of course I did not mean that Mr. Browning was an authority on the subject. I merely used that as an illustration. I think there are plenty of examples in the highest authority of all, the Bible, to prove the theory is true. For instance take this: 'It came even to pass, as the trumpeters and singers were as one, to make sound to be heard in praising and thanking the Lord; and when they lifted up their voice with the trumpets and cymbals and instruments of music, and praised the Lord, saying, For he is good; for his mercy endureth forever: that then the house was filled with a cloud, even the house of the Lord; so that the priests could not stand to minister by reason of the cloud: for the glory of the Lord had filled the house of God.'"

The young man looked at his companion in astonishment.

"Look here," he said, half laughing, "do you manufacture verses to fit the occasion? I'm sure I never heard any such verse in the Bible, though that might easily be. But you must be very familiar with that book to quote so readily. That certainly sounds as if it was made to order. If that is to be found in the Bible I'll have to give up my point. Do you mean to say that the sermon would have been better if the people had all sung?"

"Possibly," said Allison gravely, "at least we might have felt the presence of the glory of the Lord. But the verse is certainly in the Bible," she added, half-laughingly, "though I cannot claim to be always so ready with a quotation. It just happens that we had this subject for one of our young people's meetings not long ago, and I have studied it quite recently. That verse seemed so unusual that I put it away in my memory."

The others came up then and they all passed into the house.

"She is a bright little thing and knows what she is about," commented the young man to himself afterward, "and she seems to have a wide range of knowledge. It isn't all confined to the Bible either. How beautifully she recited 'The Boy and the Angel,' and how quick she was to bring in that Bible verse. It was a unique application! I shall enjoy her."

23

A Gleam of Light

Evelyn lay down in the afternoon and supposed that her guest was doing the same. Each would have been surprised could she have known that the other was studying the Bible. Evelyn had not yet returned the Bible her brother had loaned her and had it now half concealed under her pillow ready to put it out of sight in case any one knocked at the door. She wanted to see if she could anywhere find rest for her poor, weary soul. The service that morning had only reminded her of the service she had attended some months before, and she had been unable to fix her thoughts on the sermon if perchance there had been some crumb of comfort for her in it. She lay there on her bed turning the leaves in bewilderment, catching a word here and there, now and then lingering over a phrase that sounded promising, but yet not knowing how to go about the reading of so great a book. To begin at the beginning and read it through was a task she could not wait for. She tried it for a few minutes, but just now she seemed too heartsick to care how the world was formed and light and man and sin came. She did not know where to turn to find the great Physician to heal the sin-sick soul. She had gotten a little more than half through the book in a desultory way when her brother knocked on the door.

"Evelyn," he said, in what he endeavored to make an indifferent tone of voice, "if you are through with that Bible of mine I will take it; I want to look up a point."

After the book was gone she lay back on the pillow, letting the sad tears trickle down her cheeks, and felt miserable, she knew not why. Her life seemed all black before her, and yet it was not changed in outward appearance one whit from what it had been a year ago when she had thought herself as happy as any mortal living.

In the next room sàt Allison with her Bible. She did not attempt to conceal from herself that she was homesick at this hour. She was not used to Sunday afternoon naps. Her boys were gathering now. She brought each chair and its occupant before her as her classroom filled, and she went over the lesson she had begun to study when Evelyn's invitation had arrived. There were things in that lesson that seemed just fitted for Bert and Fred and a few others. How she would enjoy being there to teach it! Why was it that when one loved a work so much she must be torn away from it and sent to another place which was not congenial? True, she was having a good time in many ways, but of what use was it going to be to her? Would it not rather tend to make her own life less near to God, all this excitement and sightseeing and worldliness about her? Well, it was strange, but she must not question God's way for her. A little printed slip fell out from the leaves of her Bible. Her mother had placed it there last Sunday night as she took her Bible upstairs and had written on one corner "Dear child," and it read:

> God's plans for thee are graciously unfolding,
>   And leaf by leaf they blossom perfectly,
> As yon fair rose, from its soft unfolding,
>   In marvelous beauty opens fragrantly.

Allison studied the lines a few minutes with a gentle longing in her face which in her heart meant she would try to be what she knew her mother yearned to have her be. Then she resolutely put aside all thoughts of her class. It would not do. She must trust them to God and try to do what he would have her do here. She turned to the topic for the young people's meeting and began studying that, and then growing restless as one or two hymns occurred to her that would certainly be sung at the home meeting that evening because they fitted so perfectly with the central thought of the subject, she stole softly into the hall and down to the music room.

There was no one there as she had supposed. It was growing dusky in the room. The heavy draperies of the hall door made deep shadows and the open fire played fantastically with the gathering twilight over the keys of the piano.

Allison sat down at the piano and her fingers touched the keys lovingly. She did not need the light to show her the chords,—her hands knew where to find them. She was no skilled musician, and she knew it; but there were dear old tunes by the hundred stored up in her memory and her fingers could unlock and bring them forth in sweet melody from the instrument at will. Neither did she need the music usually to guide her. Softly she played, lest any one should hear her and be disturbed, songs she loved, touching and tender melodies, or triumphant strains. One after another they followed, flowing into their key over the soft chords, and as she grew more used to being there alone she let her voice join in softly and the words came distinctly in the quiet room:

> "My God, is any hour so sweet,
>   From blush of morn to evening star,
> As that which calls me to thy feet—
>   The hour of prayer?

> "Then is my strength by thee renewed;
>   Then are my sins by thee forgiven;
> Then dost thou cheer my solitude,
>   With hopes of heaven.

> "No words can tell what sweet relief
>   Here for my every want I find:
> What strength for warfare, balm for grief,
>   What peace of mind!

> "Hushed is each doubt, gone every fear;
>   My spirit seems in heaven to stay;
> And even the penitential tear
>   Is wiped away.

> "Lord, till I reach yon blissful shore,
>   No privilege so dear shall be,
> As thus my inmost soul to pour
>   In prayer to thee."

Before Allison had half finished this hymn she became aware of the presence of some one else near by, she could not tell if in the room or only in the hall. She had seen the faint light from the hall gas flicker out some minutes before. It could be only the butler or Marie. It might be that her little song would drop a seed of good into a listening heart. It could do no harm; she would not stop. But as she came to the last verse she felt that some one stood in the doorway by the heavy curtains. It startled her and made her voice quiver slightly, for she had been feeling the words as she spoke them, and it had been in reality, as in form, a prayer. It was not quite pleasant to be thus made self-conscious again, but she turned on the stool with the last sound and saw Richard Rutherford standing with bowed head listening.

"May I come in?" he said gravely. "I could not resist the sound; it was very sweet. Go on, won't you, and let me sit here and listen."

"Oh, no, I couldn't!" said Allison quickly. "I am not a singer, and I was only taking myself back to our meeting for a little while."

"Do they all sing like that there? Then it must be a wonderful meeting and I do not wonder you spoke as you did this morning. Please go on. Take me to your meeting too, a little while, won't you? I have never been and I should enjoy it. My sister told me of one she attended at Hillcroft once. Now you certainly must go on or you will drive me back again to my room and I do want to hear another song. You will not refuse, will you?"

Allison had been brought up to accede to requests if possible without making a fuss, and so, though she would rather have done almost anything than sing her poor little songs before this city gentleman, she turned back to the piano. After a few gentle chords, she gathered courage from the sound and went on, her voice low and sweet and tender, but every word clear-cut and distinct, in Whittier's matchless hymn:

"We may not climb the heavenly steeps
To bring the Lord Christ down;
In vain we search the lowest deeps,
For him no depths can drown.

"But warm, sweet, tender, even yet
　　A present help is he;
And faith has still its Olivet,
　　And love its Galilee."

"The healing of the seamless dress
　　Is by our beds of pain;
We touch him in life's throng and press,
　　And we are whole again."

"O Lord and Master of us all,
　　Whate'er our name or sign,
We own thy sway, we hear they call,
　　We test our lives by thine."

She touched more soft chords trying to think of another song. The music had somehow reached her soul and made her willing to go on, since he seemed to wish it. Perhaps he needed a song as well as the butler. Might she be the humble instrument through which it should come?

Suddenly he interrupted her. "You sing those words as if you meant every one from the bottom of your soul," he said curiously.

"Why, I do!" she answered, facing about toward the couch where he sat gazing into the fire. "Of course I do. I could not live if I did not believe and mean it all."

"It must be a wonderful thing to be able to believe all that. I have thought so for a long time. I would give a great deal if I did."

He spoke with so much earnestness that Allison was almost startled. She recognized at once that here was no trifler. The instinct for souls was keen in her. It was as if one of her rough boys sat before her, and she forgot her fear and awe of the city young man.

"There is a way," she said softly.

He looked up quickly. "What do you mean?"

"There is a way to test it, to make yourself sure. God has given a way. But it is so very simple that there are many like Naaman who will not even put it to the test."

"What is it?" he asked half-wistfully. "I'm afraid I don't

know enough about Naaman to know what kind of a fool you are comparing me to."

"Why, Naaman was a leper who was told to wash seven times in the Jordan and he would be made whole, and he was so angry that there had not been some hard thing given him to do that he started back home again without even trying it until one of his servants urged that it would do no harm to make the test."

"I see. He was a fool, of course. He got well, I remember now. But what is it you would have me do?"

"'If any man will do his will, he shall know of the doctrine, whether it be of God, or whether I speak of myself,'" quoted Allison solemnly, and then after a moment's pause: "'And ye shall seek me, and find me, when ye shall *search* for me with *all your heart*.'"

"And you mean that I am to go about doing the will of God just as if I were sure of it all?"

"Yes," Allison breathed softly, "and the promise will not fail."

He looked at her earnestly and steadily and said not a word. No more words came to her. She turned back to the piano and began softly playing again, and presently sang:

> *"Father! in thy mysterious presence kneeling,*
> *Fain would our hearts feel all thy kindling love;*
> *For we are weak, and need some deep revealing*
> *Of trust and strength and calmness from above."*

Evelyn was heard coming down the stairs, then, and in a moment more she spoke by the door of the drawing room which opened from the music room:

"Why, papa! Is this you sitting here in the dark? Don't you want me to ring for John to light the gas?"

The occupants of the music room wondered how long he had been sitting there in the dark.

"No, daughter. Sit down here. I have been listening to some sweet singing. Listen."

But Allison in sudden panic stopped playing and left the piano stool altogether.

"Oh, I am afraid I have broken the spell!" said Evelyn,

181

coming in. "But let us all sing something now. Father will like that, I am sure."

They sang a little while, but Richard suddenly stopped them by looking at his watch.

"Evelyn, isn't it about time we had some lunch? I have a mind to ask you and Miss Grey to go with me to hear another kind of preaching to-night, if you both care to do so. I'll warrant you one thing, you will not go to sleep, for I have heard him," and he named a preacher whose fame had reached Hillcroft long ago and whom Allison had often longed to hear.

It was something new for that family to attend church twice on Sunday. Mr. Rutherford joined them once more. It seemed to him pleasant, this little family life that had been springing up in his lonely household lately. Evelyn was growing more like her mother, or was it like his own mother, whom he could dimly remember, whose life had left its impress upon him, even though she left the earth when he was but a lad? He sat listening critically and with interest to the preacher.

Allison's face was full of eagerness. Her eyes shone with enthusiasm and her cheeks glowed. The young man by her side could not help watching her as well as he could by an occasional sidelong glance. It was something new to have some one about who took everything in this fresh, fervent way. He could see that this preacher did not put her to sleep, and that she would have a very different adjective from the morning ones with which to express her approval.

In glancing at Allison he caught a glimpse of his sister's profile beyond. He was suddenly struck by the grave sadness that it expressed and wondered what it meant. Was she too stirred by the same Jesus who was speaking to his heart? And if so, what had been the moving influence? This girl by his side? Very likely. What straightforward trust seemed to be hers! How quickly she had been able to give a plain direction, and it was simple enough too, he supposed, if one could but make up the mind to try it. Then he gave his attention to the sermon which was aglow with eloquence and earnestness.

Evelyn's sad eyes had been fixed on the preacher and she had been listening in a half-hearted way, thinking much of the time of her own unhappiness. All at once the speaker caught her attention. His voice had changed to a tender pathos. He was reciting a poem, she discovered, and these were the words that came to her ear, though she could not have told their connection with the rest of the discourse:

> *"The cross shines fair, and the church bell rings,*
> *And the air is peopled with holy things;*
> *Yet the world is not happy as the world might be—*
> *Why is it? why is it? Oh, answer me!*

> *"What lackest thou, world? for God made thee of old;*
> *Why thy faith gone out, and thy love grown cold?*
> *Thou art not happy as thou mightest be,*
> *For the want of Christ's simplicity.*

> *"It is blood thou lackest, thou poor old world!*
> *Who shall make thy love hot for thee, frozen old world?*
> *Thou are not happy as thou mightest be,*
> *For the love of dear Jesus is little in thee.*

> *"Poor world! if thou cravest a better day,*
> *Remember that Christ must have his own way;*
> *I mourn thou art not as thou mightest be,*
> *But the love of God would do all for thee."*

The words were exquisitely recited and the house was still in that hush that comes over even a quiet audience when the speaker has his hearers more than usually within his power. The few words that followed before the close of the sermon impressed the thought embodied in the last verse. Evelyn was deeply affected by it and as a drowning person will catch at anything that seems to be able to give support so she had caught at this poem; while the preacher repeated solemnly the last four lines she fastened them in her memory:

> *"If thou cravest a better day,*
> *Remember that Christ must have his own way;"*

and

> *"But the love of God would do all for thee."*

Would it? How? And how could Christ have his own way? Was she hindering? She resolved to do all within her power to discover.

24

A Visit to Jerry McAuley's

Those were happy days for Allison and sped on wings of sunshine. Not one of the troubles she had expected to meet came her way. Not a theatre was mentioned. That puzzled her, for she knew Evelyn had been fond of going. Not a card was suggested nor a dance, and as for wine, they did not even have it in the jellies and custards. She found out afterward that it was a whim of Mr. Rutherford's, not a little scoffed at by his servants, but still adhered to, because, when Mr. Rutherford said anything, it had to be so. Even her dress was a satisfaction. Marie had found a way to cut the objectionable broadcloth skirt over and turn that breadth right side up. Allison never quite understood how it was done.

They seemed to study her fancies and try to do what would please her most. There were wonderful concerts, beyond anything she had ever dreamed of, in music, and lectures and entertainments; there were picture galleries which filled her with delight; there were rides in the park and shopping expeditions, and trips to this and that point of interest. And Allison never knew until she reached home again and learned it from his own blunt questions that she probably had Bert to thank for the omission of the theatre. They knew from Bert that she did not approve of the theatre, and they showed their perfection of courtesy by not bringing it up at all.

She, on her part, was responsible for initiating Evelyn into what gave her an occupation later and much helpful thought and sad pleasure.

"There are wonderful missionary meetings in New York," said Allison wistfully. "Do you ever go? They are women's meetings, you know. They meet in their own rooms and have the returned missionaries speak to them. I should like so much to go. It may be that my brother's work in China will be mentioned."

"By all means," said Evelyn with alacrity. "Let us go. Do you know when they meet? What evenings?"

"Oh, I think they meet in the mornings, and I am not sure, but I think it is every Monday, or every other Monday. I have my magazine in my trunk and there is an article there about the monthly meeting. I can find out."

To Allison's surprise, this seemed to interest her hostess more than anything they had attempted yet. She sent to ascertain the exact hour and place of the meetings, and she attended and listened with wide, surprised eyes as she heard the stories of hardships and suffering, of pain and loss and privation, joyfully undergone for the love of Him whose they were and whom they served. Was it possible, then, that Doctor Grey had wished to stay in this country and live his life as he had the opportunity to live it, as others in his place would have done, to enjoy his own pleasure and prosperity and comfort, but that he gave it up so that Christ might "have his own way" with him, and because the love of that Christ was great in his heart and not "little" as that poem had said? Her eyes filled with tears over the thought and her heart swelled with admiration and reverence for the soul that had so cheerfully gone out away from its luxurious life that others might be helped and saved by this same Jesus.

Some returned missionaries have an idea that the people here are weary of the tales and incidents of their work abroad; indeed, one said not long ago that he was told by his Board when he came back to talk: "Now, don't tell your little stories. We have got beyond them in this country. What we want now is facts"—facts in this case meaning statistics. Let our people take heed how they stop the mouths of the missionaries in this way. The "little stories" reach the heart. Humanity is the same the world over, and the story of some heathen's conversion and willingness to take up his cross and follow Jesus may lead another brother, even though he may be white and civilized, to see the worth of the Saviour.

It was just a little simple story of a poor old Indian woman and her childlike love for Jesus that led Evelyn Rutherford at last to the light. It suddenly dawned upon her, in one of these meetings which she and Allison attended quite regularly, that this love which had been carried so far at so great expense to these heathen had also been brought to her. It had been preached to her as she walked a sunny street paved with autumn leaves one day, and on a lofty hilltop, by a missionary sent to her all her own, and was now being preached daily by the sweet, gentle girl, his sister. It was like a revelation that she could just accept Jesus so freely offered her. There was nothing at all to do but tell him so and then "let him have his own way." She smiled to herself to think how strangely the way had been paved for that by the prayer her "missionary" had taught her to pray, "Make me willing to belong to Christ." She was entirely willing—nay, eager and glad. What it involved of sacrifice or trial she did not care to ask. It was enough that she longed to have him do his will in her that she might some day be made into the completeness he had planned.

"We seem to have nothing on hand for to-morrow night," said Richard Rutherford one evening at dinner. "Miss Grey, is there anything else in New York that you have not seen that you think you would like to see?"

Allison's eyes shone with wistfulness as she owned there was just one more place which she had been longing for several years to see, and that was the Water Street Mission. She hesitated as she said it, lest they would laugh at her, but Jerry McAuley's Mission had gained by this time so much respect from New York business men that Mr. Rutherford nodded his head emphatically.

"Yes," he said, "it's a very interesting place to go."

"Have you ever been there, father?" asked the young man, looking up at his father in surprise. "Is it a suitable place for a lady? Is it perfectly safe for one to visit?"

"Oh, yes, I think so, perfectly," answered the father. "I understand a great many women go. You need not wear any jewelry and I would dress plainly; but it is perfectly safe. Yes,

I went myself several years ago, when Jerry was living, and I must say there is nothing like it anywhere in the city. More religion down there than in many of the churches, to my way of thinking."

Evelyn also seemed much interested, and so it was arranged to go the next evening.

"I wish I could go with you," said the father as they left the table. "I would like to see how the work is getting on and if it has changed any, but I have a Board meeting that I must not miss."

When the next evening came, Evelyn had developed a severe cold, which made her feel so wholly miserable that she was forced to give up the expedition. Allison was disappointed, but she tried not to show it, for she knew that Evelyn was feeling quite ill. But when Richard found out the state of the case, he proposed that he should take Miss Grey anyway, as there was to be an unusual meeting going on that night and one which he felt sure she would enjoy. He had taken pains to find out about it.

Allison looked at Evelyn eagerly. She was not altogether sure it would be the proper thing for her to do this, at least not in her hostess' estimation; but Evelyn was glad to have Allison enjoy the meeting and assured her it would be all right to go. They would be going on the cars nearly all the way. It was not like society functions where chaperones were necessary. Evelyn said she was going to bed to see if she could not sleep off her headache and cold and did not want Allison to stay and take care of her; she would much rather have her tell about the mission in the morning.

The father, hearing the discussion, said: "Why, yes, certainly, go. Two such steady people as you are don't need a chaperone. If we get through at the Board in time, I'll step around myself about nine o'clock, but it's not likely, so don't wait."

So they started.

It was almost the first time in her life that Allison had gone out alone in company with a young man who was her equal socially and intellectually. The young men of that sort who belonged to Hillcroft had nearly all gone to some city. There was little or nothing to call people out in Hillcroft unless to church and Allison had always gone there with her father or brother. Besides, she was particular about her friends and had not chosen to be very intimate with any but those much younger than herself, and these only in a helpful way. This was partly the result of her training, for her father had not cared to have her running about at night with boys, as some girls were allowed to do, before she was fully out of short dresses, so she had grown into the habit of having an escort from home whenever there was occasion for her to go out at night.

But she had dreamed of a time somewhere in the misty future when she would be taken about and have attention from some one, perhaps from more than one; but always there was a some one who was a very special one in her pretty visions of the future. And now she was realizing her dreams, in part at least. She was a young woman going out for the evening with a young man. And the young man was not the foolish, vapid fellow that she had often read about, but a truly delightful companion in whom she was deeply interested. Ever since that first Sunday evening when they had their brief talk she had been praying earnestly for him. They had never had another opportunity to speak together on the subject, but she did not forget and she hoped that sometime he would tell her that he had found that it was all true as she had said. Would the meeting at the mission to-night have any effect upon him? she wondered. She had read about those meetings, that they often reached the rich and refined as well as the low and degraded.

Allison had dressed herself quite plainly, but her escort thought her pure beauty just as great. It was not a beauty of adornments anyway, he told himself, but a loveliness of the soul.

They did not talk much on the way down-town, except about what they saw. It was all interesting to Allison. Heretofore her trips about New York in the evening had nearly all been taken in state in a carriage. Now she saw the every-day New York out having a good time. The Bowery presented a spectacle which to her wondering, unused eyes was worthy of long years of study. She would fain have lingered among the strange sights and sounds and she asked many clear-pointed questions which showed Richard that though she had never seen the Bowery before she had read and heard a great deal about it. She looked with sad, fascinated eyes upon the group of hard-faced little children who danced wildly about a hurdy-gurdy, and sighed for them, till the young man could almost read her desire to save them in her eyes.

The mission was all that Allison had pictured it in her mind. Her soul thrilled with the stories of those who testified to the saving power of Jesus. She looked at the young man by her side and saw that he was also deeply impressed. He looked at the poor drunkards as though they were his fellow-brethren and not a species of animals of a lower order. She gave a thankful sigh for that. She had believed he was great-souled like that and she was glad. Then all her attention was riveted to the face of a strangely handsome woman who in spite of her pallor and a certain sharpness, evidently had come of patrician ancestors. In her arms she carried a white-faced child fast asleep, whom she grasped convulsively while great tears were following one another down her hollow cheeks. She sat across the aisle from them near the end of the seat and presently a man who was at the end got up and went forward to speak to one of the leaders. Allison, seeing that other workers were doing the same thing, and forgetful of her escort, slipped quietly into the place beside the poor woman and began talking to her in a gentle way.

Richard looked up, astonished, when he felt that her place was vacant beside him and thereafter the meeting for him narrowed down to the two across the aisle. He could just see the sweet, earnest profile of the bent, golden head and the hardened look that came over the worn features of the woman as she grasped her child a little closer. But though she was repelled, still the gentle talk went on, and by and by he could see the fierce look grow less intense and soften and the bitter tears flow. The woman was shaking her head as if in despair, but still he could see that Allison was urging, urging, and the head-shaking ceased; the woman was considering. Allison had turned a little so he could see the yearning in her face. He wondered how any one could resist that look. He wished she would ask him in that way. He thought he would do anything for her. And now the woman was giving up. She looked Allison in the face with an expression of wonder and dawning acceptance, and a faint smile played where smiles were meant to be. A little more talk, and then the two heads bowed and Richard knew that Allison was praying in a low tone for the woman. There were other life-dramas being acted out all about him, but he had eyes for this one only. He was wishing he could hear the words of that prayer when a heavy hand was laid upon his arm on the other side, and a trembling, aged voice said low in his ear:

"Say, do you reckon he could save me?"

He started and turned to find a face bloated and wrinkled, with bloodshot eyes and features that told of long years of vice and crime. All at once his doubts seemed to leave him, he caught the spirit of helpfulness in the room, and said in clear, firm tones, "I know he could!" and then he motioned to one of the workers who was passing to give the man some help and made room for him to come in.

It was not long before the meeting broke into singing then. He saw that Allison had put her dainty white handkerchief over the sleeping baby's head to shade his eyes from the glare of light, and he saw that the mother was looking at her through her tears with eyes almost of adoration. Then he noticed that Allison's face was white, as if she had been through a long, hard struggle and he knew that the nervous strain upon her had been intense. He motioned to her that perhaps it was time they went home and she seemed glad to follow him away.

The power of the meeting was still upon them. They did not feel that they could talk just here, not till they were where it was quieter, but presently Allison drew a deep, quick breath almost as if it hurt her, and said:

"Did you see that woman? She tried to jump off Brooklyn Bridge to-day, but was kept from it by hearing her baby cry. She came there to-night to get him a warm place to sleep in for a little while—and—I think she has found Jesus."

"I saw," said Richard. "It is wonderful. An old wretch beside me gripped my arm as if he thought I was going to get away from him before I answered, and asked, 'Say, do you reckon he could save me?'"

"Did he!" said Allison, catching her breath with a little glad gasp, and then, "Oh, what did you say?"

"I told him I knew he could," was the decided answer. "And I was surprised to find that it was true."

"Oh, I am so glad!" said Allison, and then before either

could say a word or know what was coming, around the corner straight over them almost, swept a crowd of frantic people hurrying to a fire with the engine clanging and clattering in their midst.

It must have been that they had been too much engrossed with their own conversation to listen to what was going on, or their ears were expecting hubbub and confusion in this quarter of the city, for they had no warning until it was upon them. It was a wild unmanageable mob of street gamins and men of the lower class, who care not for any one but themselves, and they were excited by the cry of fire and the sound of the engine gong. Everything that was before them must go down or go with them. There was no resisting their force.

With a quick exclamation that sounded almost like a prayer Richard caught Allison in his arms and held her within a doorway, himself bearing the brunt of the hurrying throng that surged and pressed against him.

25

Enchantments

It was but for two or three minutes that they stood there, perhaps, with the wild, yelling multitude of men, women, and children, disheveled and dirty, tearing madly by, and the red glare of the engines lighting the scene weirdly, yet in that short time Allison, in her safe retreat, seemed to have changed into a new being. She hardly understood the sudden throb of joy and delight in her protector's strength that rushed over her. It was beautiful to be so taken care of. It was all a tumult below her, but she shut her eyes to the scene outside. In that doorway it was safe and peaceful.

When the uproar had passed, he drew her hand firmly within his arm and led her rapidly away.

She did not say a word. She walked as in a dream. She scarcely noticed what he did when he hailed a passing cab and put her in it.

"You poor child! Were you terribly frightened?" he asked tenderly.

"No, only at first," said Allison, with a ring of joy in her voice; "I knew you would take care of me."

He reached over and took one of her little gloved hands and held it in his own with a firm pressure. It was delightful to be cared for so tenderly. It was joy to have him hold her hand. What did it mean? She must not allow herself to love him. He was not for her. He was rich and in the great world—worldly. He was not a Christian; yes, and then the memory of the words he had spoken just before the crowd came upon them surged over her with another wave of joy and her hand trembled slightly in his. He placed his other hand over hers then as if she needed protection. It was as if their hearts could speak to one another through their hands and she felt in entire harmony with him. For a moment she gave herself up to the delight of it. Then conscience awoke and clamored loudly; but was this Allison? What was the matter with her? She who had been brought up to hold her eyes modestly from the world, who had always felt that no improprieties should be allowed, that flirting was dreadful, and had labored most earnestly with her mill girls to prevent them from dancing, on the ground that dancing permitted too much familiarity. She to do this? This was an undercurrent of thought. But she would not reason now. Several times conscience spoke loudly enough to be heard above the tumult of her happy heart and she almost tried to withdraw her hand. Once she quite succeeded in doing so and found her heart leaping in gladness that he had reached out and taken it again.

And so in this half-ecstatic state and talking both of them about the meeting and the fire and their escape, anything but the thought that was uppermost in their minds, they reached the house and were surprised to find that the cab had halted.

Allison's feet were scarcely on the pavement before her full senses returned. She turned and fled up the steps while Richard was paying the cabman, and had succeeded in bringing John to the door before the fare was amicably settled. She paused only a moment to discover that Evelyn's light was out and all was still before she went into her own room and locked the door. There she flung her wraps from her and sat down in the dark, with her burning face in her hands.

What had she done? Been just like any unprincipled girl! Allowed a man, who had not told her he loved her, to hold her hand for probably half an hour, perhaps more, she had no idea of the flight of time! It did not matter. What was time in an affair like this? Five minutes was enough to condemn her—one minute! Probably he was used to holding girls' hands. Probably the girls he knew allowed such liberties often. Her brother had told her once of a college classmate who made a practice of going around getting girls' handkerchiefs to make a collection. He had a hundred and thirty at that time. Who would want to be one of a hundred and thirty girls to share a man's—what? Not affections, in such infinitesimal parts. But he had not seemed like that. He had seemed good and noble. But then she must remember that he probably did not think anything of such familiarities, that he was just trying to be kind to her in what he supposed had been a time of fear. Oh, how she had disgraced herself and all her family! What would mother think of her? And father—father who objected to her going to a children's surprise party when she was quite young because he told her that they would be sure to play kissing games and he did not want his little girl kissed by any boy, and when she had insisted and he had yielded to her promise that she would have nothing to do with such games, lo, she had been caught by a foolish bet of one boy to kiss her just because she had declared she would not play in that way. She could remember now and feel again the remorse and anguish with which she went home with her father when he called for her at the appointed hour and confessed her shame and defeat. He had talked so kindly and gently to her about it and had explained the beauty of the purity of womanhood, and that familiarities should be saved for the time when one should come to claim her love and life companionship. She had believed it and rejoiced in the ideal her father had set before her, and now she had gone against all his teachings. How was it she had so fallen? He would think her a simple little country ignoramus, or worse, a flirt, whose talk of Christ had all been for show and whose real, inner life was against her profession. It would, maybe, lead him away from Christ, now, just now, when he was coming into the light. Something must be done. But what? Could it be explained? Could she do it? Oh, how could she speak of it, put it into cold words that she had let him hold her hand for so long and had done nothing to stop it? Her cheeks burned and burned till it seemed as if they would scorch the pillow against which she leaned her aching head. And then, as if trying to excuse herself, there would come over her again the joy she had felt. But she must not give that as an excuse. She knelt to pray, but she could only sob softly into her pillow.

Weary at last with the long excitement of the evening, and fully resolved, in some way, to make reparation for what she had done, she finally fell asleep and slept until the sun was quite high in the heavens.

It was a relief to her to find that the gentlemen had gone down-town nearly an hour since and that she and Evelyn were to be alone at breakfast. She did not want to meet Mr. Rutherford again until she could make her confession of wrong, and then how, how could she ever look him in the face again?

An hour later an escape seemed open for her. Her mother wrote that she was not very well and an invalid cousin had written that she was coming to spend a month. Mrs. Grey did not wish to hasten Allison's return, if she thought she was needed any longer in New York, nor did she want her to come if she was having a pleasant time and wished to stay a little longer, but if she felt that her visit was nearly over, they would all be glad to see her once more.

With a cry of joy Allison bent over and kissed the dear, familiar writing, and then her face crimsoned again as she remembered what a tale of disgrace she would have to tell that fond mother! Yes, she would go. She would go at once. She would take the evening train. There would be plenty of time to pack, and then she would get away from herself and forget this fearful surge of joy at the dreadful thing she had done last night, and forget this young man before she should have his image too clearly fixed in her heart, for that his companionship had been pleasant to her, she could not deny. He had but been kind to her, of course, as his sister's guest. She must never forget that again for one little instant. In some way she must plan to speak to him about last night. It was an awful, an almost impossible thing to do, but she must do it, for the honor of her religion and her family and herself.

Richard Rutherford had not been surprised that Allison did not appear at the breakfast table.

"How shy and sweet she is," he smiled to himself as he started down-town. All day long he was in a transport of ecstasy. It had been a delight to shield her from that howling mob. The ride home had been all too short. How soon could he dare to tell her of his great, deep love for her? Must he wait until he had proved to her that his belief in her Saviour was strong and true? He must be very careful, for she was a shy little soul,—he might frighten her before he had taught her to love him. What joy was this that had been given him right at the outset of the new life he had determined to live! It seemed to him like a pledge of God's faithful loving-kindness. What bliss to find another creature in the world whom he felt to be a part of his own soul! He had been used to think this would never be, and had in his heart admitted the charges of his friends that he was over-fastidious. But now here was one whom he could fully trust, whom he could love and care for with his whole soul. Would she consent to belong to him? Would she ever drop that shy reserve and give her life into his keeping, be his wife? His heart leaped with a new thrill of understanding as he pronounced that word over to himself. It had never seemed to him a particularly beautiful word before; but now what word so sweet in the whole English language as "wife"?

It was therefore with intense dismay that he learned, on coming home that afternoon, somewhat earlier than usual, that she was preparing to leave that evening and was at that moment engaged in packing.

It was Evelyn who told him and sent him out to telegraph and engage a berth for the evening train, as John had gone in another direction and there was need of haste, if Allison was not to sit up all night.

He went, of course; there was nothing else to do, but his

face was clouded over and his heart was heavy as lead. The sunshine seemed suddenly to have left the day. Had the sun set so early? Why, oh, why had he not told her of his love before, that he might have the right to make a protest now against such a hasty departure? No, that would never have done. He might only have frightened her away the sooner. What was he that he should suppose any girl was ready and willing to fall in love with him at once? It is true there had been a time in his career when many girls had seemed to be at his beck and call and he had prided himself on being popular among them and able to have any one he wished; but he was older now. Or had the light of love shown him his true self, with all its shortcomings, in a truer sense? He sighed heavily and wished the car would not crawl so slowly, but at last he was back at the house again. He must plan in some way to see Allison at once, though he knew he ought not to venture to tell her of his feelings now in such a hurry; but at least he could see her alone and tell her how sorry he was that she was going, and perhaps, but it was not likely, it would be safe to risk it yet. Still, he would see her. How? Should he ask Evelyn to send her down to the library on some trivial excuse, or should he send the maid? Ah, it would be awkward business any way he could fix it. Then he turned the key in the latch and let himself in, coming face to face with Allison herself, in the front hall, poised with one foot on the lower stair, her cheeks flaming and her eyes bright with a fixed determination.

"Mr. Rutherford, may I see you just a minute?" she said, and he knew that there was something unusual the matter. He followed her to the music room without saying a word, anxiety written on his face.

She sat down in the fire-lit room. It was growing dark now and reminded them both of the first Sunday evening she had spent there.

"What is it?" he asked in a strained voice.

"I have a confession to make to you before I go away." There was intense excitement in her voice, and her fingers worked nervously together in her lap while the firelight played over her and showed her as a pretty picture of distress.

"I hardly know how to tell you," she went on rapidly,

looking down at the locked fingers, "but I must before I go. I cannot have you misjudge my—my religion, or my up-bringing—or myself—though I did wrong. I do not know how to begin lest you will think I am condemning you also, and I am not. I know that you must think very differently about these things, and—and it would not be the same for you anyway," she gasped, choking a little at the remembrance of the miserable day and night she had spent.

"I beg that you will tell me what I have done, Miss Grey. I cannot imagine what it can be that you are accusing yourself of. I assure you I am utterly unaware of anything," he said with white face, and voice that fairly trembled with intensity.

"Oh, it is not you. It is I. I knew better. I have always despised girls who allowed such familiarities. I want you to know that I think that I did wrong. It seems dreadful to have to speak of it at all." She paused, wishing he would help her, but she saw he did not yet comprehend what she was talking about.

"It is that I let you hold my hand last night," she said desperately, her face fairly blazing and her eyes filling with tears. "I am so—so ashamed, and I have spent such a miserable night and day. I did not know that I could deliberately go on and do a thing that I knew was so wrong, but I did. And I could not go without telling you how sorry and ashamed I am."

"Did you think that was so very wrong?" asked the young man with intense voice, gripping his hat which he still held in his hand as if it were trying to get away from him.

"Oh, yes, I think such things ought to be kept for just *one*—that is—I mean that a girl should not allow—mere friends—to take such liberties." Her embarrassment was intense. In every word she spoke she seemed to herself to blunder worse. She did not see the white, stricken look on her companion's face. She was occupied with her own distress.

"I see," he said, still in that repressed tone. "But you must not blame yourself. It was entirely my fault. I remember now you did take your hand away. I should have taken the hint. It was rude and inexcusable in me. But I do not think any of those terrible things of you that you have suggested. It was not that I did not respect you. You are as pure as a lily. I beg you will forgive yourself. As for myself I shall always regret that I have caused you this pain."

"Oh, don't!" she said, and he seemed to know that the tears had come again to her eyes, and then Evelyn was heard calling:

"Allison, where are you? The man has come for your trunk. Is it ready to lock?" and Allison hastily wiped her red eyes and rushed back to her room.

The conversation at dinner was mainly between Mr. Rutherford, senior, and Allison. He openly expressed his grief at her withdrawal from the family group. He brought the bright blushes to her face by telling her that he was coming to regard her as another daughter, and neither Allison nor Richard dared look up, but each was smitten to the heart by the thought his words suggested.

Both Allison and Richard had been counting on Evelyn's cold to keep her at home. They hoped to have opportunity to finish that uncomfortable talk in some way that would not leave them with such torn hearts and minds, just how, neither knew; but each was looking forward to the ride to the ferry. Allison felt sure he would accompany her. But neither had counted on Mr. Rutherford, senior. Just as Evelyn had kissed Allison good-bye and was wrapping her own fur cloak about her for the ride across the city he appeared in his overcoat with hat in hand.

"I think I'll just go over along with you, my son. We want this little girl to understand that we are very loth to part with her and shall expect her back again as often and as soon as she can come."

It was a long speech for her father to make and Evelyn marveled at it and felt that she had done well to bring Allison into their home. Her father had shown his tenderness for her so much of late. It was growing very sweet to Evelyn. With a sudden impulse she said, "Wait," and flew up the stairs, returning in a moment with a large fur-lined opera cloak and hood enveloping her.

"I'm going myself," she said, "I shall not catch cold in this and I cannot have you all go off without me."

It was an outwardly pleasant party that rode along through the lighted streets, though two of them bore heavy hearts. There would be no chance to say anything, thought Allison, and she would have to go away remembering that grave, hurt look on his face. It almost broke her heart.

"There *shall* be an opportunity *made* for me to ask her *one* question," said the young man to himself as he ground his teeth with resolution in the dark. "Yes, even if I have to travel on to the next station for the purpose."

Quite across the ferry they went with her, and even into the train and sat chatting with her for a few minutes. Richard slipped away from them a moment to find the porter and make some little arrangement for the traveler, and then coming back grew suddenly anxious lest Evelyn would have to get off the train when it was moving. He thought he never would get them to take leave. He was so anxious about it that he almost forgot to shake hands with Allison at all himself and then did it in a very hasty manner.

Once they were finally outside and walking along by the train looking up to find her window, he suddenly remembered that he wished to speak to the porter again and rushed back in spite of Evelyn's warning that the last whistle was sounding. He cared not. He did not even pretend to look for that unnecessary porter. He strode up the aisle to the surprised Allison, who had begun to settle into the dreary retrospect that she knew would be hers during the journey. He cared not that his father and sister were looking through the window outside. He bent over her and said in low tones which only she could hear:

"Did you mean that there was some one else? Are you engaged, Allison?"

She met him with a relieved smile of astonishment. "Oh, no!" she said, in such a free glad tone, "what made you think of such a thing? Please forgive me for making you feel so uncomfortable. I cannot tell you what a happy time you have given me. And, oh, please, won't you get off quick? I am afraid you will be hurt!" This last with that feminine anguish of face and voice in which even the strongest-minded women indulge when those they love are lingering beyond the warning, "All aboard!"

He caught her hand, his face lighting up once more, and wrung it with a last good-bye, and then ran, while she watched anxiously till she saw him as the train, moving rapidly now, passed him on the platform where the Rutherfords waved her farewell.

Richard Rutherford was not very talkative during the ride home. His father and sister monopolized the conversation. He was trying to justify his heart in feeling so much lighter than it had done during the drive down. Could it be possible that he had mistaken her meaning? It had looked as though she were trying to tell him gently that she belonged to another, or at least that she did not and could not care for him. But she had disclaimed that with such a clear, true look that he knew it could not be. Also there had been something else in her face, taken unaware, when he had returned to the car, a lighting of joy. It might or it might not mean good to him. Why had he been such a fool? Why had he not explained to her that it had been honest deep love for her that had prompted him to take her hand. Instead, he had allowed her to leave his home thinking he was a dishonorable man, a man who would toy with a girl's affections for an hour and think no more of it. He never had been that kind of a man and he could not understand now why he had allowed himself to be silent. Still he had feared to tell his love when she seemed to be trying to show him that it was not for her.

But something must be done. He would justify himself now at all hazards. She must know his love even if it frightened her and did seem premature.

When he reached home he wandered up toward his own room and in so doing passed the open door of her deserted room. It was dark there, but he could see the outline of the furniture from the light in the hallway. He stepped in and sat down in a low rocking-chair and tried to think. This room had but a few hours before sheltered her. It seemed a hallowed place. He would stay here a little while and think what he would do. It might be that some sweet influence from its former occupant would show him the way. He must write and tell her, but he wanted guidance. What would *she* do? Ah! she would pray!

A few minutes afterward a light step entered the room and Evelyn stood beside her brother, her hand resting gently on his head.

"Dick, dear," she said tenderly, "what is the matter? I couldn't help seeing. Can't you tell me about it?"

He raised his head and kissed her hand. There was an uplifted look upon his face.

"Evelyn," he said, "I am going to visit Aunt Joan, and I am going to-morrow!"

26

Trouble in China

Allison had scarcely settled herself to the thought of the journey and was preparing to puzzle her brain over what those last words of Richard Rutherford had meant, when a surprisingly deferential porter stood beside her with a large box and two smaller packages. He with difficulty made her understand that they were for her, and she opened them with much delight, unmindful of the watchful eyes of her fellow-passengers. The large box contained flowers, she was sure. Yes, great, dark, rich crimson jacqueminots with long, strong stems and crisp, green leaves. She buried her face in them to hide the tears that had rushed to her eyes in spite of herself.

The other packages contained two new books that were being much discussed and a box of fine confectionery. Suddenly the fact that he had called her "Allison," in parting came forth and stood out from all other facts and confronted her. She turned rosy red, and the gentleman across the aisle who had been watching her curiously decided there was no use hoping to get a glance from those eyes. She was too much absorbed, and besides she seemed to be already secured. The dreary retrospect that had been summoned to attend her journey got off at the next station, and Allison went home in a confused state of mind, now smiling to herself as she looked from the dark window and now keeping back the tears that would come as she thought of some of the things she had obliged herself to say. They seemed rude and almost cruel now. What did he think of such a strange girl?

It was the second day. Allison had tried hard to settle into the old routine of little daily duties at home. She had unpacked her trunk and told her mother a great many things that happened in New York; not all—she was not ready for that yet—and the wise mother saw and understood and waited.

She had gone out for a few minutes to a neighbor's now on an errand and Allison was left alone in the house. It was not quite time for her father to come home for supper. She hovered about from room to room feeling a strange unrest, and chiding herself for it. She lighted the gas and went over to the table where stood a tall vase filled with roses and bent and laid her cheek upon their cool, sweet petals.

It was just at that moment that some one was coming up the walk and saw the pretty vision through the half-drawn lace curtains. He paused a moment to take in the beauty and the meaning of it for him. His roses! His heart quickened and he went up the steps with a bound and rang the bell.

Out on the street a boy stood watching him up the path. He was a handsome boy with heavy features and large, saucy eyes. He stood a moment and then took a step or two back out of the way of a tree that hindered his vision. He watched until the hall door opened and let in the stranger and then he said aloud:

"Well, I'll be whacked! It's him. It is, sure. Well, I s'pose it's got to come sometime, and he's a mighty nice feller." Then he drew a long sigh and turned up the street whistling a tune he had learned in the Sunday-school.

Allison had not lighted the gas in the hall yet, but the open door from the parlor gave light enough to tell who the stranger was when he came into the hall. She stood, looking at him almost as if she saw a vision, and unbidden by her will her lips spoke one word:

"Richard!"

"Allison!" he answered, depositing his dress-suit case on the floor and taking her in his arms. She did not draw away nor even try to take away the hand he held in one of his.

"Allison," he said, "I had to come and explain to you that it was because I loved you that I took your hand. I could not bear to have you think another day that I had been dishonorable, or playing with you. My darling, will you forgive me now?"

For answer she raised her sweet face to his, all smiles and tears, trustingly as a flower would turn toward the sun, and he stooped and laid his lips upon hers.

Suddenly, out of what seemed a clear sky to the unthinking, pleasure-loving part of the civilized world, there burst the trouble in China.

Evelyn Rutherford had not been one who cared to read the daily papers much. She would glance them over occasionally, but she had not been taught to read the news when a child and did not care for it when she grew older.

Her father and brother were talking about the Chinese trouble when she came down to breakfast one morning. She paid little attention, supposing it to be some political trouble. There were so many wars and rumors of wars that came not near her.

That afternoon she was on her way to the elevated train and the pinched face of a newsboy who was madly crying, "Here's all about your Boxers!" attracted her attention. She supposed it was some sporting news and did not care for a paper, but bought one for the sake of the little pleading face of the boy who offered it. Once in the train she leaned back and thought no more of the paper till looking down her eye caught the words "TROUBLE IN CHINA" in large letters. She drew a quick breath and grasped the paper tightly as she read. What horrible story was this? She read every word. There was little known as yet, except terrible surmise. She bought every paper the next newsboy carried when she got off the train and read with fevered haste. So many contradictory reports, so many theories and ghastly conjectures! They were all clamoring about the legations. What was the danger of the American minister, a man who had gone to China purely from business motives, or from ambition, to be compared to the dangers of the missionaries, of one true man in particular who carried the message of love and peace and who had really given up his life that he might help those brutal people? She searched hungrily for word of the missionaries. She had been to the women's foreign meetings enough now to understand a little about it. There was very little said about the missionaries in particular. They were mentioned as in great danger. In some places there was report of a general massacre of the missionaries planned, and one paper had the audacity to state that it was more than likely that the Christian missionaries were the underlying cause of all this hatred toward foreigners by the Boxers.

She reached home in a state of excitement. She plied father and brother for information and they gave it plentifully, but in language far too technical for her to gain much help. Their talk presently branched off into a discussion of the political situation of the whole world with regard to China, and Evelyn ceased to try to follow them. Her heart seemed to be settling down in dull thuds and throbs to stand the strain that was put upon it. Only one more sentence did she catch from her brother as she started upstairs. It was spoken in a low anxious tone to her father:

"I am afraid it will go hard with Grey. He is right in the midst of the trouble, and he's not one to run away from danger if he thinks his duty calls him there."

She stopped on the stairs, her hand to her heart, but heard no more. She remembered that Maurice Grey would presently stand in the position of brother to Dick. He had a right to be anxious and to speak of him. How she envied Dick! She must keep her anxiety to herself. She had no right to even feel it, and how could she help it?

She turned out the gas in her room and sat down in the dark. The slow tears trickled sadly down her cheeks and she let them stay wet on her face. She thought of the night when she had gone up to the dark attic and poured out her trouble in long sobs. She would like to cry like that again, only she could not. She was too tired. She was tired a great deal in these days. Presently she went and knelt down beside her bed and tried to pray,—to pray for the one she loved and for herself. Her cheeks had grown hot many a time as she thought of that confession she had made to herself in the attic the year before, but tonight with such grave calamities imminent she forgot that it was any shame to her to love a man who loved not her and had never even shown her any but the simplest of attentions. She forgot everything but himself and herself and the God who could care for them both. She knew so little about prayer yet; she did not know how to ask; but she prayed that she might be enabled to pray as she had prayed for her conversion.

The days that followed were harrowing ones; they were such for all the country, but so very hard for her since she must not show her feelings to any one. No, for that would be disgrace and shame to him and her both, to think that she should give her love unasked.

But she could go to the missionary meetings and she did, and found there mothers and wives and sisters who were mourning and praying and anxious for their dear ones, and sometimes she could put her arms about some distressed mother or sister and weep with her; often her tears of genuine sympathy did much to soothe and comfort. People wondered at this elegant young woman who spent so much time and money in the missionary work, and who seemed so anxious for China, and so sympathetic. Evelyn never said much nor did her deeds openly. She did not stop to question now what people would think of her changed ways, that she, a queen of society, should eschew all social haunts and instead spend her time in missionary meetings and studying about China. What mattered it to her what they thought?

"Evelyn does not look well," said Mr. Rutherford to his son one day. "She is white and thin."

"Oh, she'll be all right when the weather gets settled. It's spring fever. You know she didn't look well last spring," Richard said cheerily. He had a letter from Allison in his pocket and he was anxious to get upstairs to read it over again.

Into the midst of the days of anxiety and disquietude came Jane Bashford. She was Jane Worthington now. Her father had been strongly opposed to the match and so the young people had taken matters in their own hands and been secretly married. It had been just the kind of thing Jane delighted in, so romantic. But it was not nearly so romantic when the brief honeymoon was over and she discovered that her dashing young husband had not the wherewithal to pay their hotel bills. Jane had to be very humble and go back to her father, begging forgiveness, and the father had granted it within certain limitations. They were living quietly, Jane said, all too quietly for the young son-in-law's ideas. He made his wife miserable by calling her father all kinds of names. He intimated that he had been given to expect plenty of money, and he plainly told his wife that he cared more for several other girls but had chosen her because he supposed that she was able to command the money and had sense enough not to bawl all the time like a baby. He hated sniveling women, he declared. "And he says," wept Jane, her pretty face sad and swollen with much weeping, "that he always loved you, and that he only took me to spite you."

Evelyn's own pale face flushed deep with angry scorn. This was the man with whom she had been glad to make merry only two short years ago! From what had she been saved! "The scoundrel!" she said under her breath, while Jane, unmindful save of herself and her own sorrowful little tale, poured out the story of her wrongs.

"He often comes home dead drunk," she said with a strange hardness in her child-eyes that would have reminded Allison of the woman in the mission. She said it as if that were the smallest of her sorrows. Poor thing! She actually seemed to love him yet in spite of it all. "He talks dreadfully to me, then, and he struck me the other night," she said, showing the black and blue mark of his brutal fist.

Could she show this poor child-wife the way to Jesus? Evelyn wondered. Might it be possible to reach her through her love for her poor wretch of a husband, and show a higher, dearer love that would not fail her?

Evelyn's heart was filled with compassion, while she looked down upon her old-time friend from a height to which she had climbed in these two years. How could they ever have been friends? she wondered. What possible tastes could they now have in common? How incredulous Jane would be if she should tell her of her interest in China. China was a far-away land to Jane for which she cared not one whit.

Evelyn, with a prayer in her heart that came with the wish to help her former friend, set herself to remember all that had been said to help her to Jesus. All the steps by which she had come she would try to lead her friend. But when she attempted a little word she found she would have to begin down the ladder much, much lower than she had started.

"I don't know what you mean, Evelyn," said the weeping wife, looking up through her selfish tears. "How strangely you talk," half-petulantly. "What have you been doing to yourself? You look quite shabby and your dress is entirely out of style. Doesn't it make you feel awfully gloomy to think of such things? My! I couldn't bear it! Life is hard enough without being so poky. I go out all I can to forget my trouble. I went to the theatre every night last week. Harry likes the theatre better than anything else, only he will go back behind the scenes and talk to those horrid actresses. But then he says he always did that, that all men do, so I suppose I must put up with it. Pray? Dear me, no! I couldn't do that. It would put me in the blues worse than I am. You need a good dance to stir you up. Evelyn, you are growing morbid. Come over to our house to-morrow afternoon and I'll introduce you to some of Harry's friends. They are awfully interesting men. A little gay, perhaps, but after all, very interesting. You don't want them too slow, you know."

And so she met all Evelyn's efforts to bring her any true help, and Evelyn with a sigh concluded she would not do for even a home missionary. She determined to pray for her at least. She tried to tell her so as she was taking her leave.

"Thanks, awfully, Evelyn," she said with a stare, "but what good do you think that will do? Harry's my husband, and I don't suppose praying will make my life any brighter. Good-bye. You better not waste your time so; it will make you gloomy."

27

The Coming of the Boxers

June and July dragged their horror-laden lengths along and Evelyn grew thinner and whiter. She forced herself to read the papers from beginning to end. She read the names of all missionaries printed. Once she saw Doctor Grey's name among those who were missing, with a hint of hope that he might have been saved; but the next report of those saved did not mention him. From Allison there came anxious letters, telling of their sorrowful hearts, but showing withal a high hope in him who had power to save. Evelyn thought as she read her prospective sister-in-law's sweet words of trust that she herself was not worthy to be named among those who had faith. She could only lie in God's hand and "let him have his own way" with her and all things that concerned her. But nevertheless she envied the other girl her freedom to show her anxiety. How sweet it would be to have a right to ask and wait to be told, even though there was little hope of any joyful message on this side of heaven.

She grew still thinner and whiter in these days and her father took her away to the shore out of the city's heat, and then to the mountains, but she seemed to care as little for the one as for the other. She was sweet and gentle to him and seemed pleased with any proposition he had to make, but he could see there was something the matter with her which was deeper than he knew. He grew worried and proposed a trip abroad, but she laughed away his fears and begged to be taken home again, saying she was only homesick.

She went down to one of the missionary meetings as

soon as possible after getting settled once more. Her heart was aching to know what the workers thought or knew, but she listened in vain for any word. They spoke of the service just past in memory of the dear dead missionaries, her heart crying out against it. His memorial services and only a little while before he had been with them talking and smiling! Oh, it was terrible! She went home feeling too ill to endure it longer, and there she found lying on her dressing table a letter. It was a foreign letter with a queer unfamiliar stamp and on strange, thin paper, but the writing on the outside, though she had seen it but once before, she seemed to know at once as she had known its owner's voice and face long ago.

She calmly took off her wraps, praying the while. She knew not why she went about the little things she had to do with so much attention to detail before reading it. It was as if she were trying to steady her heart for an ordeal through which she had to pass. She did not let herself think. No question of whether he was alive or dead, or why he had written to her, was allowed to form itself in her brain. She held everything in abeyance for the reading, well knowing it might hold much of good or ill. Her door locked, she sat down and opened the letter with cold, trembling fingers.

Her full name and address were at the top of the sheet and the letter began abruptly:

I am sitting to-night in the small whitewashed room that serves for a temporary hospital. Near me on an iron cot lies a Chinaman on whom I yesterday performed a severe operation. I am sole nurse, missionary, and doctor. The others were all ordered off to-day. They had gone to Peking for safety from the Boxers, who it is rumored will be here in a few hours. The man on the bed beside me is not a Christian. He will not be in danger from the Boxers. His family think that I have cut his heart out to offer to my God and then to make strange medicine of. I also was ordered to Peking, but if I go away and leave this patient with no one to attend him now in his critical condition the man will die. It is a choice of deaths. I may be able to save him by serving him a few hours longer. Perhaps his people may come to believe in the living God if he recovers. Undoubtedly my life is in danger. In all probability I shall be cut off from any communication with the rest of the missionaries in an hour, if I am not already. There is scarcely any hope that I can be saved. It is for this reason that I am writing this letter. If I thought I should live I would not trouble you with my story. I have arranged with one of the mail couriers whom I know well and who has great respect for anything bearing the government stamp, to take any letters that he may find in a certain crack in the wall near by, known to myself and him, and he will, I feel sure, mail this. If I live I shall not put the letter where he can find it, but destroy it and so no harm will be done. If I stay quietly in this room it may be two or three days before I am discovered and by that time the sick man will, I hope, be able to get on with the nursing of the old Chinese cook whom I am instructing.

Therefore, though I feel that death is not far off I am content to-night, and I have decided to let my heart have this much indulgence.

Do you know, Evelyn Rutherford, that I have carried your image in my heart since I left you? That I hear often above all other sounds the music of your piano as you played *"Auf Wiedersehen."* I did not look the fact quite in the face that night though I felt it dimly, but I think it will be "till we meet again" in heaven. I may tell you just this once that I love you, may I not? It has been my joy and my delight when, weary with hard work and lonely, I could sit down a moment, to let the strange foreign city melt away and the Chinese jargon cease to ring in my ears while I walked the autumn-leaf-strewn street with you once more and saw the sunlight shining on your hair, or watched the shadows glancing from your lashes when you raised your eyes to mine to answer a question. Sometimes I let myself dwell on the ride we took together that wonderful afternoon. You can never know the joy of the moment when you promised me you would pray for yourself. I think I would like to stand hand in hand with you on the brow of that hill where we stopped to look, and await with you my Lord's coming. There are times also when I go back to our first meeting in New York and to the afternoon we spent in the old castle while the storm roared outside, but they are not so dear, because at those times we had not spoken of what was nearest to my heart, the love of Jesus, and I had not yet begun to pray for you, that sweet, that blessed privilege which has been my one daily pleasure. I have come to feel sure, my Evelyn, my darling—you will let me call you that for just to-night, will you not?—that you have drawn close to Jesus. Sometimes when I am kneeling at the throne of Mercy I can almost hear the echo of your whispered prayer and feel the wafting of your breath, and I think—I have dared to think—you are praying for me and my work. I have not been so wild as to fancy you could love me. I know you have no such thought. I might have dared to try to win you had I stayed in New York and attained the success which seemed to be mine for the trying. But I could not ask you to love me and leave all the life that to you would be almost necessity to come out here and suffer—nay, what I may have to suffer to-morrow or the next day. I could not be so calm about the coming of those fiends if you were here beside me. And yet, oh, Evelyn, if you were here! I tremble to think of all it would mean for me if I were to go on living and you, *you* here beside me. The wild thought has just rushed through my mind that I might have dared after all. I might have asked you. Men have done as selfish things before. Women have loved and dared, and, yes, have set their love upon just as unworthy men as I, perhaps. Thank God that I did not, Evelyn, with the Boxers coming to-morrow!

I have a confession to make. Close to my heart I carry a picture of you as a little girl, with sweet wondering eyes and a cloud of hair about your face. It was left by your brother in his college room after packing and he asked me to take care of it. Since I have known you I cut your face from the card and placed it in a small case which I always carry with me; this is since I knew you in New York, the last winter of my stay there. I do not think you will grudge me the small comfort of carrying it with me to my grave. No one will ever know who it is.

And of my love for you which has grown during the years and with the few bright glimpses I have had of you, how can I write? It is a thing to be told, not put upon paper. It is something intangible, which only eyes and lips may fully interpret. But I want you to know what your image is in my heart where no woman was ever enshrined before, and that to me you are at once the most beautiful, the most lovable, and the sweetest of all womankind. Of your queenly bearing and your many graces it would take the years of a lifetime to speak. It may be that in heaven I may tell you the meaning of it all for me, and that there our souls may welcome one another and understand.

And now, dear one, whatever your life is to be, whether long or short, joyous or sorrowful, I have told you with my last word of my great, great love for you, and I commend you to "Him that is able to keep you from falling, and to present you faultless before the presence of his glory with exceeding joy."

I shall take every precaution that this may be sent you in case I am killed, as I can hardly escape being. Do not let that part of it trouble you. I do not fear to go to my Saviour, and I shall count it all joy if I may suffer a little for his sake. It may be that through it the soul of this poor heathen on the bed beside me may be brought to Jesus in some way. I have learned to love Christ's way for me, even though it means separation from you whom I love.

Now I shall fold and address this, sealing and stamping it carefully that it may be sure to reach you if it is sent. Then I shall place it in the pocket of my coat next to your picture. If the Boxers come, as they most surely will, it is but the work of a moment to conceal this in the place appointed between two heavy stones, where even fire will not be likely to reach it. I think my courier is trusty. And be assured that I love you too much to allow this ever to reach or disturb your happiness as long as I live. Evelyn, my darling, I love you. And now *"Auf Wiedersehen."*

Go thou thy way, and I go mine;
  Apart, yet not afar;
Only a thin veil hangs between
  The pathways where we are.

And "God keep watch 'tween thee and me"
  This is my prayer.
He looks thy way, he looketh mine,
  And keeps us near.

Yet God keeps watch 'tween thee and me,
  Both be his care,
One arm round thee and one round me
  Will "keep us near."

The smarting tears dimmed her eyes so that she could not read the name signed clear and bold below as it danced in dazzling characters before her. Her pain and her joy struggled together which might first and hardest strike her. She had read slowly, dazed, and unable at first to comprehend all the love and the horror and the pity of it. Gradually, as she sat and stared at the closely written pages she seemed to see the Chinese hospital room with its whitewashed walls, the sick man lying near, the quiet figure writing, the whole surrounded by those demoniacal creatures lurking in dark shadows ready to spring when the moment came and the letter was finished.

Gradually the one who was writing became the center of the vision and everything else faded away. Then she began dimly to understand three things: that he loved her—ah, that was wonderful, beyond her understanding how it could have come about; that he was a hero—that she seemed to have known forever; and that he was dead. Slowly, slowly this dreadful fact was forced upon her. It was like having the anxiety of the summer all over again with the gradual growing certainty that there was no hope, only now it fell upon a heart fresh from his words of love and she could not tell whether there was more of joy or sorrow in being allowed to mourn for him.

There was a sound at the door now. It was repeated several times before she understood that she must answer it. She came back to the present world with a start. She had promised to go with her father to a missionary meeting in a large church that evening. She had been very anxious to go and had coaxed him. He had been somewhat surprised, but had yielded, putting aside a very important business engagement to please her. He was standing in the hall below waiting for her now. Marie called to know if she needed any help.

She folded the dear letter into its envelope and hastily put it inside her dress. The force of months of habit made her feel that she must not disappoint her father now. Her mind was not fully working, or she would have known that she could not bear that meeting in her present state, but she felt that she must go and get it done that she might earn the right to be alone in her room and think. She must understand it all before she told any one a word of the wonderful, awful news, if indeed she could ever trust the precious secret out of her own heart. She called to Marie that she would come in a moment and did not need her. Then she moved about gathering the wraps she had but a little while before placed so carefully away. She wondered now at the uselessness of the action. It did not occur to her that she had eaten no dinner and that no one had questioned it. The circumstances that had made this fact possible were unusual. Her father had taken a hasty meal at the club in order to meet some gentlemen and dispatch his business so as to be free for this evening meeting. Marie had been out for the afternoon, not having returned until a few minutes before Mr. Rutherford. Richard was away on a business trip, and none of the servants had seen Evelyn come in, as she had a key with her. When no one came down to dinner they supposed that she was invited out, and Marie had forgotten to mention it, and they did not trouble themselves further.

Evelyn's white face attracted her father's attention during the trip to the meeting. They were in a crowded car and were separated, but her large eyes had a restless, unsteady fire in them that made him uneasy. They had a few steps to

214

walk after getting out of the car and he asked her if she was quite well and still felt equal to a meeting. She answered that she was quite well, scarcely knowing what she said. Indeed, she seemed to herself to be walking through a strange, unknown land, always with that whitewashed room before her and the Chinaman stretched on the bed beside the man who was writing. Her eyes felt hot and dry, and seemed as if they were burning the lids when she let them close a moment as they came into the bright church.

They were late. The meeting had already begun. The church was crowded. The heat was intense, though outside it had been clear and cool. A place was made for the new-comers back by the door. Evelyn did not seem to see the throng of people before her; she was looking straight through them, miles and miles over land and sea, watching every moment for the creeping diabolical fiends to rush about that white room. She could see the man stop his writing and bend over to attend to the patient. She knew the very tenderness of his touch and the gentleness of his voice. She could see the earnest gaze of the sick man and knew he was judging the Saviour by his physician. Then quick to her watch again. She could see them now, those devils, stealing through the dark. There was singing all about her. Her hand held one side of her father's book, but she did not know it. Her eyes were fixed upon the dark objects. There were so many of them and they were coming now so much faster since it was all still. Some one was praying, thanking God for his martyrs; ah, that word, he was martyr as well as hero, sitting there so quietly with death standing at the door. They were a great mass outside now, and were yelling, and what was that? A shot! She saw him fall, and the ball seemed to go through her own heart. She fell back in her father's arms.

It was all confusion of kindness in a moment. They bore her out to the air and offered various assistance. Some one called a carriage and they took her gently home. A doctor who had been in the meeting went with them. She had come to herself just a moment. The young man kept his finger on the pulse. He talked to Mr. Rutherford about the meeting and the mission work, and confided his own desire to go out on the field. The father scarcely heard. He had sent for Doctor Atlee. He did not trust these young, inexperienced graduates. He was glad when the ride was ended and they had placed the still, white girl on her own bed.

Then began the reign of white-capped skillful nurses while Evelyn lay in the grip of fever and knew naught of what went on about her. Always there was that same tragedy to be acted over and over again. He loved her—and he was there—ahead of her—in danger—and she could not save him—and then that shot!

"I want to bring a former colleague of mine in to look at her," said Doctor Atlee, as he drew on his gloves one morning preparatory to leaving. "It is almost time for the crisis and with your permission I will let him watch her through. He is exceedingly skillful in such cases. I would trust him as myself. I cannot be here so constantly as I would like, and some one should be within call to-night."

"Certainly," said the grave father. "Anything you think best, doctor. We trust you, you know." There was something almost pitifully wistful in the father's appeal to the doctor's skill.

"I count it a Providence that he is here at this time," went on the doctor. "He just arrived by a roundabout way from China this morning. He was for going to his people in the West at once, but I have persuaded him to wait over and help me for a few days. He has had a marvelous experience among the Boxers; was saved as by a miracle after they thought him dead. He was nursed by an old Chinese whose child he had saved from blindness and smuggled out of the country by an unusual route and he has just landed in New York. You will be interested in talking to him. Good-morning."

"Ah, indeed," said Mr. Rutherford dryly. He did not wish to be impolite to the great doctor, but he did not wish to hear any more of Boxers or missionaries. Was it not a missionary meeting that was the cause of Evelyn's sickness? This he firmly believed.

28

A Battle with the Fever

"What! Here?" said the younger doctor as the carriage stopped. "Not Evelyn Rutherford?" and there was something startling in his voice which made Doctor Atlee look at him curiously.

"Why, yes. Do you know her? Didn't I mention the name before?"

"Yes, I know her," answered Doctor Grey, his voice under perfect control but his face white and anxious as he tried to recall everything the doctor had said about the case. There was very little hope. He remembered that. And it was an "obscure case."

It was with his own quiet manner that he entered the sick-room and looked with grave eyes at the wasted face of the beautiful girl. Her eyes were bright and restless and she seemed not to see what was going on about her.

He laid his practised finger on her wrist. For one instant her eye seemed to be caught by his, and then the restless tossing went on and a low, inarticulate moaning.

Doctor Grey studied the nurse's chart carefully.

"Her pulse is very irregular," he said in a low voice to Doctor Atlee, and then bent his head to listen to her heart. The soft rattle of thin paper caught his ear as he bent down to listen. He stepped back and called the nurse. "What is this paper, nurse? I cannot hear well because of the rattle."

"It is a letter, doctor, which she put there when she was first taken. She will not let us touch it. It makes her so much worse that we have left it there."

"It must come out for a little," he said. "Let me try."

"Miss Rutherford." He spoke in a quiet tone which usually commanded attention. She fixed her bright eyes on his face.

"I want to move this letter for a moment," he said, still in the same firm voice. "I will put it back."

Whether she comprehended anything or not she did not stir her eyes from his face as he gently took the little parcel which the nurse had wrapped in a soft white handkerchief when she found that the letter must be left in its hiding-place. He laid it beside the pillow where it could be easily given back and went on with his examination of the heart. At last he raised his head.

"I will stay," he said to Doctor Atlee, his professional unreadable mask on; but Doctor Atlee thought he detected a strange tremble to the usually firm voice.

He did not leave her side. The night came on. The father and brother came in and wrung the hand of the watching doctor with grave welcome, but daring not to ask a question. They had heard of his wonderful rescue by this time, but it was no time to speak of rescues. Death as grim, if not so horrible, stood waiting to snatch another dear one from them. They went out and each strong man sobbed in the silence of his room. They knew as if by instinct that the crisis was at hand.

There settled upon the household the hush of expectancy which always comes when the last hope has been tried and the dear one seems to be slipping, slipping into the beyond.

The new doctor was very particular, the day nurse told the night nurse. He did everything himself and seemed to think no one else knew how.

As the evening drew toward midnight he did not leave the bedside nor take his eyes from Evelyn's face. She was sleeping now and had been for several hours. They would soon know whether it was a sleep unto life or death. He had given orders that the father and brother be near at hand that they might be instantly called if there was any change. As the hands of his watch neared the hour when he expected to see a change of some sort he signed to the nurse to go and prepare some nourishment which had been previously ordered. She had scarcely slipped from the room when the great eyes opened and fixed themselves upon the doctor with

218

what looked to him like recognition. They seemed to light with a sudden joy:

"Is this heaven?" she asked in the thin, high-keyed voice of those who are almost over the border land. There was wonder and delight in her tone.

"No, dear, this is your own room," he answered gently, his heart sinking.

A shadow of disappointment seemed to cross her face. She made a quick motion to her breast as if she had remembered something and found it gone. He divined her intention and put in her hand the letter still wrapped in the handkerchief as the nurse had laid it by, but she did not seem to recognize it. Her hand kept fumbling for the letter where she had placed it, an agonized expression coming into the great, hollow eyes.

"My letter! Was it all a dream? You wrote me a letter sitting by the sick man in the little whitewashed room, and the Boxers were coming!" she said.

He was unfolding the handkerchief to show her the letter, but he started suddenly and almost lost his professional control of himself until he remembered the great necessity for care. With a superhuman effort he steadied his voice to reply as he spread his own letter before her eyes and his own astonished ones.

"Yes, darling! It is all true. The letter is here and I wrote it." His voice steadied as he spoke with the great love for her that was in his heart.

He was calling her that dear name at last as naturally as if he had always been allowed the precious privilege and had not been longing for it for months, yes, and years. But in this supreme moment no thought of it came to him. She was dying, perhaps, but she loved him. He loved her and he would save her if he could. She must be quiet.

The nurse came in with the nourishment and he gave her some.

"You must not talk," he said. "You must sleep. You have been ill."

"But you were dead," said Evelyn, her eyes still upon his face.

"No, I did not die. I am well and here, and now you must sleep and get well. Then I will tell you all about it."

She half smiled and said, "Kiss me," as a child would say it to its mother.

He stooped and kissed the white forehead, much to the amazement of the nurse, who could not understand this strange doctor and disapproved entirely of so much conversation.

Evelyn smiled and closed her eyes obediently, then opened them again and made a little groping motion with her hand.

He sat down beside her and held the wasted hand in his own. She smiled again and fell asleep as gently and naturally as a little child.

But the watcher, when he had dismissed the nurse by a sign to the other end of the room, sat immovable, scarcely daring to breathe. Gradually the truth was dawning upon him. It was his letter. He had known it at once. But how did it get here, since he had never placed it in the crack between the two stones as it said? The shot had taken him unaware. He had fallen near the sick man's cot, and the old faithful servant hurrying in had dragged him beneath the Chinaman's bed and hastily spread the bedclothes so that they would hide him as he lay. Then the faithful Chinese friend had gone out and told how all the foreign devils and the secondary foreign devils had fled to Peking and left only a poor old Chinaman who was lying very ill with his heart cut out, and begged that they would keep that quarter as quiet for his sake as possible. When they learned who it was that was sick and had sent a representative to look inside, who found it was true, they went away most marvelously and left them, so that after a few hours the faithful old cook dared to bring out his beloved doctor and friend and hide him in a little loft over the kitchen, where under careful directions he had dressed the wound and nursed him back to some degree of strength, and then smuggled him by night in strange ways until he found assistance to reach home. But the letter! How did it get to America? It must have fallen on the floor when he was shot. He had questioned the cook, but he said he knew nothing of it and supposed it must have been destroyed. A wave of thanksgiving went up from the heart of the young doctor that God had taken the matter out of his hands and sent the letter in spite of him, since it had come to a welcome here.

But his face remained the same, as the nurse from her

post of observation from time to time glanced that way. He did not change his position. He held close the small white hand, though the breathing continued steadily on and the sleeper did not move. He shook his head when the nurse, with the importance of her office which seemed to be ignored, rustled up, by and by, and offered to take his place and let him rest. From time to time his watch came out and he studied the fluttering pulse. Little by little the strain of anxiety relaxed, and he watched her face hungrily as Evelyn slept on. Toward dawning she opened her eyes, took medicine and nourishment, smiled, and slept again.

He watched her for a while, then drew a long sigh, and turning to the nurse, who had come to take the medicine glass, he said:

"You may tell her father that I think she will live."

She crept slowly out from under the shadow of danger like some ship that has almost foundered and is scarcely yet sure of her way. But close beside her day and night stayed her faithful physician.

"If anybody could save her I knew Grey could," said Doctor Atlee the next morning, and the nurse heard him and bit her lip in vexation. It was her opinion that Doctor Grey was entirely too officious.

Evelyn, when she came to herself, lay smiling and obedient, content to lie and rest and be at peace. Her Saviour had "had his way" with her, and though it had led her through sorrow, it had come out into a blossoming way of peace and joy. She did not question at all during those first days. It was enough to see Maurice Grey and to have his ministry. The vision of the whitewashed room was not with her now. It had vanished at his voice. One morning she put her white hand shyly on his as he gave her some medicine, and said:

"Maurice, I love you."

It was to them both an answer to his letter.

"Dear heart," he murmured low, and touched her closed eyelids with his lips, getting back to his dignified position just in time for the nurse to appear in the room.

The days of convalescence were sweet. He would not let her talk much of the time that had gone between this and their last meeting. He feared the excitement of recalling those sad days, but together they went back over their brief meetings and told each other all that was in their hearts.

"Do you think that I shall be too stupid to ever be able to help you just a little in your work when we get back to China?" she asked him suddenly one day almost timidly. "I would rather have died than feel that I should be a hindrance to you."

She never seemed to doubt for an instant that he would go back as soon as the way opened and it was safe to go, and she seemed to take delight in making little plans for the voyage and their home when they should reach there.

"Well, young man," said Mr. Rutherford one evening, when he had been spending a little time in his daughter's room, the first night that she was allowed to lie on the sofa after the evening meal, "it seems that you have saved this girl for us, and now the only thing in decency that I can do to reward you is to give her to you. She tells me she can only be happy hereafter converting Boxers in China. It's a good deal you ask, sir, but I guess you deserve it," and the father went out hastily, wiping his eyes.

After that Evelyn's strength came rapidly. She began to walk a few steps about the room.

After a triumphal procession one evening across the length of her room and back in the presence of her father and brother, she lay down on her bank of soft pillows smiling.

Doctor Grey turned to Mr. Rutherford, Sr., a curiously grave look upon his face. "Now, with your permission, father," he said, "I will marry her and take her down to the shore. I think the sea air would be just the thing at this time of year."

The father looked up a little surprised, but he was too practical a man to be long astonished at anything that appealed to his good sense.

"When?" he asked laconically, after the two had looked one another calmly in the eye for a moment.

"To-morrow," answered Maurice Grey promptly.

"Well, I suppose that'll be a very sensible thing to do," answered the father, after a moment's thought. "What do you say, Evelyn? Can you get ready for your wedding in one day?"

"I'm ready now, father," said Evelyn smiling, and closing

her eyes lest any one should see the too-much joy shining there, that was meant only for one.

"Well, upon my word, you are rushing things," said Richard Rutherford in amazement. "Why, here Allison thinks she can't get together enough flounces and feathers in six months to be married, and you, Evelyn, are willing to go wrapped in a blanket. I declare I never saw two such people in my life." There was jealousy in his tone and the rest only laughed, and they all separated quietly as if nothing unusual had taken place.

In the middle of the morning, with only Doctor Atlee and her father and brother for witnesses—with Marie and the nurse in the background—Evelyn was married by the same minister who had once preached a sermon to the bride and bridegroom some two years before. They had dressed her in a soft white china-silk wrapper, "Because I am going to China, you know," she laughingly explained, and when the ceremony was over they wrapped her in a great white fleecy shawl and laid her on the sofa with the windows open, so that she might get a breath of outside air while she rested. She ate her wedding breakfast of beef tea obediently and went to sleep a little while before the carriage came to take them to the train.

And so the elegant Miss Rutherford, without sound of music or profusion of presents and flowers, or heralding of cards and weary rush of dressmakers and tailors, passed out of New York society and became the unknown missionary's wife, just Mrs. Grey.

Oh, those days by the sea, where in spite of the time of year the sky was blue and the wind as soft as summer sighings, with a deep spice of life-giving power. Oh, those rides in the wheeled chair, with her dear husband to push her and to halt by her side and read aloud in the sun-parlor or Casino when she was ready to listen. It was like heaven on earth. She grew strong and well, like her former self, only with a depth of sweetness unknown to the Evelyn of old.

There were cards of announcement sent out. Richard attended to that. He was enough a part of the world yet to think of those things. Evelyn never even knew about them till she received one at the shore addressed "Doctor and Mrs. Maurice Grey," and below the regulation announcement was written in Richard's hand, "Lest you may have forgotten that there really was a wedding." They laughed over it, and were glad together that they had escaped it all. And Evelyn never even wondered at herself.

They were going home soon, not to New York, which was very dear, of course, and was home and always would be, but to Maurice's mother and father and sister. They would be there when Allison was married, and for a time afterward, perhaps, until it should be decided when they could go to China. "Back to China," Evelyn would continue to say, for since that awful night when she had watched the vivid picture of her Boxers coming and heard the shot, she said it was just as if she had been there. Whether China would look as the vision had done remained for the future.

It was down beside the sea that they told the story of the trials and sorrows and love that had grown during their separation. It was to that one tender listener who sympathized with her every heart-throb that Evelyn told the story of her visit to the attic on the night of his departure, and he in turn recounted every thought of his heart toward her in those lonely days when he had only a memory without hope to cheer him.

They went back together to New York when Evelyn was quite strong, for a few weeks before going to Hillcroft.

Jane Worthington came over in her old-time fashion to call. She looked older and worn and hard. She talked of her gayeties in so reckless a fashion that it almost broke Evelyn's heart to hear.

"Oh, yes, Harry is going on worse than ever," she said in answer to a gentle question. "He drinks and gambles away every cent he can get from me or father or Cousin Ned. Besides that, he disgraces me by running around with actresses. But I don't care any more. I have found a few friends of my own. There is one man who just worships me. Harry fairly hates him, but I like him very much myself, and I find I can have a little fun of my own. In fact, Evelyn, I'm more than half in love, to tell you the truth." She laughed in a wild, unnatural way while Evelyn shuddered.

"Oh, Jane," she said in a pained voice, "don't! I cannot bear to hear you talk so. You are a married woman."

"Married!" and Jane laughed again that empty, hard laugh. "Yes, what have I married?"

Evelyn was relieved that her husband came in just then for a moment. He had a question to ask, and he called her "dear." There was no ostentation, but the visitor could not help but see the affection in voice and look and the perfect confidence between the two.

"My, but he is fine looking!" commented Jane before he was fully out of hearing, "and he really thinks a lot of you, doesn't he? How nice. I hope it will last. You deserve it. You had a very romantic marriage, after all, didn't you? But do you really mean that you are going to bury yourself in China? What makes you? Won't he give it up? I've heard he has fine chances here if he will only stay."

"We are going for the love of Christ, Jane," said Evelyn in a sweet, low voice. Her testimony was shy, for she was not used to speaking as Allison had been brought up to do.

"Haven't you got over those notions yet?" said the caller, getting up to go. "Well, I wish I was half as good as you. Good-bye."

And Evelyn sighed as she thought of the days when she had great influence over this girl, and might perhaps have led her into better paths where she would have been saved from all the sorrows and sins with which she was now surrounded.

29

Rebecca Bascomb on the Wedding

It was the day of Allison Grey's wedding, and Miss Rebecca Bascomb was sitting by her window nearly worn out with her labors. She had watched the people as they came from the train; she had watched the expressmen as they went toward the Greys'; she had watched any member of the family that went to the post office or store, and announced to her sister at work in the next room just what shaped parcel was carried and what it was supposed to contain. She had spent so many years at the occupation of guessing other people's private affairs that she hardly ever made a mistake nowadays in matters like these.

"There goes another cut glass bowl, I'll bet a hen!" she soliloquized in her loud tone that had grown a habit with her, for her sister was nearly always in the next room when she was not running to the window to see something Rebecca pointed out.

"That's a shame, and the ceremony over and they gone! There was thirteen last night, a mighty unlucky number, for one of 'em'd be sure to get broke 'fore the year was out. But this one was a good-sized one. It was a square wooden box. O' course it might a been another clock, but what would they want with any more o' them? They've already got five, and it's likely there are a few in the house at New York, seein' the family have scraped along there for years afore Allison come with *her* fixings out. There's another carriage comin' back from the *dee*-po. No it ain't, either, it's Grey's phayton, and if I ain't beat! It's Maurrie and his new wife in it, and she's got a

226

red sack on. I should think she'd have a little sense about dressin' decent, now she's a missionary's wife. If she should go out to China with that thing on she'd draw the whole pack on her at once. Them Boxers probably don't like red any better 'n bulls."

"They'll think she's one of 'em," suggested the sister, hurrying in to peep between the curtains of the other window. "Boxers wear real bright costumes. When I was over to the Corners last summer there was a boxing match there between some college men, and they wore red and black stripes and great big gloves, and looked as much like heathens as any Chinese you ever see."

"Well, I think somebody ought to give her a little advice," said Miss Rebecca, setting her chin blandly, as if she would enjoy the task. "I wonder where Maurrie is goin'? He's turned up the road instead of down. It don't seem decent fer folks to rush around in public after a weddin' any more than they would after a funeral; seems kind of as if they was glad it was over and they was rid of the bride. I must run over in the morning and see if that really was another cut glass bowl."

Out upon the hill drive the pony flew, with Evelyn, close wrapped in warm crimson robes and furs, sitting beside her husband. When they reached the spot where they had stopped that day and paused to look down as before, Evelyn laid her face against her husband's shoulder, and he put his arm around her and held her close.

"This is what I would have liked to do before, darling, if I had dared," he said, looking down into the sweet eyes upturned to his. "Do you know those lines of Mrs. Browning's:

"Nevermore
Alone upon the threshold of my door
Of individual life, I shall command
The uses of my soul . . . What I do
And what I dream include thee, as the wine
Must taste of its own grapes. And when I sue
God for myself, he hears that name of thine,
And sees within my eyes the tears of two."

She looked up to meet his smile, her own eyes dimmed with tears of joy.

"Maurice," she said, "I have been thinking; suppose I had not come to Hillcroft that time. You know I did not want to do so. Suppose I had had my own way. Then I would never have met you again, perhaps, and you would never have told me about Jesus."

"His way is best always, isn't it, dear? Shall we try to always let him have it with us? Now we must turn back, for it is growing cold, and mother will be wondering what has become of us."

Novels of Enduring Romance and Inspiration by

GRACE LIVINGSTON HILL

☐ 23500	**IN TUNE WITH WEDDING BELLS #13**	$2.50
☐ 23805	**MARIGOLD #15**	$2.50
☐ 23317	**WHITE ORCHIDS #28**	$2.50
☐ 23810	**COMING THROUGH THE RYE #32**	$2.50
☐ 23361	**DAWN IN THE MORNING #43**	$2.50
☐ 23429	**THE STREET OF THE CITY #47**	$2.50
☐ 24124	**THE PRODIGAL GIRL #56**	$2.50
☐ 23856	**THE HONOR GIRL #57**	$2.50
☐ 24238	**MIRANDA #60**	$2.50
☐ 22903	**MYSTERY FLOWERS #61**	$2.50
☐ 23558	**CHRISTMAS BRIDE #62**	$2.50
☐ 20286	**MAN OF THE DESERT #63**	$2.25
☐ 20911	**MISS LAVINIA'S CALL #64**	$2.50
☐ 24736	**AN UNWILLING GUEST #65**	$2.50

Prices and availability subject to change without notice.

Buy them at your local bookstore or use this handy coupon for ordering:

SPECIAL
MONEY SAVING
OFFER

Now you can have an up-to-date listing of Bantam's hundreds of titles plus take advantage of our unique and exciting bonus book offer. A special offer which gives you the opportunity to purchase a Bantam book for only 50¢. Here's how!

By ordering any five books at the regular price per order, you can also choose any other single book listed (up to a $4.95 value) for just 50¢. Some restrictions do apply, but for further details why not send for Bantam's listing of titles today!

Just send us your name and address plus 50¢ to defray the postage and handling costs.